THE START OF EVERYTHING

EMILY WINSLOW

THE
START
OF EVERYTHING

A NOVEL

DELACORTE PRESS | NEW YORK

Copyright © 2012 by Emily Winslow

All rights reserved.

Published in the United States by Delacorte Press, an imprint of The Random House Publishing Group, a division of Random House, Inc., New York.

DELACORTE PRESS is a registered trademark of Random House, Inc., and the colophon is a trademark of Random House, Inc.

ISBN 978-0-385-34290-2

Printed in the United States of America

Book design by Casey Hampton

For CB

who is always cheerful, knows absolutely everyone, and shares.

PART I

CHAPTER 1

MATHILDE OLIVER

I rubbed my finger along the envelope's triangle flap. It was sealed all along the V, except for a small gap at each corner.

I pulled the letter off the pile and down into my lap, under the table. No one saw. Everyone had their own work. I slid the tip of my smallest finger into the puffed-up right corner.

The printer stopped. It had been spitting pages for thirty minutes. Without the noise of its grinding and rolling as background, a rip would scream.

"I have to leave," I said, standing up. It's important to explain abrupt movements. "I have an appointment." I pushed the letter into my bag, then threaded my arm through the handles to shut the bag between my ribs and upper arm.

I always sit at the end of the table so I can't be trapped or nudged. Table legs touching mine are completely different from someone else's knee. But today someone had already been in place at the end of the table, with papers spread out for sorting. Not only had I been made to sit along the side; I had to sit well in. Then she made her stacks, creating space again, space that got filled before I noticed it. Trevor had sat down next to me. Now he leaned onto his chair's two back legs. There was no way past. I waited, bouncing my elbow against my bag.

"Oh, sorry!" he said, and pulled his chair in. I squeezed past, holding my breath. The back of my skirt rubbed against the windowsill. The tips of his dark hair brushed against my shirt buttons. I popped out into the small open space next to the copier. The door was only five feet away. If I lay down across the carpet, I would push it open with the top of my head. That's how close it was.

But Lucy squatted in front of the filing cabinet, blocking the door. She did it deliberately.

"Lucy!" Trevor hissed. She looked up, and he stifled a laugh.

She closed the drawer and stood but was still right there. I turned sideways so I didn't graze any of her body as I opened the door.

I was unobstructed from there. The corridor was empty. The receptionist in the entrance never speaks to me. I charged outside into the courtyard and stopped. The spring sunlight was so bright that I closed my eyes. The letter crinkled against an apple in my bag.

A hand came down on my shoulder. I shimmied to throw it off. *Too close, too close.* I snapped my eyes open.

George is a big man. I took a step back.

"Er, Mattie?" he said. "Where are you going?" He rocked from one foot to the other.

"What?" I said. Another step. My heel hit the bottom step behind me.

"Mattie, I was coming in to get you. It's your father. He's had another heart attack. He's been taken to hospital. I should bring you."

The hospital. It would be full of people. There would be rules I don't know.

"No," I said.

"We'll stop by your house first. We can pick up some things for him to . . ."

He reached out, and I smacked his hand. The contact shocked me. I don't like to have to do that.

He made two fists at his sides.

I retreated up the steps, back into the Registrar's reception area. "Would you tell him to leave me alone, please?" I said to the woman at the desk. I stood sideways to her, facing a wall. But she knew I was talking to her.

George followed me. "Her father's been taken to Addenbrooke's," he explained. "He's Dr. Oliver, from Astronomy."

"Miss?" the receptionist said, asking me if it was true, or if I cared.

"I don't have to go," I said. "There isn't a rule."

"No, there isn't," she said. She lifted the phone, as if she might call security. Or not. It was up to George.

He rocked back and forth again. He pushed air out of his mouth. He turned and left.

"Are you all right? Do you need an escort?" the receptionist asked. She leaned forward. Next to her hand was a calendar that had just the number of today's date on it, and a dictionary definition of the word "anodyne."

"No, I—"

Trevor was suddenly there, next to the desk. He must have finished the filing. It must be lunchtime. He had a jacket on. "Mathilde, a sandwich?"

"No," I said.

"You left your notebook on the table." He jerked his thumb back towards the office.

"It's in my bag," I said, squeezing the canvas mouth more tightly shut against my ribs. It had to be in my bag.

"No, you left in a hurry. I can get it for you if you want."

"No!"

This is just the kind of thing my father doesn't understand. He thinks that because the lists I keep aren't embarrassing, they aren't private. But they're mine. That makes them private, even if what I write down is ordinary. It's not anybody's business what I keep track of.

"I'll get it," I said. I walked forward and stopped.

"Mathilde?"

One of Trevor's buttons had a wild thread unravelling through it. It was right in front of my face.

He backed up until there was space for him to move sideways, and he let me pass.

CHAPTER 2

CHLOE FROHMANN

The building that houses Major Investigations is unlabelled, just another bland office-park rectangle weighing down the hem of a village. Inside, desks and testosterone take up all the room. I work my way around both and take off my coat.

The ordinary, diffuse buzz of talking and typing unites into an animated babble of welcome. I look up. It's been months.

DCI Morris Keene is back. I've seen him in a hospital bed; I've seen him in his home. It's good to see him in work clothes again, in work *mode* again. But it's hard to pin what's changed. He's not older. His injuries aren't visible. It's in the way he carries himself, I finally realise: He seems wary.

He accepts the back-slaps, and nods at each "welcome back," but doesn't linger at any of them. He heads straight for me.

"Detective Inspector," he says. He remembered my promotion. Does he notice the looks shooting around the room? Some people think I don't deserve it.

"I'm glad you're back," I say. I put out my hand.

He hesitates. I take his hand and shake, just to complete the greeting. His fingers are slack inside my grasp. I let go. "Sorry," I say. He retracts his hand, slots it into his trouser pocket so no one else will try.

I'm shouldered out of the way as he's surrounded by well-wishing colleagues. They're not just pleased to see him; they're shutting me out. They think his hand is my fault.

They're not wrong.

"These from you, Chloe?" Keene asks. He means the flowers on his desk. The bouquet is tall and bright, tied with a straw bow and squeezed through the neck of a glass vase. Its too-sweet smell brings acid up my throat.

"Not me." I have to avoid stereotypically feminine gestures at work if I don't want to be taken for an admin or a Family Liaison Officer. "They're from Claudia Cole." Our Superintendent's wife. She hand-addresses all of their Christmas cards. She runs marathons for charity. She is a feminine marvel.

Superintendent Cole promises to pass Keene's compliments on to Claudia. Then he plucks Keene out from the middle of it all and barks at me to follow. In his office, he says, "You've got a first-day-back treat. Decomposing body caught in a fen sluice gate. A young woman, it looks like. Keep the press off it as long as you can. We need an identity fast." The pathologist is already en route, north towards Peterborough.

Keene smiles at me. "Good to be a team again," he says.

I curve my mouth back at him, my best effort at returning an expression I don't feel. I keep my head down on the way out.

"I'll drive," says Keene, aiming his key. He clicks a button and headlamps flash.

"Posh," I say. I get in and suppress a gag at the tangy "new car" smell inside.

"Not posh. Just new. I needed an automatic." Still outside, he reaches in through the open driver's door to insert and turn the key with his good left hand. Then he slides in under the steering wheel, belts himself in, and, foot on the brake, puts it in reverse. After all that, his good hand joins the other one on the wheel. His right palm rests on it while the thumb curves under to hold on. It's only the fingers that are useless; the thumb works.

He turns a look on me that dares me to comment. I don't take him up on it.

Once we're on the road he says, "You'll have to take all the notes."

"My handwriting's better, anyway."

He laughs. My eyes crinkle in a real smile. *Wow, that's been a while.*

"Everything all right while I've been gone?" he asks.

I say yes while my head shakes. I hate it when my body tells the truth without my permission.

Keene was watching the road. He believes my "yes." The white, bumpy scar across his fingers stands out in the daylight. It wasn't so obvious in the hospital. The wound to his abdomen had seemed so much worse. . . .

I get it over with. "Some people feel that I let you down. That you shouldn't have been alone."

He glances at me, indignant, then back at the road. "Who said that?"

"It doesn't matter who said it. Everyone thinks it."

"They think I can't interview a witness on my own? Because that's what I was doing, interviewing a witness."

"I know, Keene, I—"

"I didn't know, and you didn't know, what was going to happen. I don't need a nanny, for fuck's sake."

"You do realise that this misplaced concern isn't aimed at you but at me? I should have been there. Two of us, and it wouldn't have happened the way that it did."

"You can't . . ." He shakes his head, eases into a roundabout, and continues once on the other side: "You can't control everything. So my physiotherapist tells me, between exercises. You can't control everything, or always know what you're going to need, until you need it. You didn't know; I didn't know. The only person who did something wrong was the one with the knife."

My muscles unclench. Relief blurs my eyes. All this time I thought I'd been feeling outrage at the accusation; I'd actually been feeling guilt.

"It's not so bad," he notices. He turns the wheel expertly, having obviously practised the manoeuvre.

I know what's being said. They're wondering if they should trust me to partner with Keene again. Not that any of them wants to partner with me now. *No, that's not fair.* It's not everyone. But the ones who aren't doing the complaining are still doing the listening.

I breathe deeply and remind myself: *There's nothing anyone can do with the Superintendent on my side.*

I know why Cole put me with Keene again. It isn't because he trusts me, though he claims he does. He knows I'm an outsider right now, and the promotion widened the gulf that was already there. He knows I need to watch my step, and need his backing. He wants me to keep an eye on Keene and report back candidly about his capabilities. He wants me to spy on my partner.

———

The fens are reclaimed land. A massive drainage effort centuries ago turned marsh into land, but every winter the water creeps back. It has to go somewhere. Systems of ditches, sluices, embankments, and pumps divert the river overflows to their designated washes. Here, now, the river Nene is receding from its winter swell.

Spring warmth had bloated the body to the surface, and it was caught in a sluice gate where the lock keeper found her. There isn't enough soft tissue on the skull for us to discern a face, and the skull itself is so damaged that a reconstruction doesn't seem possible. Jensen guesses late teens to early twenties, with the caveat that he'll be more sure after a proper exam in the lab. A person this age likely has local parents looking for her, for a generous definition of "local." We're close to the county border; if nothing obvious pops in the immediate area, we'll have to look to Lincolnshire for their missing persons as well.

"Where do you think she went in?" Keene wonders.

I look around. The wash is thin and shallow now, but a couple of months ago its width reached far. The water here connected with the river Nene, with the B1040 road, with branching ditches. "How about *when* she went in?" I suggest. "Not recently, obviously. But . . . after this year's flooding started? Did she fall in alive and drown? Or was her corpse dumped into the water—or dumped in a dry ditch, later dislodged by the flood?"

"In other words, wait for Jensen's report."

I nod. The body will narrow things down.

We look out over the wash. Even when it's dry, it's mainly unoc-
cupied land, waiting for next year's flood. Alongside it, farmers' fields.
The main road has been underwater since January. Not many people
around. "Do you think we have any potential witnesses?"

"The sex shop?" He points with his chin. It used to be a Little
Chef. You still see those restaurants on the motorways, full of tired
families stretching their legs and their bellies, but I haven't eaten at one
in years. This one must have been comical to convert, those wide windows fronting a place where, presumably, the current patrons value
privacy. Those windows are now filled with display lingerie, both to
entice and to block a look in. No shoppers are here, anyway. Only police vehicles occupy the vast, empty car park today, clustered under the
pink sign.

Keene answers himself: "The trees block any hope of a view. Besides, she didn't go in here."

We don't need Jensen to tell us that. If she had, she would have
been found much sooner. She would still have a face on her. A sudden
shout from near the body; I tense and ready to run, but it's just Jensen
shooing a crow off her.

"Keene?" I say. He's gone pale.

"I'm thinking," he snaps. "Bloody hell." I follow his sudden tantrum, pushing through thin branches. The trees here seem to reach for
one another, weaving into a net. He finally turns, and his turning re-
leases a tense branch to spring back at my face.

"Sorry," he says. His voice isn't sorry.

His mobile rings. He reaches for it with his right hand, can't grab
it, then quickly switches to the left. I look away. He's due his privacy
while he adjusts.

He finishes the call and flicks his phone shut. "The Missing Persons
Bureau will get us details for all the young women reported missing in
the last six months, priority to Peterborough-area cases." He gives me
some statistics.

"That's not bad," I say. *No, not bad at all.* Three quarters of missing-
persons reports resolve themselves within forty-eight hours; the number of cases left for us to deal with is manageable. Jensen's analyses will
further narrow things down. Some sorting, some interviews. "We'll
have an identity within the week," I tell Keene.

We return to the sex-shop car park, where Jensen is supervising the transport of the remains. The body is rolled past colourful bras splayed against the windows. Handwritten posters promise "sale prices" next to smiley faces. I catch the eye of a mannequin; it's stuck in a permanent wink.

CHAPTER 3

MATHILDE OLIVER

In the office, Lucy was talking with the new girl, who brought a newspaper in with her every day. Sometimes she spread it out on the table and it would overlap some of my envelopes. I don't like to touch newsprint. On this one, the greasy ink made a generic picture of the river Nene in flood, near Peterborough. The words said a body had surfaced in the water there.

Lucy called the short girl Enid, which is how I learned her name. She said, "Enid, that's disgusting!"

"That's what water does. They have no idea who she was or how long she's been there, really. Less than a year. More than a month. There were some hairs left to say she was fair. . . ."

I couldn't see my notebook. The paper was opened wide, not even folded once. My notebook had to be under there. I looked for its outline, but the page about the dead person lay lightly. It curved. Anything could be under there. Or nothing. The other side, the rest of the news, lay thick and flat.

"Hi, Mathilde," Enid said. "We'll all have to be more careful. Someone doesn't like girls with fair hair."

I have fair hair. Enid's hair is shit brown.

"She's joking," Lucy said. "Seriously, Enid. There's nothing about any other victims."

Enid shrugged. "Just haven't found them yet."

"Mattie, are you looking for this?" Lucy took my notebook off the seat next to her. She held it by its binding, which left the pages to flap.

I couldn't speak. I willed her to put it down. Instead, she stood and walked around the table, holding it out. I didn't move. "I'll just put it in your bag," she said. The bag had slid down to my elbow. It hung open there. The letter poked out the top.

I swung at her with the bag and took the notebook with my other hand. "Jesus Christ," she said, jumping back. No one was in the way. I got out.

It took twenty-seven steps to get away from the office, out into the courtyard. I stuck to the edge of the building and slipped round the corner. In Senate House Passage, I kept to the cobbles that bubbled along the edge of the otherwise flagstone path.

Around the corner on King's Parade, tourists aimed cameras at the chapel. I needed to cross the street to get behind them. But a car nosed out of Trinity Street, condensing pedestrians back onto the pavements, and me against a stone wall. There aren't supposed to be cars here; bollards at the entrances to this part of town guard against all but taxis and ambulances and police cars. For those, they sink into the ground. But this wasn't any of those. This one had no right to be here. I clenched my hands into balls at the ends of my arms.

Easter holiday is always a difficult time. Children are off school, and families glut the city centre. Tourists move about in herds.

After the car passed, I rode the pedestrian tide over the road.

I know the system here. The homeless man selling magazines and the fudge-shop barker always speak to me, but they don't expect me to answer. They say the same things to everyone. I stiffened but kept walking. I forced myself. Ahead, a new crowd formed.

Six months ago, Corpus Christi College unveiled a new clock. Pedestrian traffic patterns were now permanently clotted by it. People clumped and goggled in front of the glass. They don't even keep to the pavement. They spill back into the street, leaning and stretching to see around the interfering reflection of King's College's famous façade.

I hate the crowds. There were things I needed to do.

The envelope had been addressed the same as before: *Katja, Corpus Christi College, Cambridge.* Routing insufficiently addressed University mail is my job. Usually it's enough to match initials or single names with a college or department list. But if it isn't (and I found no student or Fellow called Katja at Corpus), I open them for additional information. We're so good at getting mail to its intended recipient that some students test us with deliberately vague addresses.

This one wasn't a test. This Stephen was desperate to find her.

In the first letter, he'd written:

Katja—

You know I lied when I agreed I wouldn't try to keep in touch. You had to have known.

I've got to see you again. Please write. I'm at a friend's farm in Truro. The address is on the envelope. I'll be here for two months more, and then who knows. I'm midway through the new book.

Please write. Please.

—Stephen

I'm only supposed to look at the salutation and signature for clues. But I read it all. I copied it into my notebook. Then I put it into a file of work-in-progress back at the office.

The second letter came eleven days later.

Katja—

Imagination can be a terrible thing. You haven't responded, so of course I've imagined why. I miss you.

I didn't tell you about my book, because I wanted you to be impressed with me, not my reviews. I see now how ridiculous and falsely noble this was. I'll be quite happy for you to adore me for my literary success. The Times *loved it. There, I've said it. Will you reply now?*

—Stephen

Lucy noticed me reading the last one. That's why I had to get out of the office, instead of trying to read the new one on my lap. But the crowd was in my way. Why would anyone want a photograph of something so ugly?

This new clock is based on an old pattern. A grasshopper escapement is a wide sideways X on the top of a clock's main gear, turning it exactly one second at a time. But this one isn't merely an X that squeezes and opens like the legs of a hopping insect. It's an X made into a monstrous robot grasshopper that rides the massive clock face, blinking and biting and lolling its tongue.

The mouth snaps each minute. That gave it its name: The Time Eater. The tail lifts every quarter hour. Then, every hour, it stings. I've tried to find a pattern with the eye blinks, but I think they're random. Every time I pass, I wait for a blink before I go by.

It took fourteen seconds this time. I counted the pendulum swings.

Another car intruded from Bene't Street onto Trumpington Street, nudging the front row of gawkers up onto the kerb. This one wasn't a police car, either. It was an ordinary car and had no right. The rest of us were squeezed back, feet tangling at the bottom of it all. I bit my lip. It felt like hours, which was the point of the clock. It keeps irregular time. It's exactly right only once every five minutes. Sometimes it runs briefly backwards, then surges forward to catch up. It's meant to represent the subjective experience of time, the sloppy lie of what people feel—pleasure passing too quickly and agony lasting too long—instead of what time objectively is. I hate it.

The crowd sprang apart. It always happened this way. The gathering, the press, then the release, over and over. I launched myself into the road and ran, following the college wall until the gatehouse breached it.

Cambridge is laid out opposite to the universe.

Light takes time to travel, so the farther out one looks into space, the further back in time one sees. Our view of the moon is just over one second old. Our view of the planets is minutes old. The sight of even the closest stars is years out of date. Distant ones, ones that have even died by now, show us their infancy, millions of years ago, as the structure of the universe coalesced out of the gases of the Big Bang. If you want to see old, look far.

Cambridge is the opposite. The oldest colleges, shaped around courtyards and entered through formidable stone gateways, cluster in the centre; only when one squints and looks to the city outskirts does one find the glass and concrete of recent colleges.

Corpus is one of the central, old ones.

I sucked in a breath before entering through the massive portal. The last time I'd come here had been for my interview. I'd practised everything I was supposed to say. I'd eaten toast for breakfast and ironed my blouse. But when the student volunteer waved me over to join the group, and all the other applicants turned their heads to fling smiles at me, I seized up. "I have to leave," I'd said, the way I'd taught myself to do, before running. Louis had been a porter on duty then. He was on duty now.

"Mathilde! I don't think your father's here right now."

"I know." Of course Dad wasn't there. Louis must not have known he was in hospital; or, Louis knew and was keeping it from me, thinking I didn't.

He didn't say anything else. I hate when people wait for me to keep talking.

"I'm looking for someone called Katja," I finally surrendered.

"Kate? Professor Jarvis?"

"No, not Kate . . . Katja. K-A-T-J-A. Does someone by that name work here?" She hadn't been in the database of students and faculty, but maybe she was a bedder or in catering.

"No, love, I don't think so. Why do you think she works here?"

"Someone told me she did."

"Why don't you ask your father?"

"No," I insisted. We haven't been speaking. When we've been home at the same time, I sit in the bathroom, where he won't try to talk to me. I fell asleep in there two nights ago. I woke up with marks from the bathmat against my cheek.

Dad wishes I were at university. And I am. I'm starting with the Open University next term, online. He wishes I were studying at a physical uni. Not Cambridge, necessarily, though I know he'd like that best. I didn't tell him that I'd scheduled an interview, but I know he knew I was expected. After I didn't turn up, he came home and shouted at me. I hid under the bed.

I don't know why he'd thought it was going to work. I hated school from the start. The small tables in my first classroom had had two children crammed together on each of the four sides. All those feet kicking underneath. We'd had a communal pot in the centre for pencils, which were never put back right. I brought my own pencil, and I remember the girl next to me not knowing it was mine. She made me put it in the communal pot at the end of an activity. She actually grabbed it out of my hand and said I was stealing when I tried to get it into my pocket. I slapped her, and she bit her lip, which made it look like I'd hit hard enough to draw blood, which I hadn't.

"Mathilde?" Louis said. He always wore the same suit, or ones that looked the same. I like Louis. "Do you want to leave a message for your father?"

"No," I said again. "May I leave a message for Katja?" It was my responsibility to find her.

He gave me a piece of stationery. I wrote that I had mail for her, and asked her to contact me. I folded it and wrote "Katja" on the outside. He promised to pin it to the announcements board.

Louis doesn't mind if I sit. He never minds. I made sure he wasn't watching.

I took out the new letter. It had been folded in three to fit in the envelope, and the paper was so stiff that it popped open when I pulled it out.

Katja—

I rearranged the furniture today. I pushed the small table up against the wall, just under a window, just as it was at Deeping House. I don't have Internet and purposely didn't bring any books. This was supposed to force my mind to work, but I've only found other ways to procrastinate.

I used to look out my uncle's window at you. You made me smile.

If you were in this garden right now, I'd climb right out of the win-

dow. If I turned my back to go out of the cottage door, who knows
whether you'd still be there once I got round the back.

I don't want to lose you again.

—*Stephen*

I read the new letter twice. *Deeping House.* Perhaps they would
have a home address for her in a guest book. I stuffed the page back
into its envelope.

"Would you care to take your father's mail?" Louis asked me. He
said Dad's pigeonhole was full. I didn't say no, so he gave me the stack.

Three journals, wrapped in plastic. Two thick padded envelopes.
He's been getting a lot of these, from members of his childhood boarding school's "Old Boys" society. Alumni were submitting memorabilia
for an exhibit Dad was coordinating. Dad had loved school.

The letters on top had mostly typed or stickered addresses. They
were announcements, invitations, conference materials. One was
hand-addressed. I notice these things since working at the Registrar's
office.

I dumped the rest into my bag and held on to that one.

I wanted to open it, but Louis would see. I slipped outside.

A tourist group had gathered at the mouth of the college gate, one
of those whose leader carries a distinctive oversized umbrella. This one
had a pattern of birds all over it, flying in a swirl as though they're
being sucked up a cyclone. The group blocked the exit, so I stepped
through into New Court. Courtyard grass has rules. No one but a college Fellow is allowed to cross it. I had to walk all the way around the
huge rectangular lawn, even though the chapel was right across from
where I'd started.

The chapel is stone-cool and symmetrical, and empty most of the
time. Sometimes an organist practises or someone prays, but no one
was there now. I sat in a back pew. The chandeliers weren't lit, or the
candles, but the vast stained-glass windows sprinkled coloured light all
over.

The envelope had been sealed only at the point of the fold, so it was
easy to pop. The letter inside was wrapped around half a dozen photographs.

The pictures were old. Dad and Amy Banning took them of each other on a narrowboat trip, laughing as they pushed the beam or wound the windlass to pass through locks. Some must have been taken by strangers on the towpath, because they're together, touching. The boat was called the *Adorabelle,* which isn't a word.

The letter read:

Dear Tobias—

I'd wondered if I might hear from you. It was strange coming back to Cambridge, to drop off Luke. Memories rushed at me. I'm sure you understand that they weren't all happy ones.

I married three years ago. You would like Bernard. We're very happy.

For that reason, I don't feel right keeping these photographs. But I appreciate the effort and the apology. If you're indeed ready now to move forward in life, then I wish you luck.

I never told Luke what you had accused, so you needn't worry about any awkwardness if you run across him. He has only ever thought highly of you.

Sincerely,
Amy Banning Harrow

Luke. He was only a year older than I was. He would have started at uni already, apparently here. I was twelve and he was thirteen when Dad was going to marry Amy Banning. Luke was supposed to have become my brother.

I pulled out my notebook and copied the text of the letter into it. I wrapped the page around the photos again, and slid them back into their envelope.

The last time I saw Luke, Dad had rented us a film. He asked at the video shop what twelve-year-olds would want, a boy and a girl. I didn't like what was on the screens. I went outside while Dad paid.

Dad had told me four times that I should be friendly to Luke, and that I should leave Dad and Amy alone while they were in the kitchen.

Luke sat on one end of the couch. I sat on the footrest for the leather chair. The TV was small, so Luke moved closer when the film started. I stayed where I was.

The movie started with slow music. Luke reached across me to aim the remote and turn it up. I tucked my elbows in, out of his way. Music rumbled, then horses galloped. The hooves matched Dad and Amy chopping vegetables. Then the music and horses got louder than the kitchen work. Only Amy's laughing was louder.

Dad had said I needed to stay and be nice to Luke. I covered my ears but I didn't get up.

Luke said something to me. I couldn't make it out through my hands and the horses. I shut my eyes. He shouted "Mum!" so loudly that I jumped.

Dad pushed past Amy. "What is it now, Mathilde?"

And, overlapping him, Amy said, "I think the volume is a little loud, Luke."

Dad adjusted the TV, then went back into the kitchen with Amy. Luke moved closer and leaned over to hear it better. His leg almost touched mine.

"Don't do that," I said.

"What?"

"I said don't do that!"

"Do what?"

I grabbed the footstool underneath me with both hands and lifted it, so I could crab-walk out of his range.

He picked up the remote but put it down again. The sounds from the kitchen now were of frying and talking. The horse in the movie fell to the ground. His snorting nostrils were six inches big on the screen, blowing dirt around with panicked exhales. I gripped the footstool again, to make myself stay. Dad had made me swear to be good.

"Are you all right?" Luke had come close again. He was so close his nostrils were as big as the movie horse's. I could smell that he'd eaten Doritos.

I twisted my head away from him as far as I could, but it wasn't enough.

"Mum!" he called again. I didn't have my hands over my ears this time, and he didn't bother to face the kitchen door. His mouth was right next to me when he shouted.

"Stop it!" I shouted back. I pummelled him with my fists. I pushed and pushed his chest until he was back on the other end of the couch, where he had started. Dad pulled me off him. He wrapped his arms around my chest and lifted me up. I kicked backwards, pounding my heels into his thighs.

He carried me into my room and dropped me onto my bed. I bounced. He didn't sit on the mattress with me or even turn on my light. He got out and closed the door. I got up and put my ear against it. "I'm so, so sorry," he said, but not to me.

Back in the present, the chapel organ blasted a chord. My bag fell over and spilled my notebook out. The apple used it as a slide.

The organ blew louder and louder. I grabbed up my things and ran at the glass doors, sliding on the patterned tiles. I pushed through into the courtyard. The grass faintly glowed, the way aggressively living things do.

The door swung shut, keeping the organist in. I breathed through my nose. I've learned to do that, to slow everything down.

The tour group had moved on. I scurried past Louis, back out onto Trumpington Street. I looked back at the corner, at a new crowd gathered in front of the clock.

I turned the other way, towards the hospital.

CHAPTER 4

CHLOE FROHMANN

Cold water protects a body. As a medium, it slows decomposition, though you wouldn't know it from the end result. It's not the water that makes the flesh fall off the bones; it's the fish, and the buffeting. At first Jensen thought the damage to the skull could have come about postmortem as likely as being the cause of death. But, upon examination, the several markings embedded in the skull turned out to match one another. Looks like a single weapon, taken to her face and head, is what killed her.

We still don't know who she was.

IS THIS YOUR DAUGHTER?

Cambridgeshire police are investigating the identity of a young woman whose remains were discovered by a fen sluice gate near Wisbech last week.

Do you know her?

She would have gone missing within the past year, most likely three to six months ago.

She is approximately five-foot-five in height, with a size-five shoe.

Blond, shoulder-length hair.

Gap jeans: size 6.

Red sweater, with a blue stripe at each cuff, hand-knit, personal label.

THE POLICE NEED YOUR HELP

The notice ends with the number for the Crimestoppers hotline. I shove the newspaper across the desk towards Keene. "We don't *know* she's blond," I say. "We strongly *suspect* that she's blond." The hairs we have were from her sweater, not her head. None of her scalp had been left.

"It's a starting place," sighs Keene. "We have to make some assumptions or the field is too wide to do anything."

The dump point was likely along the B1040. Its flooded segment has been searched, but nothing relevant found. Jensen's report has done little for us. Recent missing persons—ours and Lincolnshire's—aren't matching our girl. Yes, late teens to early twenties, as had been originally assumed. A handful of teeth, none of them with dental work. We thought the sweater, with its custom label, was our ticket. "Knitted lovingly by June Marks." We actually found June Marks, on an Internet knitting forum. She'd made the sweater for her nephew seven years ago. He'd offloaded it to an Oxfam charity shop in Leeds. Dead end.

It's hard to get rid of a body completely. But if you obscure it enough, you don't need to.

"Soon we'll have hundreds of call-ins to cull, thanks to the press.

Most of them worthless." I tap my pen against my lips. "Where is her mother, her boyfriend, her classmates or coworkers? We should know about her already. She's probably a sister and a cousin and . . . How does someone just . . . disappear?"

"Not everyone has family." Keene shrugs.

"Maybe not close family. But everyone lives somewhere. Somewhere, there's a her-shaped hole. It's five and a half feet tall, and it's been empty since around Christmas. Do you think she's not British?"

"I don't want that headache. For now, for my sanity, I'm assuming British."

"Someone the world doesn't realise is missing, right? Maybe estranged from her family?" A friend of mine works with prostitutes in Peterborough. I'll ask her to check around, see if anyone isn't where she usually is. "Maybe someone who's grown out of foster care?" Identifying the criminal is supposed to be the hard part. Turns out that identifying the victim is a hundred times worse. There's no starting place, just a puddle in Wisbech.

"If she's not local, what was she doing there?" I wonder. "Who visits the fens in the winter?"

"It's a day trip from London. For all we know, she was killed in London and driven for the dump. Killed anywhere."

I shake my head. "No. No, for *my* sanity, it isn't random. Killed elsewhere? Fine. But think about it: You're dumping a body. You're scared. Do you go someplace where you have no knowledge of the layout? No knowledge of who might be watching? Our girl may not be from around there, but I bet our killer is."

"Maybe we should ask the press for call-ins about *him*: 'If you know a homicidal maniac in the Wisbech area, call Crimestoppers at . . .'"

"Ha!"

Cole leans between us, wants to know the joke.

"Brainstorming, sir," Keene says smoothly.

We catch eyes, suppress smiles, like teenagers caught passing notes.

Keene's phone rings. He reaches with the wrong hand, fumbles it, grabs it up with the left. It's stopped ringing. He turns his back to check the number and return the call. He has some difficulty with the buttons.

I busy myself as if I don't see. I fold the newspaper; I check my own phone for messages. More Crimestoppers tips.

"Split up for this," says Cole. He doesn't usually micromanage. But in this case, it's not a command; it's his blessing on it. No one will be able to blame me if bad comes from it.

We get around. It's solid work, even if none of it goes anywhere. One Peterborough man's wife has been missing for two years. He clings to the possibility that she drowned rather than left him. She had a badly broken leg in her past that doesn't fit our bones.

A woman in Whittlesey is looking for her little sister. The family disowned her when she fell pregnant. The last she heard from her was a photo of the baby, a chubby one-year-old, at Christmas. No return address. Our body had never given birth.

We know what she didn't do: break her leg, have a child.

I pester Jensen: "What *did* she do? Can you please Sherlock Holmes this for me and tell me her job and marital status by some forensic magic?"

He knows I'm joking. Still, he takes offence at the word "magic." We're all spiky now, all defending our lack of progress: *not my fault.*

———

I kill trees printing out the relevant database results. Paper piles make the work look comfortingly solid, despite our pursuit having, as yet, no tangible result.

We're sorting. It's a slog.

". . . Not a language student; too far from Cambridge. An au pair?" I muse. Lots of those from the rest of Europe, pouring into the UK otherwise unattached. Nothing with the reported missing women is panning out. We're brainstorming for who could sever attachments and not be noticed as missing. Yes, her friends would notice she's gone, but if she's between jobs, they might just assume she got one. Mum might complain about no phone calls, but she wouldn't be the first parent to bemoan an uncommunicative child.

Keene says, "Gwen's sister used one. She worked with an agency. But there are websites, too. It's a haystack."

I click the top hit on Google.

Welcome to Au Pairs for You, where we match families and au pairs for the short and long term, for household help and language learning support.

Are you a family? Are you an au pair?

I click that I'm *a family,* because I want to search for au pairs. They offer me a drop-down menu asking where I live: *the UK.* At the next menu, I choose that I'm willing to accept an au pair from *anywhere.* I don't tick any boxes. I don't care if she smokes or isn't willing to care for pets. Start anytime, any pay grade. I do tick that I'm looking for a woman. Then I untick it, because the third option besides male is "couples," and she could be half of a couple.

We have found you 1,478 matches!

Each one has a photo and short personal statement. Contact information is withheld until I register. Even then, there's no proof required of anyone in this scenario. Anyone could claim to be a happy family looking for childcare. Anyone could claim to be a young woman on a gap year who "loves babies." None of this is vetted. The website requires a registration fee but doesn't screen users.

Lena, 18
I'm a friendly girl. I love to dance, and I love babies. I will love to find a happy family and play with your children. I also clean and keep a very neat house.

Zennia, 24
I'm a happy woman with sweet disposition for family care. I love older children and dogs and have especial skills with arts and crafts. I am responsible and outgoing and looking for the right family to become a close part with.

Collette, 20
I have looked after my nieces since they were born, and now that I am graduate school I hope to see the world and work for you. I

plan to study teaching and for now want to better my English with
a happy family with children.

"Look at these photos. Would you let your daughter put this on the
Web?" I say to Keene. Collette is wearing a tight tank top and leaning
forward towards the lens.

"I tell her not to be stupid. And then I don't look. Weren't you a
teenager once?"

"Of course. I put my tits in one guy's face at a time, not up on the
Internet. And not on a job-application website." They're not all like
that. Plenty of them are hiking or hugging a toddler, in a sweatshirt or
blouse and jeans. Most of them are pretty; at that age, almost everyone
is. But the glamour shots, the school-dance ball gowns, and the pouty
ones make my heart ache. I can smell the adolescent desperation.

"I feel sick," I say. I excuse myself and retch into the toilet.

On the way back to my desk, Cole pulls me into his office. He wants
to know how Keene is handling things. I tell him, "He's frustrated that
we're no farther on than we are. Same as me."

"And could that be due to his . . . incapabilities?"

Anger on Keene's behalf bubbles inside me. "No, sir," I say. "He's
fully capable." I add, "It was his hand that took the cut, not his brain."

"I appreciate the anatomy lesson, Frohmann. Thank you."

I return to my desk. Keene heads for home.

An hour later, he calls me from the side of the A1198. He's bab-
bling. I make him repeat things. I catch that his car is off the road and
he needs me.

I dash to my car. Familiarity washes over me. Yes, this is how it was.
I was driving when the message had come through: Keene down, ambulance dispatched, suspect in custody. I rushed to the hospital instead
of to the scene. I was waiting when he arrived. He was conscious; he
was bloody. The medical staff shooed me to a waiting area. I used
Keene's phone to call his family.

Cole was there, too. And Mitchell. We were all on the same side
then.

Cole's a bloody idiot if he thinks he can flip me now.

CHAPTER 5

MATHILDE OLIVER

I'd been to Addenbrooke's before, years ago, to meet with a counsellor after Dad broke up with Amy. At first he'd been angry with me. Then, when I tried to explain, he latched onto a word. I said Luke had *touched* me.

I meant he had been too loud and too close. But Dad grabbed the word "touched." He thought Luke had tried to be . . . like a boy with me. That's what he accused, when he broke up with Amy.

I knew Luke hadn't, but later I wondered what that would have been like. Once, I lay on the couch, the couch where we'd sat, with a pillow tucked between my legs. I squeezed it there, thinking, and suddenly everything skewed, and my legs kicked in little spasms. Dad came in to see what was wrong. I pretended to have fallen asleep.

"Miss?" This person put a hand on my shoulder. I got still. "Can I help you?" she asked.

I looked around. I didn't know where Dad would be. "My dad's ill," I said. Her hand got heavier. I shrugged it off.

"Does he need help?" she asked. "Or is he already here?"

"I think he's here. I think he had a heart attack." I told her his name and where we lived. She went to the large desk and typed things into a computer.

I stayed where I was, which meant she had to come back around the front of the desk to talk to me again. She came again with the hand. It landed hard. "And he's your father?" she asked, trying to make me look at her. I looked at my other shoulder, the unweighted one. I nodded to answer.

"Dear, I'll have his doctor come down to speak with you. Why don't you sit . . ." My head was still going up and down, and so I changed it to side to side. I was all right standing here. I'd chosen my safe place at Addenbrooke's Hospital.

Dad thinks I'm the way that I am because Mum died, even though I was myself before she died. But he doesn't pay attention, so he wouldn't know. Six months after she died, I'd had a growth spurt and needed new clothes. He took me to Marks & Spencer. There was a sale going on, and it was mobbed. I hid in one of the dressing rooms, but so many people were waiting that they checked behind the curtain to hurry me up. I bolted outside and ran all the way to Chesterton Road and along the river. He called the police to look for me, but I was already home.

The doctor put his face in front of mine to get my attention. I jumped.

"Tobias Oliver is your father?"

I said, "Yes."

He took my upper arm and steered me towards some chairs. I didn't resist; it didn't seem allowed. This is why I don't like hospitals.

"Sit down," said the doctor, pulling down on my arm to try to make me.

I pulled back. "Is my dad here?" I asked, looking around. This isn't where I would keep a patient, but why else would he bring me over here?

"Not right here, no. Please, sit."

I sat. Rules were everywhere in this place.

"What?" I asked. I hadn't been listening.

He said it again.

"All right," I said. "Thank you." I stood up.

"Miss?" He was trying to make me stay for something.

"He's not here," I said. "He's dead." Which he'd just told me.

"Yes, he is. Would you . . . ?" He waved at the nurse at the desk.

"Thank you," I said, walking away. He couldn't make me stay. I ran out. Behind me, the revolving door kept spinning.

———

I carried all of Dad's books from the dining room and put them in his study. I took his slippers from the lounge and his coats and wellies from the hall closet, and put them into his bedroom. After an hour or so of transfers, I closed the study and bedroom doors. They didn't have locks, so I put tape across where the doors met their frames, just by the knobs.

In the kitchen, I cooked rice and sliced an apple.

When the Big Bang was first theorised, it had been shocking because it implied a start to the universe, which had until then been generally assumed to be eternal and static.

Now everyone's adjusted. It's scientific fact: Something exploded, and that explosion contained everything that we know of, still rushing outward.

But that doesn't mean everyone accepts that that explosion came out of nothing. Penrose posits a cyclical universe that expands and contracts and expands out again, over and over. Hawking suggests a multiverse, where an infinite number of randomly composed universes exist; it's not surprising that at least one resulted in life and intelligence. Turok also lives in a multiverse, and he puts forward that our Big Bang was the point where two higher-dimensional spaces bumped into each other.

The point is, there's no such thing as a start, no matter how far back you go. There are only continuations.

I laid out my clothes for tomorrow. I set up my bag by the front door. I waited until it got dark, and then I went to bed.

———

Trevor knew. When I returned to work the next day, he whispered it
to Lucy, who whispered it to Enid, who gasped. She rushed over to
where I was sitting. She leaned over me so far that everyone could see
past her ruffled collar right down her shirt.

"I'm *so sorry* about your father," she exhaled. I slanted to avoid
her.

Trevor patted her shoulder. "Come on," he said. "I think Mattie's
all right."

She reached to take her newspaper out of my way, but I shot my
hand out. "Is this the same body?" There was a sketch now, of a young
woman from behind. The height, hair, red sweater, jeans, and shoe
size were emphasised. It was all they had.

"You don't need to see things like this," Lucy told me. Lucy was
always telling people what they should and shouldn't do. Lucy always
thinks she knows what's best.

"You're not my father!" I shouted. I stood up, panting. Everyone
jumped, even Enid.

"Why don't we all just try to get some work done?" Trevor suggested. Enid folded her newspaper.

I sat back down. The mail in my inbox was mostly advertising.

I moved to the database terminal and typed in "Katja" for the whole
University. There were none at Corpus Christi, but St. John's had two.
King's had one. I emailed all three to ask if they knew a Stephen, a
Stephen who might think they were at Corpus.

Probably they all knew Stephens.

I tapped keys idly. "Tobias Oliver" appeared in front of me letter by
letter. I clicked search, and his entry popped open. It'll be weeks before
he's excised from the database.

I typed "Luke Banning." It corrected me, by offering Luke Banning Harrow. He must be fond of his stepfather. He was at St. John's.
He was reading Maths. Dad had told me he liked maths. That's why
he'd thought we would get along. In Dad's fantasies, we helped each
other with homework. Enid passed behind me, pretending she needed
something from the file cabinet. I minimised the browser window
until she left.

This was when I pulled up Google and poked around for Deeping

House. The only reference I found was a six-year-old application for planning permission to convert Deeping House, a listed manor, into flats. The owner was named, so I Googled him, too. Ian Bennet. I got his phone number to go with the Deeping House address. The only other place Ian Bennet came up was in reference to his protest of the conversion of a nearby Little Chef into a sex shop.

The hard edge of a folded note nudged my little finger. It was attached to Enid, and nipped between two pink-tipped fingers. I quickly minimised the browser window again, but not before she saw what I was reading. The news article was one of those sites that has ads triggered by the topic; the sidebar had a photo of a near-naked woman talking on a phone.

"It's a mobile number," she said, tapping her note. "Before you came in, a man called George had phoned for you. I told him you'd be in later. I got his number for you."

"Thank you," I said. I didn't want it, but if I didn't take it she would keep poking me. "I don't like using the phone," I added, in reference both to George's call and to whatever she thought I was reading on the Internet.

"It's all right to be sad," she said. She didn't leave. She had a perfume on. She smelled overwhelmingly like Christ's College's jasmine tree. Sick climbed up my throat.

"I know," I said. The scent gathered strength. "Thank you," I added. Still she hovered. I pulled out my phone. That worked.

I didn't want to call George, but I had to call someone, to keep Enid away. I faced the wall and phoned the number I had found for Ian Bennet, the owner of Deeping House.

A teenage girl answered, which I wasn't expecting. She said Katja had worked for a family upstairs, as a nanny, but she wasn't there anymore. "Of course not," I said. "I know that. I want to know where she is now." She said that I should call Mrs. Finley upstairs and ask. She hung up. This is why I don't like telephones. You don't know when you're supposed to talk and when you're supposed to listen, and abrupt things happen.

Real people can be abrupt, too, but you usually see or hear clues first. Lucy must have walked the long way to come at me from behind.

"Mathilde, we're going out later, just for a drink. Would you like to come along?"

She'd never asked me that before. The only thing different is that my father is dead.

"No," I said, putting my phone up against my ear again. I felt like if I took it off my head they'd try again.

So I looked up the Finley number. I got the woman who is the nanny now; she told me the name of the service Katja had used. Then another woman grabbed the phone and demanded my name. She said that if I was thinking of hiring Katja I should think again because she has *poor judgement.* She said that multiple times: *That girl has poor judgement.* I hung up, but the phrase kept repeating in my head.

I wanted to go home, but it wasn't time to leave yet. I had planned to leave at four o'clock.

There was no new mail. I wondered if they were withholding it. That would be like them, to think they know what I need. *I'll work whether they want me to or not.*

I dialled the number for the au pair agency. The woman didn't tell me anything useful. She said she couldn't dispense private information. *Dispense,* like a pharmacist.

Now it was four o'clock. I left.

The next day, fresh mail was delivered to the office. I read it in my lap.

Katja—

I've had a horrible day. I helped Alistair to deliver a calf. I'd no clue how to go about such a thing, but I'm willing. I thought it would be an experience I can use in the book.

It had died inside its mother. We didn't know. The leg broke off in Alistair's hand. Then he pulled the head out. It was birthed in stiff pieces. He got the rest of it out with a rope.

I'm back in my cottage now. Curtains drawn, blanket over my knees. I probably shouldn't tell you what a coward I am that that sent me reeling, but I need you to know it happened. I need you, full stop.

I can't help but wonder why you're doing this. It's not right to start something and just drop it. It's not right to treat a person like a new hobby you were trying out, like knitting or tatting that you can give up

on and leave in the basket if it bores you. If you don't want to see me
again, say so. But it's not right to say nothing. It's not right to go silent.
    You know what to do.

—Stephen

I put down the letter and cried, because it was horrible that the calf
was dead.

CHAPTER 6

MORRIS KEENE

The car door opens only a few inches. I suck in a breath and slide out, holding my arm across my stomach. My scar is only a small lumpy line, but I coddle and protect my abdomen as if I have a baby in there. I force myself to stand up straight; my natural posture bends in the middle now, like a page that's been folded too hard in the past.

I push the door shut. Even my dead right hand can do that. My fingers don't bend anymore, but it's a fine paddle. I can slam, slap, and wave. Amazing how infrequently I need to do any of those things.

"It wasn't my fault," I tell Chloe. I have to make that clear.

"I get that, Keene. Not your fault. Now, can you clarify what 'it' is?"

The tow truck pulls my car away. There's only a smashed headlamp and bumper damage; I could have driven it home safely, but that would have been unlawful. I did everything right. I called for a tow and called the police, right? Chloe's the police.

"It's not funny," Chloe says. She's right. I stop laughing. "How did it happen?"

"It wasn't my hand," I clarify, truthfully. "It was an idiot over the centre line. A lorry pulled out of that lay-by"—I point—"so the car coming towards me swerved into my lane. I ended up going off the road and hitting a post. It's his fault, no question. No question. I have his plate number, and we exchanged insurance information." I hated giving him mine. But I'd already grandstanded my name and rank; I couldn't fake out of it.

"Then it's all right," she says. We get into her car. "Straight home, or a pub? You look like you need a drink."

I haven't even called Gwen. I'll catch hell if I choose *pub*.

"Is everything all right at home?" Chloe asks me. "Is there a reason I'm the one picking you up?"

"I'm sorry, I shouldn't have asked you to—"

"Keene." She puts her hand on my arm. "I've got your back." Then she waits.

"I didn't want Gwen to see me like this."

"Like what? You did everything right. You said."

"On the side of the road. Waiting for a tow truck that I couldn't even sign my name for."

If the insurance company thinks my hand was partial cause, they could question my right to drive at all. I manage fine with an automatic. I'll get adaptations installed if they want. But they might not believe me. "What happens if I can't drive?" *When did my voice get that squeak in it?*

She doesn't get it. "I'll pick you up tomorrow morning. It can't take more than a couple of days to get your car fixed."

No, no, no. I'm not worried about this week. I'm worried about every week that comes after. What happens if I'm not allowed to drive? What if I *shouldn't* be allowed?

"So, home?" she says. Right, of course. She wants to get on with this. She wants to get home herself. I nod.

I reach back to pull the seatbelt forward and across me. I can't pass it off to my right hand, though, and it slips out of my grasp just short of connection. It slithers back over my chest into its origin. I pull again;

Chloe reaches across me to grab it. Just like that: She extends her arm across my body and grabs for the metal tongue. We tussle and then she gives up, turns away. I'm panting. Once again the strap snaps back into its slot over my shoulder.

"Sorry," she says, not facing me.

I must have deployed The Look. I've never seen it myself, but there have been a few times since I got out of hospital that I've made Gwen cry without saying a word. I think it's a look of horror and disbelief—at least that's what I'm feeling. I'm not a child in a five-point restraint. Hell, even children in five-point restraints can buckle themselves. When Dora was maybe four, she—

"That was insulting of me. I really am sorry," Chloe says.

"You meant only to help. I know." I pull the strap and glide it right into place, no problem. I just needed to get used to the different car. This strap's at a different angle from the one in Gwen's passenger seat. Obviously, it's the opposite side from the one in my driver's seat. "I need to do some things for myself."

I pep-talk myself while she belts herself and sets the indicator flashing. This isn't as bad as it feels. People have minor accidents every day. People with two good hands have them. They're on the road again the next day, or even just drive away. This is nothing thousands of people haven't already gone through just fine.

We join the cars heading for Cambourne. It's a comforting procession. There's been traffic on this route from the Romans onward. We just slip into the queue.

————

I mean "I hate this" as a kind of apology. But Chloe takes it the wrong way.

"You're welcome," she says. It's morning. She's come to get me. She's doing me a favour.

"No, that's not—" I say. *Never mind.* If she doesn't get it already, I can't drag her there. She can't be happy with the situation, either, having to cart me around. She can't be happy that we have to follow up on the Crimestoppers calls together. She's waiting on my seatbelt. "Getting there," I say. When the *click* finally comes, I fall back against the seat, stupidly exhausted, stupidly victorious.

THE START OF EVERYTHING

More rambling interviews go nowhere. At the end of the day, traffic thickens into the home commute hours, and we've gained nothing from our day's work.

"How do you want to do this?" she says, about whether to drop me home or elsewhere.

"My brother said I could borrow his car for a few days. It's an automatic."

She looks sceptical. Insurance should have given me a hire car, but the hire company wants me to take a test to prove I can safely drive without adaptations. My car will be ready before their bureaucracy runs its course.

"I'll be fine," I say, infusing those three words with the absolute requirement that she not give me shit about this. I've been driving for over twenty years. The accident hadn't been my fault.

"I know you can drive, Keene. I just didn't think Richard had a car."

Of course. Why would he when he lived in college as a Life Fellow? But now he's commuting in from a village, living under a thatched roof with his new wife. He's had to learn. He figured an automatic would be easier than training to shift gears at age forty-two. It's about time he lived out of college, where bedders change his sheets, and meals are served at the Fellows' high table. Maybe besides driving, he'd learn how to make up his own bed and to boil an egg.

"He lives in Pampisford now," I tell her. "He figured an automatic would be easier for teaching an old dog new tricks. You can drop me at Magdalene." The University's oldest colleges are named after their royal founders or after Bible figures, like Mary Magdalene. God himself gets five of them: Jesus College, Christ's College, Emmanuel, Trinity, and Corpus Christi, all clustered within the city centre. "Richard's parked it there for me. Alice will pick him up." That's his wife.

"Suits me." She shrugs.

She drops me in front of Magdalene's porters' lodge. I cross the street to the college's parking structure. Richard's car is supposed to be in the open area behind. I don't see it.

So I keep looking. See, this is Richard. He doesn't let anyone down. Did he leave it inside? That wouldn't make any sense. I don't have a card to open the gate. Even so, I lean against the grille and squint. I don't see it in there.

Where the hell is it? I start to sweat despite the chill. *Maybe he parked it on the street?*

But there isn't any parking on Magdalene Street, or Northampton Street. I jog down Queen's Road, just in case. But there's no flash of yellow in the nose-to-tail chain of vehicles lining its whole length. Yes, crayon yellow. He'd bought the car used; he didn't have a choice about the garish colour.

I just keep going, past the most ornate colleges: Trinity and Clare and King's. Grand trees lining the avenue dip their heavy branches towards my shoulders. This is far beyond any semblance of "behind Magdalene," but I don't know what else to do.

He would have phoned me if there had been some inability to find a space where he'd expected. He would have phoned. Chloe could have dropped me home. *Now what?* I lean forward and splay my left hand over my stomach scar.

Don't make me do this. Don't make me beg. I call his number. I count the rings, then it trips into voicemail. I hesitate, then: "Richard, it's Morris. I thought we had arranged . . . Clearly, you've made other plans, I . . . Sorry."

I'll have to call Gwen. Maybe she's already in the car? What time does Dora get out from school on Tuesdays? There might be a practice. Getting all the way here, then back again in the commuter traffic, will take more than an hour. I could get a bus. . . .

I hit redial. Richard's voicemail again.

"I should never have trusted you, should I. You . . ." I ring off before it gets worse. There's a lot I want to say, but there's no point. My physio says that I need to evaluate whether a given action is going to be *helpful,* not just whether it's *justified.* We talk during the exercises, and sometimes she says, "Does that help?" It's hard to know if she means the exercise or whatever I've just been going on about.

No, blaming Richard isn't helpful. But this isn't like when we were teenagers and driving meant getting away from home for an evening. This is my work. This is my first case since I've returned to the job. If I can't handle this, they'll give it to someone who can.

"Without Richard's car, what will you do?" Gwen asks me for the hundredth time, opening and closing drawers on both sides of me. She's going away as a "parent helper" on Dora's choir trip, and thinks I can't manage on my own.

"What are you looking for?" I'm rubbing an electric shaver around on my face because my left hand can't manage a blade.

"Floss. I always forget to use it at home, but if I don't bring it I'll get something stuck in my teeth. What will you do when you're not working?"

"Walk, call a friend, call a cab." A taxi would only be prohibitively expensive for commuting or work. I don't give her my real answer: Stay home. Then she'll worry about *that*. My physio says I have to be careful not to isolate myself.

"Call Richard again. I'm sure it was a misunderstanding."

I agree that I'll call. I don't agree that it was a misunderstanding.

Dora hollers from downstairs, something about shoes and sheet music and being "horrifically late." They drop me off.

Chloe lives with her fiancé, Dan, in a repurposed Victorian almshouse. It's picturesque, even twee, just a lounge and a kitchen and a bedroom upstairs. There are waiting lists for these now-chic little dollhouses. Dan invites me in for coffee.

His vast drafting table takes up one whole end of the lounge; he's an architect, working part of the time from home. The dining table is a fraction of the size, crammed against the opposite wall, built for two only. Chloe takes up precisely half the space of it, clearly experienced at sharing it.

I follow Dan to the kettle. He makes up the cafetiere.

"Here's yours, Coco," Dan says, bringing Chloe a mug.

Chloe shrinks back and raises a hand. "All yours. I'm not having any." Dan gives it to me. "You feeling all right?" he asks her.

"I just don't want coffee," she snaps. Then she concedes, "I don't feel great."

I want to say, *You need a break?* But I can't. Because if she doesn't come, how do I get around?

"It's not a problem," she says. I can see from here that her toast has nothing on it; there's no butter shine or Marmite smudge.

Dan's chopping carrots. There's a slow cooker on the counter, so I'm guessing he's working on dinner. He turns to me to say, "She's tough." He gestures with the knife. I flinch. My left hand catches the counter. Everything fades, just drains of colour and stretches out. . . .

Then snaps back into focus. Dan's back to *chop-chop-chopping*. It's like he didn't notice.

Chloe did. I wave her off. See, waving has its uses. My right hand's still good for something.

———

I paw at my pocket, unable to get hold of the buzzing phone inside it, until my left hand scoops it out and snaps it open against my ear. "Keene," I bark into it. It's not my brother. He hasn't explained himself yet.

Forensics—pardon me: the CSI team—have new evidence. Their title was changed recently, so that real life can more closely conform to American TV. A hammer and bloody shirt have turned up in a brook running along Trumpington Road in Cambridge.

"That's nowhere near our case," Chloe says.

"And the strands of long hair wrapped around the hammer head are dark, not fair. But comparisons have been made with the damage to our skull, and the hammer fits as a possible weapon."

"Maybe we're wrong about our victim's hair," she muses. "Maybe the sweater was only borrowed from a blonde."

Or maybe two separate people with longish hair have been beaten about the head with the claw end of a hammer.

"And the bloody shirt?" Chloe asks. The hammer had been wrapped in it.

"Blue sweatshirt. Small pocket. Nothing distinctive." And no DNA or fingerprints from any of it, thanks to the water. It was as much a dead end as the victim's red sweater.

Traffic congeals in the direction of Cambridge. The smell of exhaust tinges the air.

Chloe swerves. She pulls off to the side and flings the door open to be sick on the roadside.

"What's wrong with you?" I say, but that's not what I mean. I touch her back. Spasms undulate along her spine. When she finishes, she springs back up to sitting and wipes her mouth. She tells me there are tissues in the glove box.

I reach with my right hand. "Shit." I reach with my left hand and pinch the latch. It takes four tries to make the door pop. I hand the packet over and she cleans up her shirt.

"You'd better go home," I say.

"I'm fine." She crumples up the used tissues and stuffs them into the door pocket.

Of course she can't take even half a day off. I can't get the job done alone.

"I'm fine," she repeats.

That's exactly what I say when I fumble my mobile. I say it when I struggle to write left-handed, when I have to be driven instead of drive. My right hand is useless, but I'm "fine." I have regular physiotherapy. My left hand is compensating. I manage. I won't give her less respect than I demand for myself.

"Get back on the road, then," I say.

She stamps down the clutch and seizes the gear shift. The car jerks, then hurtles on towards Cambridge.

CHAPTER 7

MATHILDE OLIVER

Like Corpus, John's is a succession of courtyards. A stone path cuts across the vast lawn of First Court, makes a plus sign in the lawn of Second Court, then outlines the rectangle of Third Court's smaller lawn. On the other side of Third Court is the river.

I pressed both my palms against the stone balustrade of the Kitchen Bridge. One Katja had replied to me. She didn't think she was the person my Stephen wanted but had agreed to meet here. She was late.

Just upstream, the river curved away; just downstream, the river's only enclosed bridge, the Bridge of Sighs, filled my view. Across the water, wide lawns stretched out along the banks, and St. John's post-card building, rightly called "the wedding cake," loomed in a fussy froth of pinnacles. They rise up all over, like the points you make to test the stiffness of egg whites.

It wasn't just the path I needed to mind. Riverside grass isn't pro-tected like courtyard grass; people walk and sit and lie on it, so I had to keep both paths and greens under surveillance. Katja told me she had long blond hair. The dead girl had hair like that. I couldn't shake the sketch from the newspaper out of my mind. I pictured this Katja in a red sweater. That's why I missed her. I didn't think it was her at all. She had to say, "Mathilde? I'm Katja. Are you looking for me?"

I was. But then, over her shoulder, I saw him, cutting across the lawn. He was bigger now. Still skinny, but taller and lumpy now with muscles. It had been six years, six growing-up years. But I think it was Luke.

"Yes, yes, I'm Mathilde," I said. Then, "Do you know Luke Banning?" popped right out of me.

"I thought this was about someone called Stephen."

"Yes." I blinked. *It was, but—*

"My little brother's called Stephen. He's eleven."

"No, that doesn't—"

Luke jogged up the steps into the wedding cake. His figure stuttered in and out of view as he passed behind the row of pointed windows.

"There was a boy in my sixth-form class called Stephen. Does that count?"

"What?" I pulled my head around to face her again.

"A boy called Stephen. Back home in Exeter."

"Is he a writer? Has he written a book?" I willed myself to pay attention.

She honked one loud *ha!* "No, he's dense."

I turned again. Luke had crossed onto the enclosed bridge parallel to ours. I squinted to follow his form behind the arches.

"Look," she said, "I really don't think I know any Stephen who would write to me at Corpus. That doesn't make any sense. . . ."

I sprinted over the bridge and across the lawn and up the stone steps. I swung right, down the Gothic-windowed corridor. It narrowed into the enclosed bridge. I barrelled in and stopped at the crest of its stone hump. But for me, the bridge was empty. Katja gaped at me from the open-air Kitchen Bridge.

I cupped my hands around my mouth and called through the crisscrossed iron bars that cover all the glassless arches: "Katja?"

She waved me off and carried on.

"Katja!" I shouted. I surged over my bridge, too. I spilled out into

Third Court, the one with the unbroken rectangular lawn, and caught her up as she rounded the corner. "Do you know Luke Banning? Or Harrow, Luke Harrow? Was that him?" I panted, open-mouthed.

"Who?"

"The man on the bridge just now. Was that Luke?"

"I don't know him. I didn't see any—"

"He's at John's. You're at John's," I accused her. "He was just on the bridge." I pointed behind me. I stamped my foot.

Her mouth hung open at me.

"What's wrong with you?" I demanded. I rubbed my back up against a stone pillar. I covered my face with my hands. When I pulled them down, she was gone.

I returned to the Kitchen Bridge and, again, pressed my palms on the stone balustrade. The coolness and solidity steadied me.

Punts glided underneath me. One chauffeur pushed his pole against the bottom and told lies about the empty clock faces on the wedding cake's central tower. There's a legend about a race with Trinity College to build the taller clock tower, and only one would be allowed to have an actual clock. It isn't true. Anyone can have a clock in Cambridge. John's could have a clock if it wanted. It has four blank, round faces instead. It chooses to not mark time.

———

I followed the path past the wedding cake and slipped out the back gate onto Queen's Road. I crossed St. John's sports ground, which was empty except for a gardener on a ride-on mower making stripes in the grass. In the middle of the field, a few trees huddled round the path. Two cigarette butts nestled among the roots. The miasma of their smoke still lingered.

The University expands to the west. This part of town is an ongoing construction project. Maths, Physics, and Computing build out here because advances in their subjects require new facilities. Astronomy and the Vet School have always been out here. They chose isolation, so the animals would have room and the astronomers would have darkness. Now new buildings spring up next to horse paddocks, and even Astronomy is building, crowding itself.

I cut through Maths. I crossed the car park and then Madingley

Road. Growling traffic followed me until I reached the turnoff. A cool avenue of trees culminated in the bright red door of the astronomy library.

I ran for the red door. Behind it, I U-turned into a stairwell. You have to turn immediately around to see it; most people don't even know it's there. The stairs wrap around and up. I breathed through my nose so I wouldn't taste dust.

At the top, there's a square half-height door, only a little bigger than an under-the-counter refrigerator. Its keyhole glowed red.

I took the key from the ledge on the wall. I stoppered the red light with it and twisted, hard. The door popped. I squinted and cupped my hand over my eyes. Sun shone hard on another red door; that's what had made the keyhole bright.

The abandoned copper telescope dome over this red door was green with age, and ringed with a delicate filigree. It had been important once, but it wasn't kept locked anymore. I entered and let the door fall shut behind me. I had a torch in my bag. I switched it on.

All was as I'd last left it. There was no telescope in here anymore; it was just an empty shell. There was only an awkward homemade table no one had wanted. Hundreds of wasp carcasses huddled in the corner where I'd swept them. The table was clean. The long beach chair I'd brought from home leaned, folded, against the round wall. I unfurled it and lay down.

I'd been living here since taping up Dad's doors. I didn't like seeing the tape. I brushed my teeth in the ladies' room in the Hoyle Building; I'd done it two mornings already and no one said anything. I had clothes in a plastic bag. There were three more outfits in there before I needed to wash anything.

I'd deal with that then. For now, I closed my eyes.

———

"George!" I whispered. He couldn't hear me. He was too far away.

The ground between us had been raked up by diggers. Plastic fencing ringed the resulting pit. On weekdays, the old buildings vibrated from the machines.

But today was Sunday. A white hard-hat rested on a seat. Caterpillar tracks pressed their zigzag patterns straight down into the mud.

People weren't supposed to be here. Only the academically diligent and the cleaners were supposed to be about, in their own corners.

But I'd stepped out the red door to find more than a hundred strangers milling. They had nothing to do with the University. Children waved foam balls painted to look like planets and posed for pictures with characters from space movies. My father had once taken me to such a "family day." He thought that because I liked science I'd welcome hands-on activities. Families are frightening. Kids shove, and dart, and jabber. Parents push monstrous buggies and swing massive bags from their shoulders. Wind blew the smell of grilling sausages at me. "George!" I hissed. I couldn't see him anymore; a crowd around a roving R2-D2 filled up the space between the two white tents. I needed him. He was the only person in the crowd that I'd recognised.

There had been no reply yet to the note I left at Corpus for Katja. I'd left messages at departments as well, wherever there was a place to pin one. I put one up on the board here at Astronomy. I checked it every day.

I tried to go in when it was uncrowded, avoiding the twice-a-day teatimes and open evenings. Only once had someone stopped me to talk about my father. She'd said she was "so sorry." She'd scooped up my hands and squeezed them. I let my fingers hang there until she let them go. People will do that if you wait it out. That's another trick. Fighting or yelling only attracts more attention. I hold very still. Sometimes I count. I counted now: one plume of cooking smoke, two white plastic Stormtroopers patrolling the crowd . . .

"George!" I called out. He was still in there somewhere. I followed the path between the telescope huts. No scientists use them anymore; kids and amateurs look at Saturn's rings. Dad used to let me lie underneath the big one, in the cushioned bed made for a time when human observation was necessary, before cameras and computers. Once he let me pull the rope that swivelled the big domed roof, to position the opening. I think that was one of the first things I liked after Mum died. It was surprising how lightly that big metal roof turns with just a tug. They were pets to me, those great telescopes. I used to stroke the side of the big Northumberland.

Now children jostled in lines for their turns to look at the machines and pull the ropes. Like it was some sort of zoo.

"Mattie, what are you doing?" George snapped.

I lifted my shoulders up and down. "Nothing."

He pulled me off the path, onto the scraggly grass. "I've been phoning. You never answer. Are you all right?"

"I need you to check something for me. I put a note on the board last week. I need you to see if it's still there. Or see if there's anything for me."

"What kind of note?"

"It isn't any of your business. It's written on lined paper and folded. I wrote it with a pen. I wrote the name 'Katja' on it."

"All right," he agreed. "All right, but I need you to do something for me. I need to get some things from your father's study. I need them. I've been phoning you."

"No, no, no," I said. "The door has tape on it," I explained.

"Tape? Like police tape?"

"Tape. I taped it."

"You taped the door?"

I don't like answering questions. "I taped the door. It's my door now. I need the note."

"We all need things, Mathilde. I'll get you your note, if you untape that door."

"No, no, no," I said. Because it was the second time I said it, I said it louder.

Darth Vader interfered. He walked up and said, "Are you all right?"

George backed off. "She's . . . never mind," he said. Darth Vader stood between us until George got inside the main building.

I waited for a long time, but he didn't come back.

I had to wash my hair.

No one told me I had to, but I knew.

My hamper bag was full, and my small cache of wearable things had dwindled to my nightgown, which is all right to wear over and over again. I squashed the bag of dirty clothes inside the suitcase. I folded the beach chair and leaned it back against the wall.

Normally I would walk the straight line down Madingley Road to

Chesterton Road, but I wanted to see if Luke would be at John's again. I cut through Maths instead.

The Maths complex is symmetrical, six pagodas flanking the main building. *I could work here,* I thought. There are porches with tables and benches and sunlight, but no one was outside. They were hunched at computer screens or in lecture-hall chairs. Or off with clubs or societies, but I wouldn't have to do that. No one would make me. I could just work, if that's what I wanted to do. Skinny open staircases dangle down from bridging walkways and a sloping rooftop lawn, also empty. Up there, up on that lawn, I saw him. I thought I saw him. I had to be sure. I dropped my suitcase. I ran.

I grabbed the thin, wiry bannister and skittered up the stairs, up, all the way up to the roof. I ran so fast I had to breathe through my mouth, like a dog.

There was no one. I whirled around. No one behind me, either.

That was all right, though. That was as it should be. Maths first-years don't use this building. They take lectures in the Arts School.

I walked up the building's prow, between two lawns slanting down from either side of an ascending pavement. I walked up it to the tip, and leaned over the railing.

A man was right underneath me. I felt suddenly warm.

He had brown curly hair. He didn't look quite like he had on the Bridge of Sighs. I'd been foolish to think that had been Luke, anyway. Hundreds of students are at John's. The bars that criss-cross the arches had mitigated my view. This Luke was bigger, hunched a little to hear what some girl next to him had to say.

She had long black hair. It was longer than her T-shirt, and hung in a shiny slick down her back. He stroked it, from her neck to her waist, and left his hand there.

He looked behind himself, and ahead, over her shoulder. He didn't look up. Thinking they were alone, he put his hands on her cheeks and kissed her.

There are moments when the grasshopper clock groans to a pause, then rushes backwards, once around the dial, then hurtles forward around again, catching up, because some minutes are longer than others. This was a long minute.

———

John's playing fields and courtyards blurred as I rushed through. I rounded shops and dodged buses. I slowed only when I was past Jesus Lock. The river changes there.

The river's shallow middle part, snaking through the colleges, is crowded with tourists and students in skinny, flat punts, which are so numerous on the water that they nudge and bump and rub. The upper river, in the south above the Mill Pond, is quiet except for a few kayakers. But this part, my part, in the north beyond Jesus Lock, is deep enough for proper narrowboats.

Narrowboats are long, floating houses, brightly coloured and ostentatiously curtained, and they wear elaborate gardens on their roofs. Most of the country is navigable by narrowboat, because of the system of locks that lifts and lowers them. They moor along both sides of the river here, completely lining the banks. In the early, early mornings, the thin sculls and long oars of college rowers practise between them.

Here, set back from the water but peeping around Queens' College boathouse, was home.

A dead plant blocked our door. It had a florist's envelope tied to it.

I pushed it away with my foot. I stuck my key in the door, but it stuck when I tried to turn it. I tried it the other way; the bolt clicked into place.

I sprang back. The house had been unlocked. But I hadn't left it that way.

I made myself reach and touch the key again. I twisted it to pop the bolt and opened the door. I had to push hard to shove the accumulated mail back against the wall.

The streetlight through the front window lit a tumble of baskets in the living room. Videotapes and old issues of the *Radio Times* spilled out of them in a streak.

On my right, the dining-room furniture was in silhouette. The back garden security light glowed all the way through the back door and kitchen to halo the sideboard, the drawers of which jutted out like a pregnancy. In the kitchen, curtains wafted. Sharp shards glittered on the floor.

A change in air pressure slammed the door behind me. I jumped up, straight up, and bumped my head on the hall light.

I flapped my hands to get feeling back. There was no sound. No traffic outside. No squirrels on the roof. Nothing even ticked; the wall clock hadn't been wound; it lied about it being half-two.

I charged past Dad's office, where the tape dangled and the door gaped. I pounded up the stairs and reared back when I faced the open door of my room. The wardrobe had blurted my clothes all over the rug. My bed stuck out diagonally from against the wall.

I stumbled forward. Dad's door hung back, and his mattress tilted off the bed frame. The file boxes he kept under his bed had been opened and the contents strewn. Some of it, I realised, was already under me. I tried to kick it back into the room but slipped on an old bank statement, waving my arms, until I landed on my bottom. From the heap of his clothes, a striped sleeve reached out to me; ties slithered over the top. Empty upended suitcases looked right back at me.

A *ratatatat* exploded nearby. Fireworks. It wasn't bonfire night, or the May Balls, or anyone's graduation. The neighbours had no right. But there it popped again—a fizzy tattoo. Maybe a college boathouse was celebrating. The noise battered my head. I covered my ears.

———

Water sloshed behind the little window, while the whole machine vibrated with a dull buzz. The first load of clothes made circles. It calmed me down. I washed all of my clothes first, then Dad's. While they swirled in the machine, I cleaned up the kitchen.

I swept the shattered glass and blocked up the broken window. I herded and restacked rolling tins that had been pushed out of their cabinet. I sorted the corkscrew and can opener and grater and wooden spoons back into the cooking drawer, and the forks, knives, and spoons back into their correct slots in the utensil drawer. The rubbish bin hadn't been disturbed by the intruder, but it stank. So I put the bag out.

That was the start. That was the realisation that there was work to be done besides restoring what the break-in had put wrong. I bagged rotting celery and leftover rice and grey meat from the refrigerator. As Dad's shirts and underwear and socks came out of the dryer, I bagged them separately, for the charity shops. I carried my skirts and shirts back upstairs, hanging or folding them, then filled my arms with Dad's shampoo and soap and toothbrush and razor. All of that came with me downstairs into the dustbin bag with the rotten food.

I'd have to sort through the household paperwork later. I refiled it all and slid the boxes back under Dad's bed, which I'd righted and stripped. I boxed up the work papers from Dad's study for George, and reshelved all the books. I sorted the mail. Most of it was for Dad and would never get to him.

That was the first moment I twigged that Katja might be dead.

My shoulders waggled in a shiver. I hadn't yet had the shower I'd come for. I made it as hot as it would go.

It was when I was under the wet rush that the notes of the doorbell pealed. When we first moved here, the doorbell that came with the house upset me. I'd cover my ears and stomp, and not even hear when it stopped. Dad let me pick out a new one. We went to the shop and I pressed the button for each one twice. This one made a sound pattern, down-up-down-up, as if it were tracing the constellation Cassiopeia.

I padded wet footprints while pulling a knot into the belt of my dressing gown. My hair was clean but dripped. I opened the door and pushed my head out into the cool evening.

"Hello?" I ventured. No one was there. There were no new parcels on the step. No coupons through the mail slot.

I retracted my head back into my shell and shut the door. The knocking felt like it came instantly. I hadn't stepped back into the hall yet. It rattled the door.

I turned the bolt to keep it shut. Then I stood on my toes to fix my eye at the peephole.

A man looked back. I reared from the lens.

"Mathilde?" he said, muffled by the door.

He knew who I was, so I squinted, and stretched again to reach the peephole.

It was Luke.

Not the Luke from the Bridge of Sighs, and not the Luke from Maths. This Luke was a little smaller, and with shorter hair and glasses. This was the real Luke, who'd come through this door six years ago with Amy Banning. He was right here. "Mathilde?" he said again. "I'm Luke. I'm Amy's son. I don't know if you remember me. . . ."

I unbolted the door and pulled it towards me. Then his smile fell askew and he looked away.

"Oh!" I said. I pulled my dressing gown together around my neck. "I'm going to get dressed. You can come in."

I padded up the stairs, in the still-wet footprints on the carpet. I put on an outfit that was still somewhat damp from our underpowered tumble dryer. It was a skirt and a blouse, over knickers and a bra. I held my wet hair back with a clip. I listened for him downstairs, but he wasn't doing anything I could hear. The soft spring of the old couch, the couch we'd sat on all those years ago in front of the television, wouldn't travel upstairs.

I put slippers on my feet. "Luke?" I said, to warn him I was coming back.

He was still standing by the door.

I looked back and forth between him and the television. "I thought you'd sit on the couch," I said.

"Oh, I—"

"I didn't mean you have to. I only thought you would." No. Dad and Amy weren't in the kitchen. He was nineteen years old. We weren't watching a rental video. "What do you want?"

"I heard about your father. Mum's come back with me, for the memorial." Of course the others hadn't been Luke. Of course. Students go home for Easter. Stupid of me, *stupid* . . . "I'm so sorry. I should have come sooner, to see him, but—" He swallowed, and leaned his head over his shoulder. "I didn't know for sure if you still lived here," he said. "And university's tougher than I thought, and I—"

"What do you mean?"

"What?"

"How is uni difficult?" I tilted my head up to look right at him. I didn't blink.

"It's just—" He opened and closed his hands. "Work. It's hard."

"Oh." I looked at my thin slippers and he ducked his head to catch my eyes.

"Was that the wrong answer?" He tried out a smile.

"I'm at the Open University. I might apply elsewhere. Maybe."

"John's is good."

I waved my hand in front of my face as if scattering flies. "So many tourists."

"I know. I live in the Cripps Building, though. Not so many round there." Cripps funded a lot of Cambridge architecture in the sixties. It's not what people photograph.

"Are you doing all right, Mathilde? Is there anything you need?"

We were still standing in the hall. I covered my cheeks with my hands. "I'll get us some tea." He followed me into the kitchen.

I'd taken all the rubbish out, but a mound of black bags by the back door looked like I wasn't hygienic. "That's all for the charity shops," I explained.

But he was more concerned about the window. "What happened here?"

"Somebody—but it's all right. They're gone now." I put water in the kettle. I plonked cups onto saucers.

"Somebody what?"

"Somebody broke in to the house." The damp clothes caught up with me, and I shivered. "But I cleaned it up."

"Have you called the police?"

"No!" I said. "Nothing's gone."

"Then why do you think—"

"Maybe they ate something?"

"Mathilde . . ."

"I don't know! But the house being messed with isn't the worst thing that's happened recently, so forgive me if it's not the first thing on my mind!" Tears bubbled over my lashes just as the kettle shrieked.

"Mathilde," he said again.

I fiddled with my collar, bending and unbending it.

"Is there anything I can do?" he pressed.

He was so close that I could feel his voice on my face.

I shook my head. I didn't need anything. Not anything, but: "Would you like to stay the night?" I said.

It just popped out of my mouth. It got out and I couldn't take it back.

"What?" he asked, looking from side to side, even though there was nothing in particular on either side of him.

"No," I explained. "I didn't . . ." I rubbed my cheeks.

"Mathilde . . ." he said. I started undoing my buttons. "Mathilde, no," he said. "Stop!" He pushed my hands down, and I wrestled away from him. My shirt fell open between us.

He looked at me. I was leaning forward, and he was above me, looking down. I put my hand on my breast, covering the white bra cup. My breathing lifted and dropped my chest, over and over.

"I'm sorry," he said. He slammed the front door.

I lifted back the corner of the living-room curtain. He mounted his bike. He pedalled in quick, forceful bursts out of the yellow lamplight.

CHAPTER 8

CHLOE FROHMANN

The CSI team is already at work in the brook where the hammer and shirt were found. Their full white coveralls cover, well, all of them but the face. It's unlikely they'll find anything. The blue unisex sweatshirt had been wrapped around the hammer and the sleeves knotted to make a tight parcel; the person who did that wouldn't just throw something extra in on top. And anything from their person—hair or fabric caught on a branch in the wild tangle on the banks—would be impossible to link, even if it's lasted this long, which itself is remote.

Commuter traffic shuffles along beside us on Trumpington Road. On a sedate parallel street on the other side of the brook, a line of schoolchildren marches towards the Botanic Garden. Teachers try to distract the students from looking at us, but it's impossible. As they pass, they become little owls, heads turned nearly all the way around to keep us in view.

"Why here?" Keene wonders. All those schoolchildren, all those commuters, the tall terraced houses overlooking the brook. It hardly seems a safe place to dispose of something anonymously. But at night it must be a different place.

"Had to be in the dark," I say.

"Yes, but why? Why here? I can think of a hundred secretive places in preference to this. Maybe someone chose here because they couldn't get much farther. Someone without a car?"

That would be almost all the students in Cambridge, a fifth of the city's population. "But you wouldn't want it near you," I insist. "You'd put it where it couldn't be attached to you. You'd walk. You'd ride a bike. Anything to get it far."

"Or you'd put it where you could keep your eye on it."

I look around. *Is someone watching us now?*

We sort through the latest Crimestoppers tips in my car. Too many of the reports don't fit our profile exactly. People are lazy, or desperate. Here's one: Ashley Abington, seventeen, runaway. Had an online-only relationship with a supposedly seventeen-year-old boy in Cambridge. Missing since October. Dark hair.

We visit her parents. They suggest that Ashley could have dyed her hair blond. I assure them that the hairs found with the body were not dyed. The mother crumples in relief.

We don't mention the dark hairs on the hammer.

Twice that week I hear from them, pressing me about their missing daughter. I assure them that Sergeant Spinola is doing everything he can, to remind them that this is his case, not mine. They don't believe me. I start to regret being so free with my card.

————

At home, I rummage through our tools. The weight of our household hammer had sifted it to the bottom. I fish it out and heft it in my hand. This one is wood-handled. The weapon one is metal-handled and heavier.

The spatter pattern on the bloody shirt positioned it as worn by the attacker. The hairs wound around the hammer claw indicate the target was the victim's head. Any traces of who had once grasped the hammer handle were obliterated by its long soak.

A heavy footstep presses on the floorboard behind me. I turn fast, both hands on the hammer grip.

"Whoa." Dan takes a step back.

I apologise. I breathe deeply.

"What's up?" he asks, waiting for permission to come close.

I drop the hammer back into the box and shake out my hands. Once the press is on to something, I'm allowed to tell him. "She was killed by a hammer," I say. Whether the hammer from the brook is the same hammer is up for grabs.

Dan touches my shoulder. "Don't let it in," he says.

I know that. Letting it get to me isn't helpful. If I'm emotional, I can't do my job right. A good job takes a clear head. "Our forensic results have been compromised by the water. Not much to go on. So I'm . . . acting it out," I say. Under what circumstance would a hammer be the weapon of choice? Did the killer bring it, or was it to hand?

My first thought it that you'd have to be angry to swing a hammer like that.

My second thought, based on my reaction when Dan unexpectedly entered the room, is that it might be enough to be afraid.

———

Keene gets the call, as usual. I'm behind the wheel. Funny how the same day has been on repeat for the past week.

"Train station," he reports to me, flicking his mobile shut. "Cambridge city centre. Someone jumped."

"Who's on the scene?" I ask.

"Two transport police are there. Three uniforms." He shakes his head. "And almost two hundred bystanders, from the platform and the train. Names and witness statements are being noted, but it's not practical to hold the whole crowd."

"Was it a man or woman?"

"Woman. Maybe girl. They found her bag. It had a library card. No credit card, no driving licence."

That sounds like a teenager. "Jesus," I mutter.

"I know. She'd been harassing people on the platform. Could have been a push, maybe."

"Maybe." *Probably not.*

I change lanes. Normally I'd hate to be distracted from a bigger case. For a suicide? An accident? But our fen girl remained as anonymous as that winking mannequin in Wisbech, peeking out the sex shop window.

"At least this will be straightforward," I say.

In the back of my mind, the memory of that mannequin face hovers: *wink*.

CHAPTER 9

MATHILDE OLIVER

I pressed the red STOP button. It had been fastened onto the post wrong, reading sideways. I pushed it down hard, covering the error with the pad of my thumb. A distant bell pinged to alert the driver. "I have to leave now," I said. The girl next to me had an iPod, but the man behind me might have wondered. A mother with a pushchair tilted it to make a token space for me to fit through. The baby's hand flailed, cracker crumbs flying from his dirty fist.

I leaned on the button again, then pulled my hand back to my chest. The driver has a mirror. He'd know it was me. We're not supposed to hit it twice. That's why the red letters at the front of the bus light up: S-T-O-P-P-I-N-G. They light up so we know the button's been pressed already.

I breathed in through my nose. My heartbeat slowed with the bus. We'd already passed Corpus, now Pembroke College, and the Fitzwilliam Museum. Something reflective in their new sculpture garden flashed light in my face. I covered my eyes.

I'd had to come by bus, because the box was too heavy to carry any great distance.

I jolted forward when the driver braked. I stood up. A government poster in front of my face advised "Slow down—don't drown on Fenland roads." The picture was of a flooded road, but all I could think of was the sketch of the dead girl from the newspaper.

"Are you all right?" the driver asked, because my box was so heavy it hunched me over. My legs waddled so my knees could hold up the corners. I moved gingerly, one foot down onto one step, then the next.

The box slipped out of my arms onto the pavement, *umph*ing heavily onto its flat bottom. The bus pulled away. I'd taped the top together, so nothing could fly out. But damp could climb up from the ground. I tilted it up with my foot and got my fingers underneath. I heaved it up again, leaning back for balance.

That's when I noticed the police car.

It was one with a flashing light. It was parked on the quiet residential street on the other side of the brook, running parallel to the traffic of Trumpington Road. The houses there were all tall and terraced, rubbing up against one another to the point of shared walls. I felt squeezed just looking at them. George's was one of those.

A little farther down, people in white coverall suits prodded the shallow waterway. They looked puffed and padded and bald. Their hands were purple rubber, and their heads were white hoods pulled tight with elastic. Their mouths were wide paper ovals, big with surprise or horror.

I turned around. I counted. I counted cars, which doesn't work, because they move. So I reduced it to red cars only, which I can keep track of, even when the light turns green. I counted people inside red cars. I counted people with beards in red cars. There was exactly one.

I turned. The white suits were still there. They bent. They had poles and a bucket up on the bank. A uniformed officer watched from the footbridge.

I looked past them. George's was one of those terraced houses behind the brook. I plopped the box back down onto the pavement. I pushed it up against a brick wall. I got a pen out of my bag and wrote "George Hart-Fraser" on it, and the number of his house.

I ran up Trumpington Street, then flattened my back against the college wall. Down the road, the white-suited police were searching the water.

Up the road, another crowd clustered around the grasshopper clock.

———

I don't like answering telephones. I'd been letting the one at home take messages and keep them. The recording is of my father's voice. He says who we are and that we aren't home. It was strange to be sitting right there and hear him say I'm not home.

I still had the number Enid had written on a slip of paper for me. I called when I didn't think he would be home, to tell his machine where I'd left his box.

That evening, the phone in my house rang.

I counted to four. That's how many times the phone is supposed to ring before the machine picks up.

Five.

That wasn't supposed to happen. Six. Seven.

It kept ringing. My fork clattered onto my plate, bouncing up once then landing on my half-eaten pork chop.

I wiped my mouth with kitchen roll. I got up and stood in the hallway.

I watched it ring.

———

"I've been phoning you," George said.

He blocked my way down Senate House Passage. I was on my way to work.

"I don't like phones," I said.

"I got the box."

I nodded. I'd filled it with Dad's work. George could use it.

"Where is it?"

"You got the box," I parroted. How could he ask me where it is if he's just said he got it?

He got close to me and hissed right down at the top of my head. "The watch, Mathilde. Your father promised it to me. We had an understanding."

My eyes were right in front of his neck. He swallowed.

"All right," I said, to make him go away. "I have to go to work now."

He didn't move. He swallowed again. "You'll bring it tomorrow?"

"Yes!" I said. I hunched my shoulders up around my ears.

He stepped aside, pivoting on one foot like he was a door swinging open. I pushed through, my feet churning on the slick, round cobbles.

———

I opened up the charity-shop bags. They were still heaped by the back door.

I looked inside every pocket and every sock. Dad's watch wasn't there.

I looked upstairs. None of the empty drawers had a watch in it. It hadn't been filed with any papers. It wasn't under his mattress.

I sat on the braided rug with my back up against Dad's bed frame. I rested my forehead in my hand.

Dad's watch. It had a leather band. The little hairs on his wrist had curled up around its edges. He always wore it.

I whipped my head up so fast that I cricked my neck. I galloped down the steps.

My bag was on the chair in the lounge, where I always dropped it when I came in. Some things stay the same. I always drop my bag there. My bag always has my wallet and my notebook in it. I carry pens. Every day I add an apple. It's not often that I take something away.

The hospital had sent me a small padded envelope they called Dad's "effects." It had surprised me that you could fit the effect of a person into an envelope. But I knew what they meant, really. It contained his things.

I scrounged it up from the bottom of my bag. I'd willed myself to forget it was there.

I uncurled the top of it, and spilled the contents onto the coffee table: his wallet, his wedding ring, and his watch.

I put the watch back into my purse, for George. He could have it. I didn't care.

I picked up the wedding band and looked through it. The only time Dad had taken it off was when he dated Amy Banning. Then, after the video evening with Luke, he'd put it back on again.

———

The next morning was Friday, the day of Dad's memorial.

I was supposed to wear black. I had a black dress. I had black tights. I had only brown shoes. I didn't know if that was allowed.

I put everything on and rubbed the shoes with black shoe polish. That only made them look dirty.

I scrubbed my hands under a rushing tap, wrapping them around the white soap bar over and over. I added a cardigan, because it had suddenly gone cold out. The sweater was so dark a blue that it was almost black. I'd done my best.

I went to work. The service would start at half-three at Great St. Mary's church across the road. Enid wore a black blouse and said she'd worn it specially. Lucy and Trevor also said they would come, but they didn't have black on.

There was another letter from Stephen.

Katja—

I apologise for my previous letter. I was distraught. It was only a calf, after all. I retract my desperation.

Alistair has lodgers coming, so I'm moving on. I've a signing in London for the new paperback. I'm able to divert to Cambridge on the way from there. On Friday 19th I'll be catching the train from King's Cross to get into Cambridge at quarter to four.

Please meet me. Wouldn't it be good to say hello? I won't try to steal you away from your work, or from whomever you're close with now. I only want to see you again. Don't you want to see me?

It can be whatever you like. But please come.

Wear my red sweater. I like that you kept it.

Stephen

I accidentally jostled Trevor's coffee. "Sorry!" I said. "Oh, sorry!"

"It's all right," he assured me. He dabbed at a splash with a tissue from the box on the windowsill. "Are *you* all right?"

Trevor looked hard at me. I folded the letter in half. It wasn't his job to read them. It was mine.

I bounced my chin on my neck to tell him *yes*.

He turned back to his work. I unfolded the letter. I read it again. Today was Friday.

And the red sweater. I knew, right then I knew.

"We should go now," Lucy said, standing straight in front of me. She knows I don't like when people talk at me from the side. Everyone was being nice today.

"You go ahead," I said.

I think she was going to say more, but Enid pulled her away. The three of them left.

I waited until they would be well ahead, then put my jacket on. It was black, too, by chance. My bag wasn't. It stood out against me. It had the watch in it, for George. He was welcome to it. I don't wear a watch.

Great St. Mary's church is near, just at the end of Senate House Passage. People milled in front of it. I hung back in the passage. My breath puffed in front of me, made visible by the unexpected spring chill.

I thought of the inside of the church, packed in with people my dad had known. A lady in a green skirt was handing some paper out as more entered. I pushed my eyebrows together. She shouldn't have worn green. *I* didn't.

I counted the people I knew. Not the green-skirt lady, or the two men in college gowns. *One, Dr. Ogilvie in a black suit. Two, three, the sisters who cleaned for us, in elaborate hats.* Not the clutch of students wearing jeans; I didn't recognise them. *Four, George.* I was supposed to give him the watch.

Five, Amy Banning, in a dress. Six, Luke.

Luke. I batted my fists against my cheeks. Not the four men entering together; I didn't know them. Not the student sailing past on a bicycle. I looked and looked for someone else, someone to count after Luke.

He and his mother stopped to talk to the green-skirted lady. He looked uncomfortable in his suit, hands in pockets. He leaned and looked around, in every direction from which someone might come: down both sides of the church towards the market, down King's Parade, down Trinity Lane. I curled myself up around the corner when he looked down here.

Seven. Dad's ashes were inside the church.

I turned and ran back down Senate House Passage. I stopped at the bottom, panting. If people were sitting in the pews already, then Stephen's train was coming. It was inexorable.

I ran up Trinity Lane. I ran to Bridge Street and then down, down, down its straight line, through all its changing names: Sidney Street, Regent Street, Hills Road. I knew I could make it in time. I stopped only for crossings, rocking from foot to foot while I waited for each green man to appear.

The Cambridge train station is situated far down Hills Road, built there so it won't tempt students to London. The front of it is blocked by bus stops and a taxi stand. My view was further obscured by a sudden flurry. Snow blew into my face, like the sudden fizz from a shaken Coke bottle.

The waiting-room floor had already gone slippery from footprint slush. Some people curled around their mobiles, calling for lifts, making an obstacle course for the hurriers pushing through to secure their places in the taxi queue and inevitable traffic snarl. Shoes slid and churned against the wet. I hung back.

The three-forty-five train lumbered in. I advanced, turning my shoulders this way and that, to slide myself into the spaces between other bodies.

The train had six cars, each with doors at both ends. I imagined Stephen to have blond hair but knew there was no basis for this. I looked for young men, and there were dozens, new dozens every moment.

"Stephen?" I asked. I touched arms and pulled men around to make them hear me. "Stephen?" I asked. Not him, nor him. Some of them had got through the station doors already. I ran down the length of the train. My elbows knocked against newspapers folded in the hands of tall men, and the head of a child. I grabbed a man's arm to steady myself, near skating on the wet concrete floor. Not one of them was Stephen. "Stephen?" I said to everyone. I had to tell him why Katja wasn't there. I had to explain. I couldn't let him misunderstand. I couldn't let him think she'd meant something by not coming, when she hadn't even known. When she hadn't been able to know. I was sure that Katja was the dead woman in the water, in the red sweater. I had to tell him.

Near the end of the roofed platform, I couldn't tell who'd come out of the train and who was waiting for the next one. There were women and a boy and three older men. One big man was there. I knew him, of course, but I didn't say his name. I said, because it's what I'd been saying, "Stephen? Are you Stephen?"

His hand jutted out, flat and perpendicular to the ground, as if he were saying "stop." It punched between my breasts, shoving me out into the now-thick snowfall. Cold bit at all my bare parts, my back burst into pain, then my body flopped and dragged over gravel and metal bumps. The world inverted: Snow sprayed upward, pricking me hot rather than cold, raging little stars in fountains on either side. "Sparks," I tried to say out loud. I recognised at last that the hot ones were sparks.

CHAPTER 10

CHLOE FROHMANN

Two dozen commuters had been held for us in the waiting room, because they had something to say. The rest had given their contact information and been let go. There's no place to sit in the room, just floor space for a winding ticket queue, and the witnesses are clearly irritated at the time they've been kept standing for us. We both step forward. They all look to Keene.

"She was asking for someone called Stephen," a teen in school uniform volunteers, his mother gripping his shoulders protectively from behind. "She pestered everyone who came off the train." Agreement echoes in the small space. Mathilde Oliver—that was the name on the library card—had been looking for a Stephen, haphazardly. She'd accosted men of different heights and builds and colouring, all coming off that train. So she'd known his expected movements, but not what he looked like.

"Any of you called Stephen?" Keene asks. All shake their heads.

Sergeant Robinson, in the bright yellow vest of the transport police, steps in. "There were two Stephens on the bystander list. One waiting for a train, the other from off a train." The officer coughs apologetically. "We didn't know that was important when we let them go."

"Right," Keene says. "Anyone here see it happen?"

A woman in a vivid purple blouse and thick gold jewellery raises her hand. "I was next to her." She shudders. "I heard it. I had my back to her. Thank God."

"Anyone else?" Three other people shuffle forward. A man in a business suit, and an older couple dressed for an evening out. They'd been near but paid attention only after she was falling.

"Had she been bumped into? Was it an accident?" Keene asks.

They all deny that they'd had physical contact with her, and they hadn't noticed if anyone else had.

I'm making notes on the list of names Robinson gave us. Keene keeps prodding them with questions. "Who else was nearby? Is this everyone?"

"I remember a man in a suit pushed past me, away from the tracks, when I turned at the sound of the screams," says the purple-blouse lady.

Keene raises his eyebrows at the only man in the group in a suit. "I didn't push anyone!" he insists.

"It's not an accusation, sir. We're just trying to ascertain who was nearby."

"I already said I was nearby!"

"Right. I've got that. What did you do when she fell? Did you push past . . ." I hold the list up to him and point. "Did you push past Ms. Delphy, Mr. Birnbaum?"

"I didn't push past anyone. I froze," he admits.

"All right. Ms. Delphy, do you see the man who pushed past you here?"

She looks around. "No," she said. "Or maybe I do, but all I saw was a suit. A white man in a dark suit. Dark hair." She points at Mr. Birnbaum. "He's the only one in a suit here now. Except for you, of course," she clarifies.

Robinson leans in. "There were lots of men in suits, Inspector. Dozens. At the time, it didn't seem necessary . . ."

"Yes, I know," Keene says. It wasn't feasible to keep two hundred cranky commuters detained and organised in this small station. Even if we'd wanted to, they had started leaking out the exits as soon as the screams faded.

Robinson adds, "We have everyone's name and address, sir. At least, everyone who stayed about. There was a certain amount of confusion." I stifle a laugh. That was an understatement to describe a train station at four on a Friday afternoon. "We've got two camera phones. People took pictures."

Of course people took pictures. And there was the station's CCTV. We'll see who was wearing a dark suit. Keene confabs with Robinson. I leave them to it and step out onto the platform.

The train is still on the track. No more will come through this evening; commuters are being diverted onto buses. The driver sits on a bench on the platform, still stunned.

"I braked, but she . . . There was little chance," he says.

"Of course. No one holds you responsible." I sit next to him. "Was anyone close to her on the platform?"

"A dozen people! That time of day, the station is swarming. . . ."

"Could someone have pushed her?" I ask.

He shrugs. "I wasn't looking at her until she came at me. How she got to be that way, I couldn't say."

I catch the eye of the officer who's been discreetly looking after him. "His wife's on her way," she says, so I move on.

Keene joins me on the platform edge. We go up to the blue-and-white tape but don't slip under. The CSI unit is doing their hopeless best with footprints in the slush near the lip of the platform. "Was the snow before or after?" I ask.

"Concurrent," one of the team answers. *All right, maybe she slipped. Maybe this was an accident.*

"Is she still down there?" I stretch my neck. The tracks are several feet below the level of the platform.

"Not much point getting her to the hospital in a hurry." Keene skirts the taped-off area and leans around.

Jensen, the pathologist, is down on the tracks. "She died from being hit by a train," he deadpans.

"Did she have a ticket in her pocket?" I ask.

"I can tell you that later." He hasn't even rolled her over yet.

"Any thoughts on pushed, jumped, fell?"

He shakes his head. "There's not much in the aftermath to distinguish one way of having got here from another."

"Anything inconsistent?" Meaning: *Any damage that doesn't look train-related?*

"Not from here. I'll call you if I find anything."

A young woman from the CSI team brings me the articles that had been strewn from, presumably, the victim's bag. No train ticket, but a notebook and a letter. The letter is to a Katja, from a *Stephen*.

Keene leans over my shoulder and reaches. "Gloves," I chide, having already pulled a pair on myself. He stuffs his hands in his pockets. I wait for them to come out again, but they don't. It comes to me: *Can he even pull latex gloves on anymore?* I angle the letter so we can both read it.

"It's not to Mathilde," I point out. "It's made out to someone called Katja. And the notebook has drafts of other Katja/Stephen letters, or transcriptions."

"Interesting," he says. "Could the library card be wrong? Could she be called Katja?"

Robinson inserts himself. "I don't think so, sir. A tag was sticking up out of her collar. It had 'M. Oliver' on it."

"Christ, Robinson, how close did you get?" The disgust in Keene's voice is new. *Since when did he become so squeamish?*

"I had to be sure she didn't require assistance, sir," Robinson says delicately, as if appalled that anyone would wonder.

A shudder brings Keene back to himself. "Is there an address?"

"Not much of one," I answer. "Just 'Corpus Christi College, Cambridge.'"

"How did Mathilde Oliver have this letter? Was she at Corpus, too?"

Robinson is on top of things. "Her father was at Corpus. It was his memorial today."

"As in dead?" I ask.

He nods. Suicide was a vivid possibility, then. Grief.

Keene is satisfied. "All right. Likely there was no wrongdoing, but we'll let CSI and Jensen comment before we let it go. In the meantime,

I'll check with the college. Chloe, you view the station's CCTV footage."

"Wait," I say, skimming the words one more time. "Stephen's written to Katja several times. He complains of no reply. And he writes that she has his red sweater."

"The sweater's been in the news. If Mathilde made the same guess we are . . ." Keene rubs his jaw, working out the coincidence.

If Mathilde made the same guess . . . If she looked for her, and perhaps came close to finding her . . . then the crimes could be related. Maybe Mathilde Oliver didn't slip in the snow or end it all in grief.

CHAPTER 11

MORRIS KEENE

I push the car door shut behind me. Chloe has dropped me at the Market Square; she's off to view CCTV footage in the basement of the Guildhall. I jog around to Bene't Street, the corner of which is lit pink by the new clock. I stop in its glow, under the robot grasshopper, to phone Richard again, but again there's no answer. I swear, and resist the impulse to hurl my mobile against the pavement. Nothing to do but keep walking.

The Corpus porters' lodge is just around the corner. I knock, push open the door, and lean over the counter.

"What can I do for you?" asks a man in a neat black suit. The porters' names are displayed on the wall beneath photos, and *Louis* is his.

"Good evening, Louis." I have my warrant card ready, in my inside jacket pocket. I pull it out left-handed, with a gesture I'm gratified to notice is becoming more natural, and introduce myself and my rank. His chin tilts up.

"I'm looking for someone called Katja," I explain.

"We don't have any Katjas at present," he tells me, "but we have a great many people looking for one."

"Really?" Now, that's interesting.

"A young man this evening insisted his friend Katja is a student here. He tried to describe her to me, but I hope you understand that telling me she's pretty and twenty and dark-haired isn't going to get us anywhere." I ask him to describe the young man, and "blond ponytail" is the sum of him. He goes on: "And Mathilde Oliver has been after Katja as well. She's not a student; her father was a Fellow here."

"Mathilde Oliver?" I repeat, trying to keep my voice bland. Louis takes me over to a bulletin board where "Katja" is written neatly on a folded note. He unpins it and hands it to me. It's a request to be contacted, nothing more.

"Do you know what she wanted to say?"

"No. No, I told her there's no one working or studying here by that name. But she was quite determined. I hated to disappoint her. It's terrible what she's been through."

"Her father?" I prompt, remembering what Robinson had said of his recent death. I never used to trust myself without reference to my notes, but since I've been unable to write things down I risk on my memory more. It gives me an almost giddy feeling, worrying and exhilarating at the same time. I throw out another question: "And what about her mother?" I ready myself to catch the answer and keep it, using only my head.

"Her mother died years ago. Her father's memorial service was this afternoon. She's quite alone in the world. Is—is she all right?" he asks, with a surge of realisation. "I thought this was about someone called Katja?" He looks me full in the face. I lie right at him that we're only gathering information, and that I'd love to ask Mathilde about Katja.

"I haven't seen her today. I'd hoped she would have attended the memorial, but . . . I suppose I didn't really expect her to."

"When and where was this?"

"The service started at half-three at Great St. Mary's."

She was hit at 3:50, in the middle of the service. But I had to be thorough—the pews of that memorial would have been full of dark suits. "Would you do something for me, Louis? Would you write down for me who was there?"

That is my new tactic. Sometimes it's not appropriate, but it's funny how differently people think when writing instead of dictating. They guess less, I've noticed, and sometimes reveal something interesting in the way they organise the information or circle a name. "Would there have been a Katja there?" I add. "Or a Stephen?"

The door slams open so hard it whacks into the counter and bounces back onto the hand of an anxious young man. "It's her. I found her. I told you she was here," he announces. His hair is wild and his jacket askew.

Louis leans across and whispers, "Perhaps you should give him a badge and a hat. Apparently he's found Katja for you."

The young man walks us around the corner and prods his finger against glass. "There," he says triumphantly, pointing at a portrait taken of Corpus College's May Ball last year. In it, the students who made it all the way through to breakfast are propping one another up, tipsy, haggard, and grinning. Ties are loose, high heels discarded, bright dresses garish in the morning light. I remember once being so young that I could pull off that kind of night and still smile.

It's the window of a photography studio displaying graduation portraits, team photos, and the like. His finger touches a tiny image of a dark-haired woman in a shiny dress. Our dead girl, as far as we know, had been fair-haired. At least, the hairs on her sweater were fair.

Louis pulls glasses out of his pocket and peers. "You're mistaken, young man," he chides as he straightens up. "Her name isn't Katja. That's Grace Rhys."

"No," the young man protests.

Sometimes women lie about names to get rid of a man, but he doesn't seem angry or insulted. He wags his head gently, baffled by Louis's pronouncement but certain of his own. "That's Katja."

"Katja who?" I ask.

He shoots me a sideways look. This changes something in him.

"We can solve this," I say. "Louis, is Grace in college right now?"

"She's not with us any longer."

That phrase chills me. I immediately jump to assuming he means death.

"She graduated?"

Oh, dear, the boy is like a puppy, so eager and hopeful.

"She degraded," the porter admits. Her decomposing remains come to mind. I shake my head. "Degraded" is an academic term. It means she temporarily dropped out. "Maths is a difficult subject," the porter adds kindly. "It was a difficult term for her."

"When did she leave?" I ask.

"This past November."

A difficult term. That could mean a lot of things. Academically difficult? Socially difficult? Family problems?

Louis answers without my having to ask: "She's a young person, and did what young persons do. Some handle it better than others. I often noticed her head out for the evening. She was rarely back before we locked up."

That's not that late, honestly. Eleven, perhaps? "Do you know that she always did come back? Did she have a boyfriend? Or girlfriend?"

"I wouldn't care to speculate. She had friends."

We're back at the college gate.

The young man's face lights with realisation. "If she wasn't here, she never got my letters, did she? She couldn't have done, could she?"

Well, that's a kind of lemonade, I suppose. "How is it that you got her name wrong, do you think?" That's a whopper. *If it was a one-night stand, did he call her that in bed?*

But he ignores me. He's happy again. He's come chasing a woman who apparently ignored him, and it turns out he actually hadn't yet entered the game.

We follow Louis back into the porters' lodge. "Can I have her address?" he pounces as soon as Louis is behind the counter again. "No, no, of course you wouldn't. But would you send her *my* address? You can do that, can't you?"

"Slow down," I interrupt.

He comes to a complete halt and finally notices that I'm not with the college. "Who are you, anyway?" We make a mirror, he and I, both in our dark suits and suspicious expressions. Well, he's wearing a dark blazer over jeans. Not quite a suit, but it's close enough to mistake in a crowd.

Louis commands with a glance before he even speaks. "That's the police, young man, so you'd best do whatever he says."

"Police? Is she all right?"

"Do you mean Katja?" I ask. "Or Grace?"

He presses his lips together. "I knew her as Katja," he insists sourly. "She had a holiday job over Christmas, up near Peterborough."

Peterborough. That's the closest city to where we found the body.

"And what's your name, sir?" I have a feeling I already know.

"Stephen Casey," he says.

Stephen. Of course.

———

I consider recording the conversation, but I'd have to ask permission and that might put him off. "Mr. Casey. Tell me about this woman. Tell me about Katja." *Tell me about Grace.* Louis allows us to use the Head Porter's office. I take the steady straight-legged chair, leaving Stephen to wobble and roll in the one with wheels and a loose reclining back.

"She's . . ." Stephen swallows. "She worked as a nanny, for the Christmas holiday. My window overlooked the climbing frame in the garden. It was more interesting to watch her play with the children than to struggle through the chapter I was trying to write. Look—I just want to say hello to her. I'm not stalking her, if that's what you're thinking."

"Why would I think that?" This feels good. This is the right thing to say.

His voice tightens up. "Because that's your job? To be suspicious? Right?"

"I'm not suspicious. I'm curious. Do you think there's a difference between the two, Mr. Casey?"

He's untwisted a paper clip into a long, straight wire. He taps it, puncturing the desk blotter. "You know there is."

"It would seem you wrote to her a number of times."

"How do you know that?" he asks, forgetting he's already admitted writing to her.

"It's my job," I quip. I smile.

The door hinges scream. Louis pops his head in. "I have the list," he announces, referring back to the list of memorial attendees I'd asked him to write. His long arm hands it through to me. At the same time, my phone sounds. My momentum with Stephen is already interrupted, so I tell him to stay put. I take the call outside, under the college gate.

It's Chloe. "I've got him," I announce. But she's already talking.

"The footage was near useless," Chloe says. "Can't tell whether she jumped or was pushed or fell. You can see a man in a dark suit jacket, like the witness said, but not his face. It was just too crowded." I try to barge in with my own report, but she doesn't pause. "I'm following up on the Stephens now, the ones who were on the platform and gave their names. One of them's at home and the other one's at a pub on King Street. He was a bear to track down, but—"

"No," I say. Sweat bubbles up on my forehead.

"What?"

I hear laughter and cars around her. She's probably on King Street already. "No," I repeat. "Stephen's *here.*"

"What?"

"He's at Corpus. Come to Corpus. Please."

"You should have called me," she says icily.

"I'm perfectly capable of conducting an interview on my own." I sound like a teenager.

"Of course you can, but perhaps you'd spare me wasting my time following up with people we don't need to." A driver on her end leans on his horn.

I bite back a sarcastic retort. She's right.

She rings off.

I phone Richard again, out of habit. Ringing, ringing. After four more I'll be offered the chance to leave a message. I know the routine off by heart.

I squeeze the phone between my ear and shoulder while I glance over the porter's list. And there he is: *"Dr. Richard Keene, eulogy"* on the list, and, suddenly, at last, answering his mobile.

"Where were you?" I demand. I'd practised my indignation all day. "I showed up at Magdalene as we'd agreed, and the car wasn't there."

"I know. I'm so sorry—"

"I've been phoning you ever since."

"My mobile's been off."

"I know your bloody phone was off. I figured that out. Did you think, when I asked you for the car, that I was asking on a whim? Because this isn't a whim. This is my work. This is—" I almost say "my life." I catch myself. "This is *important*."

"It is important. I know. I know." He and Chloe keep saying that they *know*.

I remember the list. "Did you deliver a eulogy today?"

"What? Yes. Why?"

So he hasn't heard. I don't tell him. "Was there anything unusual about Dr. Oliver's death?" I ask, pacing.

"Not that I know of."

"What do you know about his daughter?"

Someone says something in the background, on his end. He says, "It's Morris." She, presumably his wife, Alice, says something unintelligible.

He gets back to me. "Mathilde. She didn't come today. I hoped she would, but she didn't."

"Did you know her?"

"Not well." There's another muted exchange in the background.

"And her mother's dead?" I confirm.

"What?" he asks, having been listening to Alice, not me.

"Is Mathilde's mother alive?"

"No, no. Mathilde was very young when she died."

Suicide is seeming more and more likely. It was only the urgency of her hunt for Stephen that made it strange. And why did she have that letter at all?

He at last loses his patience with me. "Why are you asking me all these things?"

"I'm asking everyone. She's dead."

There isn't even breath on his end. Nothing—except a door slamming in the background.

"How?" he asks, and then, "I have to go."

"You promised me the car."

There's a long pause. Then, "I'll ring you back."

The dial tone is a shock. He's not the sort of person who does that.

I need to know more about the letters. I step back into the porters' lodge, but Louis has transformed. He's a younger man with a massive barrel chest and a cheerful smile. "Good evening, sir," he greets me.

"Where's Louis?"

"Just gone off duty. Can I help?"

I shake my head and blink. How had he done that when I was on the phone right outside the lodge door?

I reach for the door to the Head Porter's office. The new porter rounds the counter to stop me, but I'd reached with the wrong hand, anyway. It might as well have been a paw.

"I'm a DCI with the Cambridgeshire police," I explain, reaching again for my warrant card, which, somehow, is no longer in my jacket pocket. I have the correct hand going for it but can't find it anywhere. I pat myself until I finally find it in my trouser pocket. I hold it out in front of me, almost into Louis's—yes, it was Louis's—face.

"DCI Keene," he says pleasantly, while wrapping a yellow scarf around his neck.

"Yes," I say. I blink. "I was just speaking with your colleague." The other porter pops up from whatever he's doing underneath the counter. Stacking parcels, fixing a chair leg?

"It's the end of my shift. I was just getting my coat." Louis's eyes flick towards the back of the room, and a tall coat stand in the corner. That's where he was, donning his coat. Nothing's off except for me.

"Right," I say. "Right. Louis? You said Mathilde Oliver's not a student?"

"Oh, no, no." The porters share a look. "She works at the Registrar's office," Louis says. "Part time." He explains, in brief, her role with insufficient addresses. The Katja letter would almost certainly have been one of those. "And," he adds, halfway out the door, "did you notice the name I starred? George Hart-Fraser?"

The page had gone into my pocket with the phone. I pull it out again and shake it open. There, in the middle: *George Hart-Fraser**

"George worked closely with Dr. Oliver, Mathilde's father. And he was Grace Rhys's supervisor. He would be a good person to talk to, if you want to know anything more about her time here." His office and home addresses were written in neat block letters beside the name. Knew them both? That's certainly of interest. And his address: Brook-

side, one of the quiet streets parallel to the traffic of Trumpington
Road. That's where the hammer and shirt had been found. . . . "He was
late," the porter sniffs.

Dead? No. Not that kind of late. I had to get it together.

"He was late to the memorial. It was incredibly rude."

And he would have been wearing a dark suit. There's going to be
very little we can do to prove that Mathilde's death was murder, but if
it had been done because she'd got too close to the identity of the body
in the fens, we could at least catch the man for that one.

I thank him, but it's suddenly Chloe in the doorway, not Louis anymore. I flinch. Somehow I'm failing to follow transitions. My life has
become a homemade animation, where the picture changes drastically,
just once every second, instead of a hundred incremental times. "Where
is he?" she wants to know. She means Stephen.

I look towards the Head Porter's office. The door is shut, as I'd left
it. The new porter—I check his name on the photo board; he's
Jonathan—says, "Louis tells me you have a guest with us." He reaches
out and turns the knob. The door falls open.

I blow out my pent-up breath. Stephen is still there, still in the rolling chair, now hunched over the desk, reading an open newspaper.
He's shaking.

"Stephen?" I prompt him. His head swivels round on his neck. The
look in his eyes keeps me back.

"I lent her my red sweater. Blue-striped cuffs. I'd bought it at an
Oxfam in Leeds," he says. "It had been 'lovingly knitted by June
Marks.' I always thought her son or nephew must have been a shit for
discarding it. Jesus Christ."

He looks like he's going to be sick. Chloe and I pull him up to standing, and guide him outside to her car, to take him to Parkside station
for questioning.

PART II

CHAPTER 12

GRACE RHYS

There were a lot of locks.

The huge wooden doors at the college gate always shut at seven p.m., leaving a normal-sized cutout door within one of them for use until eleven. Then that's locked. That's what the college A20 key is for, and also for the post room and laundry room, and the door out the back of college onto Free School Lane. Then there was my room key, a key for my cupboard in the kitchen, and my uni card for getting into the new library. I had a key for my bike lock, which is one of those heavy D-shaped ones that can't be cut. I had a key to our house at home in Milton Keynes, but, with Mum and Shep on a long-deferred honeymoon, that was rented out. Altogether my keys made a sharp, jangling lump in the corner of my bag. I could hear them.

I just couldn't get my fingers round them.

I slumped onto a sliver of stone step in front of the college doors; November cold chilled my bum. I dumped out my bag—lipsticks, phone, wallet—into the hammock my skirt made across my lap. I don't usually wear a skirt, but it was an evening out. I'd made an effort.

A capless pen, four pound coins, a cluster of safety pins. Then the flimsier stuff: a folded photocopy of lecture notes, a hair slide, an emery board. Business cards from two men in the pub who'd bought us drinks. They'd given them round before we split up at the end, like passing out sweets. I don't think they minded which of us might call which of them, but it's not like any of us were going to. I scraped around the crumbs and scraps at the bottom; nothing. But I could still hear the metallic rattle of the keys.

At last my finger caught a rent in the cloth lining. The keys must have worked their way through there and got stuck between the cotton and the leather. I had to tear the hole worse to get them out, fingering it till it widened and pulling the sharp cluster through. *Victory!* I leaned back against the door, just for a minute. *Don't sleep.* I hadn't drunk that much. One pint and some wine. I just hadn't been getting enough rest.

The CCTV camera hummed, swivelling to change its view. That's the same camera as outside my room window. It's been set to never look in; it aims at the Corpus College gate, the pavement alongside King's College, and down towards Silver Street. Not ever into my room. It even looks down if it just has to sweep across from one target to another. It looked down and swept across me now.

I got up. The bolt made that hard *click,* and I eased open the cutout door in the main gate. My second foot caught on the lip and I landed hard on the first. Balance, hop, slippery stone. I got my feet together and swayed just a little.

No one noticed. That was the normal way of things.

I don't know why people don't see me. I don't eavesdrop on purpose, but people talk in front of me. Katja thinks I like listening in because I didn't watch enough television when I was a child. She's wrong; I like listening because it's easier than talking myself.

The courtyard spread out in front of me, all grass lawn and stone walls. I was lucky, right? I was a Cambridge girl. I was through the door. I was in.

CHAPTER 13

CHLOE FROHMANN

I don't remember feeling this way before Keene's injury. Was he less pushy then? Or was I content to be his sidekick? Maybe it's the promotion gone to my head, but I lean right past him and start in: "What makes you think Grace Rhys is the Katja you knew?"

Stephen sulks. He tugs on the ends of his hair. He doesn't like being in the police station. "I recognised her."

We have Grace's family's contact information from Louis the porter, but the phone at her family's home has rung unanswered. We'll be able to track down more about her in the morning. For now, Stephen is all we have.

We collect a sample of his hair to compare with the hairs found on the sweater. His hair is long for a man, and fair, which is consistent with the sweater being his. He confirms that her hair had been dark and shoulder-length, which is consistent with the hair on the hammer from Brookside. No chance of DNA from our waterlogged evidence and body, so "consistent with" is the best we can do. "Consistent with" is a dressed-up way of saying "maybe."

"I—I've been trying to get in touch with her. For a few months now. We met over Christmas. She was nannying, and I was borrowing my uncle's flat. Look, can I have something to drink? Nothing fizzy. I have a sensitive stomach. Just—is there water? Do you have any water?"

"Sure," Keene says. He nods at me to go get a plastic cup of water.

"Sink's broken," I say. I ignore Keene's incredulous glare.

Stephen blows air hard out of his mouth, like he's trying not to hyperventilate. "I really cared about her, right? I really knew her, and now she's dead."

"I'm guessing she deserved it," I say.

"What the fuck?" Stephen explodes. "What do you know? No one deserves what happened to that poor girl. No one. What the fuck?" he finishes, leaning back in the chair and crossing his arms over his chest.

"It must have been an accident, then," says Keene gently.

"I don't know."

"You just tell us what happened, and we'll figure it out together," Keene promises.

Stephen shakes his head. "I didn't do anything. She was fine last time I saw her. She was happy," he insists.

"Then what makes you think she's the person we're looking for?" I ask. "There are lots of red sweaters in the world. Lots of young women who wear them. Is it just that she didn't give you her real name and number? A woman doesn't chase you, and you think it must be because she's dead? Is that a relief, better than rejection?"

"I wanted more than anything to see her again!"

"Yes, your letters make that quite clear. Do you make a habit of stalking women who don't reply to you? We can check on that, you know."

"I've never stalked anyone," he insists. "Letters aren't stalking."

Keene interrupts, all good-cop: "Why were you trying to meet up with her?"

"We were friends. Maybe more than friends. I don't know."

I can't let that by. "What do you mean you don't know? Did she say no? Did she fight back?"

"Jesus fucking Christ," Stephen says. "No! No. We met, and then I had to go to Cornwall. I wrote her letters and she didn't answer. I figured she had a boyfriend. But I didn't know. I just wanted to see her again."

"You cared about this girl, right? So do we." Ah, the pretence of intimacy. *Well done, Keene.* "We're going to get the person who smashed her face in. We're angry about it. And we have to know if we can trust you. We push you, because that's how we find out what you don't want us to know. If you did this to her, we need to know that. That's what you want, isn't it? You want us to do what needs to be done?"

"I do," Stephen says to Keene, still narrow-eyed at me.

"You passed, all right?" Keene says, but I'm not so sure. "We're all on the side of the angels now, together. All right? Tell us about *her.*"

Stephen tells Keene, "I thought she was called Katja. I know she was! The children called her Katja. Every day."

"Children?" I interject.

"She nannied over the Christmas holiday. We lived in East Deeping in a converted manor house. Not together," he clarifies. "We weren't living together. It's flats now. I was staying in my uncle's flat while he was in Tenerife. I'm working on my next book, and the first one isn't quite paying the rent yet. He said I could use his place while he was away. She and I overlapped by only a month." Face in hands, he gets himself under control. "I was supposed to work, but the climbing frame was right outside my uncle's window. I'd see her playing with the children.

"The work wasn't going well. I was stuck, and she was pretty. She was distracting. Finally, after a few days, I got up the nerve to write her a note, but she wasn't interested."

I snort. I didn't mean to; it just came out.

"The last day I saw her, that day was a mess with the weather. It was a Saturday, with the snow, remember?" I know the one. Today's had been just a flurry, but the one in January had been a proper snowfall, rare enough that it pinned a date precisely. "Everyone was stuck in together. The parents were with the kids, so she didn't have to work. I invited her into my uncle's flat for a cup of tea. I don't know what had changed, but she . . . she took off her clothes. . . ."

"Just like that?" I start laughing. Keene's giving me a kick-under-the-table sort of look, but really? He's accepting this?

"So you're saying she was willing," Keene clarifies politely.

Stephen shifts position, away from me. "Yes! I wouldn't—" He stops short, not wanting to even use the words. "After that, I had to wash the sheets again, for my uncle. He was coming back. The laundry's across the hall. She took a shower. She was gone when I came back. That was my last day. When I packed up, I noticed my sweater was gone, and her college sweatshirt was still over the back of the chair. That's it. Really. I left. I didn't have any idea, until today, that anything might have happened to her."

We quiz him on the particulars: the address of this manor-house conversion, his uncle's full name, the names of the other residents, which he didn't know. And her name.

"It's what the mum she worked for called her, too. I heard her. If it was a lie, I wasn't the only one she lied to."

"She didn't tell you her last name," I point out.

"No. I didn't tell her mine, either. It didn't come up."

I bring the problem into focus: "Don't you find it strange that you're the only one to have missed her?" We all think about that for a while. "If she was our body, then where was the family she'd worked for, where was her own family? Shouldn't their concerns have been raised by now?"

"Did you know that someone was looking for *you*?" Keene pulls out a photo of Mathilde that had been in her wallet. She wore the navy jacket and skirt of a school uniform, next to, presumably, her father. Both stood straight, and not touching. "Do you know her?" he asks.

"I don't think so," Stephen says. He takes the photo and bends to examine it. I lean in, too. She was petite and serious, her blond hair held back by an Alice band.

He shakes his head. "Not at all," he says. "Why would she be looking for me?"

"She's been receiving your letters," I say.

"What? Why would that happen? What did she do with—"

"She tried to meet you at the train."

"No, I—I didn't make the one I'd planned. My train into London had run late. I felt awful. If Katja had come, I wouldn't have been there. I would have been just half an hour late, if the trains had been running properly. Just half an hour, but she wouldn't have waited, would she? And then I wouldn't know if she'd come and left or never come. . . . That's why I went straight to Corpus."

"You went nowhere else? Corpus first?" Keene clarifies.

"The train stopped, and we were diverted onto buses. Track maintenance or some electrical nonsense. By the time I got to Cambridge, it was certain she wouldn't have lingered for me. . . ." He trails off. "Of course, that doesn't matter now." Then, "Why did this woman have my letters?"

"She'd been trying to get them to Katja. Then she tried to find you, coming off the three-forty-five train. Then she fell in front of it."

"My God, was that why the station was closed?"

"She might have been pushed. Do you have your ticket?" I ask. If he really did catch the later train, then he wasn't on the trackside with Mathilde. But so far we have only his word for that.

"No." He squirms.

"Did you buy it with a credit card?"

"Yes."

"Can you give it to us to check?"

"No! I don't have to do that."

I raise my eyebrows to Keene at that bit of non-cooperation. Keene tosses him a kindness. "Would anyone on the bus remember you?"

"Yes! Yes. Thank you for asking," he says primly. "I signed an autograph. There was a woman reading my paperback."

"Makes you feel like a man, does it?" I prod him.

"Makes me feel like a decent success, yes. Why not? Anyone ever ask for your autograph, Detective?"

"So you'd have her name?" Keene interjects, expectant.

"Adrienne!" Stephen blurts, victorious and half-rising. "She spelled it: *i-e-n-n-e*." Then he drops back to his seat. "No, that's her mother. She had me sign it for her mother, Adrienne."

I can't help the laugh; it just pops out. How deflating to offer to sign a woman's book, and she turns it into a gift for her *mother*.

"What's so special about Katja or Grace?" I ask. "You didn't know her well enough to even get her name right. What makes her worth chasing?"

"It's not chasing, I . . . Never mind."

"No, no, please tell us," Keene says, leaning forward.

"It's not chasing. We had a connection."

It comes to me, what could account for the intensity. "Were you a virgin, Stephen? Is that it? Did she deflower you?"

Keene pushes his chair back, getting out of the way. Stephen sucks in a breath.

"Or did you imagine the whole thing? Are you still waiting for it?"

I wait for denial, swearing, rage. Stephen looks down. His hands grip each other on the table, vibrating.

Just one more push: "You always repress anger like that? You look ready to pop."

"I don't want to talk to her anymore!" he says to Keene, pointing at me, whole arm extended.

Keene offers to have him dropped off somewhere. He doesn't need a lift; the bus station is down the street. He gives up the address of where he's staying next, house-sitting for a friend up in the Lake District.

"Anyone might lose their temper if you say that, whether it's true or false," says Keene with maddening quiet, after Stephen has gone.

"That's my point. Everyone has a temper. What if he tried it on with her, and she laughed at him? *Bam,* there's your temper. Everyone has one, and some of them kill."

Everything Stephen's described could be a twisted version of what's really a stalking. I spell it out for Keene: "Watching her through the window. Supposedly intense relationship without any solid information to show for it. Those letters? Rehashing and elaborating a ridiculous fantasy. She just had to have him, huh?"

"Women aren't necessarily sentimental about sex. It could have happened the way he said."

"Thanks for the lesson in feminine sex drive, Keene. I thought we were all virgins on our wedding days." Sure, I've thrown myself at a man or two. Well, if those overgrown boys I knew at uni count as men. "Things could have happened the way Stephen said, they could have. We just shouldn't rely on his word alone."

"He's a public—well, minorly public—figure. We can track him down," Keene assures me. "But we had no reason to hold him. Not yet, anyway," he adds. Nice of him to throw me one crumb. "You sure did scare him." He chuckles.

"One of us had to remain objective."

"I was good cop! You didn't think I really trusted him, did you? We don't trust anyone. Right? Just each other?" He leans back in his chair. He smiles.

Just like that, just for a moment, we're back to the way things were, before the knife.

"I can drive you back to Cambourne," I offer.

"No. There's one more bus."

I tap East Deeping on the wall map. "I'll pick you up at eight tomorrow. We'll head for the house early, catch people before they're out for the day."

He nods but won't look me in the eye.

"What happened to your brother's car?"

He pumps out a resigned laugh. "I've no idea. The bigger question is what's happened to *him*."

He's right; Richard is never unreliable. "Are you sure you understood him?"

He turns on me. "Oh, you're right, Richard's error can only be explained by me having incorrect expectations. Not possible for him to make a mistake. Thanks, Mum."

I feel as though I've been punched in the belly. *No, he doesn't know. He's just being sarcastic.*

"Morris," I begin.

"I'm fine, remember?"

"Morris, don't try to do it all on your own. Stop trying to impress us. Cutting me out doesn't make me think what a great man you are. It makes me angry. Work with me."

"You sound like my physio."

Shut up about the damned physio. I hear more about her than I do about his family. "Morris." I take a breath. "I've been letting you just barrel on, but not much longer. There's only so much coddling—"

"Coddling?"

I throw my hands up. "Oh, never! I'm only pulling your rickshaw all over this investigation. The driving is mine, the paperwork is mine. In interviews I have to fight for my share. You're not the only one with struggles. You're not the only one off-kilter." Tears burble out of my eyes. *Not now, not now. Damn.* "You're not the only one whose body is out of control." I rub my fists on my eyes to make it stop. "Do you have any idea how vast a difference there is between a man who takes time off to recover from injury in the line of duty and a woman who takes time off to have a baby?"

"You're—"

"You're so sure that no one understands what you're going through, that no one else has ever made an adjustment or had a physical change. Well, I'm hungry and sick and exhausted every day. My body's going to inflate, my pelvis is going to crack open, and I'm going to push out a parasite that requires me to feed it twenty times a day. If my challenge were limited to my fucking hand I don't think I would even notice it!"

My chest heaves. I close my eyes.

"I'm sorry, I—"

"Just deal with it. You're the hero who took a cut to bring in a killer. You're golden here."

"No, I'm—"

I walk out. There's no right thing for him to say. He doesn't understand. He *can't* understand.

I can't believe I told him. I haven't even told Dan.

CHAPTER 14

GRACE RHYS

I'd made it through the college gate. My tights were laddered from tripping through the door. I looked rubbish. My head pounded.

My staircase is off First Court, in the corner. I jogged up the steps to get my heart going, up past my floor, past the toilets and shower. The kitchen is at the top. I had to have a coffee.

I put on the kettle and unlocked my cupboard for a jar of instant, Fairtrade and dark. A sugar packet would add an extra jolt. The kettle made that snorish rumble it does. I leaned onto my elbows and stared outside; the light across the road was still on; it was something to look at. *Eyes, keep open. Look.* That light has been left on for two days now.

"What are you staring at?"

I jumped. "Oh!" I said. "Nothing."

Ainsley knelt down to the fridge. "You shouldn't look in other people's rooms." She didn't even face me to say it. I glared at the back of her pink T-shirt. She straightened, and it still hung to mid-thigh on her. She was dressed for bed. "What time is it?" I asked.

The kettle wheezed. "A bit late for caffeine," she said.

I mixed the coffee and pulled a milk out of the fridge.

"Is that mine?"

I looked down at my hand. It was a half-pint, organic, skim, the kind of short plastic bottle with a little handle. There: "Ainsley," in black marker on the label.

"Crap, I'm really sorry," I said. "So stupid." I pulled out a box of almond milk and poured that in instead. That box said "Caroline."

"You really should get your own milk," she told me. She had her glasses on, which she never does during the day. They made her eyes huge.

I shrugged. I pushed my hair behind my ear, then quickly tugged it back.

"You wouldn't like it if someone looked in your room, you know," Ainsley said.

I thought of that camera outside my window. "It's not a big deal. She's left her light on." I knew it was a girl who lived there, because most nights I saw her at that desk, reading. I knew she was a Maths fresher, because I recognised the books from my previous year. "It's not like I ever saw her do anything but read." Pretty much every night until a few days ago, actually. "She's probably staying with a boyfriend or something."

"It's not your business." Her popcorn finished in the microwave. She emptied the bag into a ceramic bowl and picked out the unpopped kernels to bin them. Ainsley is kind of a control freak. "What are you smiling at?" she wanted to know.

I poured the sugar sludge at the bottom of my coffee down the sink and shook my head, hard. My hair was wild; I could feel static haloing around me.

"Nice earrings," I think she said. It was hard to tell; she said it as she went out the door. I clapped my hands over them and pulled them off. Their clasps had squeezed my lobes; I rubbed to bring the circulation back. I crammed the earrings into my jacket pocket. *Stupid.* I should have taken them off before I left the pub. What if it hadn't been Ainsley? The jagged rhinestones bulged through the fabric a little.

I rinsed my cup with Fairy Liquid and upended it in the drainer. The light was still on across the road. Her desk was as she'd left it, with a book splayed open, text down. The title font was unreadable from here.

This book was different. All the previous ones had been first-year textbooks.

The back of this one was a face, presumably the author, looking serious in black-and-white. He was youngish, and handsomeish. It looked like a novel. Maybe some free-reading had inspired her to take a break from working so hard. Maybe she got to a sex scene and flung the book down to go and try it out herself. Yeah, she didn't seem to be sleeping in her bed anymore, so that's probably what happened.

"What are you looking at?" This was Chao. He unlocked his cabinet and chose from among the dozen small boxes of American cereals he keeps in there. This one had coloured marshmallows in, and a cartoon leprechaun on the box. He used Ainsley's milk.

I patted down my hair. I pulled it over my ears, but the earrings were in my pocket. "Nothing," I said. I didn't want another lecture. I looked at myself in the toaster. I'd chewed off my lipstick, and mascara had rubbed off under my eyes.

Down the stairs. In my room, I laid my books out all over the bed so that I couldn't give up and lie down.

I got the lecture notes out of my bag. There were three problems to work out for tomorrow's supervision. The camera outside my window changed position. Below, the music from the college bar pulsed. The rhythm lulled me. I tilted my desk lamp to hurt my eyes a little.

My head bobbed to the music, hitting my chin against the thin gold chain my grandmother had given me.

I'd never told her that I was tired or bored or desperate to do anything else besides read to her. My only excuse to ever leave was "I have to study now, Gran." She understood that. She was so proud of me.

I'd been the one to find her, on a Sunday morning this past summer holiday. It had happened in her sleep. I don't know how it is I told the difference between rest and absence, but she was cold. I knew that without touching her.

Mum and Shep had been married three years but never had a honeymoon. Gran lived with us, and everything had been scheduled around her care. Mum is a whiz at organizing, and put the funeral together with the same practicality and detail with which she'd kept

Gran alive. Then she put her hand to a round-the-world itinerary for her and Shep. There had been enough in the life insurance to help me with uni and give Mum and Shep this treat. She had a photo place make me a calendar of pictures of where they'd be every month. Because she made it before they left, the photos were impersonal and iconic, symbols of places. I looked up. November: Australia. The fruit-segment shapes of the Sydney Opera House stuck out a bridge like it was a tongue.

I tried it out: "I have to study now, Gran." But I couldn't trick myself. Gran didn't need us anymore; we could do anything. Mum could go to Australia. I could stay late at a pub.

I pushed the books to the side of the bed and stretched out on it. The desk lamp lit my empty chair. The song downstairs changed. *"Baby, yeah,"* I joined in. It didn't mean anything; it was just an excuse for a good beat. *"Uh, uh, uh,"* I sang. I kicked off my shoes. I curled up, arms across my chest, knees to elbows. I shut my eyes. I could do whatever I wanted.

————

There's a path from the Bursar's Garden into the Master's Garden that you'd never guess was there. It takes going right for the corner, rushing at it like the Harry Potter platform at King's Cross, to get close enough for the optical illusion to reveal itself: The walls don't meet. It looks like a corner, but it's not. Through there, a narrow corridor crowded with rubbish bins leads to the Master's Garden, and through that to the room where I had my supervisions with George Hart-Fraser.

Pip was already there. Her whole name is Philippa, but she always chirps, "Call me Pip!" You can hear the exclamation mark. I assume we were paired up because we're both girls. She was the only other girl in our year in Maths at Corpus.

She always wears skirts. In the cold, she adds leggings underneath. She uses a curling iron on her long hair and smells like watermelon-scented hairspray. Her charm bracelet tinkles.

"Hi!" she said when I came in, *tinkle tinkle* as she waved. I entered the scent cloud and sat in the chair next to her. The chair across the table was empty.

"He's late," she whispered, as if saying it were scandalous.

"George isn't the type to oversleep, is he," I observed, stretching my mouth in a yawn.

"He's in Chile, silly," she said, pronouncing "Chile" to rhyme. Mum and Shep are going to South America in February. They're going to Carnival in Rio. "Where were you?" Pip asked.

"I was asleep," I said. "So who are we waiting for?"

"Dr. Oliver."

I stiffened. Dr. Oliver was our Director of Studies. Failing to have done the work for a supervisor was bad enough; in front of Dr. Oliver, it could cause me real trouble.

"Luke warned me he might not show," she said. "He was meant to take over George's lecture to first-years this morning, but he walked out."

Luke is Pip's boyfriend. He's in first year Maths at John's.

"Luke said they got about five minutes in. Dr. Oliver caught Luke texting. . . ." Here she pouted her lips, so I assume he was texting her, "and told him off. Luke said he apologised, and Dr. Oliver looked him in the face and walked out. Just like that. Luke's worried he might be in real trouble. I told him he couldn't be, not for a small thing like that. But Luke said Dr. Oliver seemed upset."

"What else did Luke say?"

She looked up and squinted. "Nothing else," she finally reported. I don't think she got that I was teasing her. *Luke said, Luke said, Luke said. . . .*

"Why is George in Chile? Is it a conference?" I asked. He must have told us, but I don't always listen.

"For the VLT." *Ah. Lucky.* He got to deal with the literally named Very Large Telescope. He'd come to astrophysics by way of maths, which is why he was supervising us. I'd considered physics when I was younger, mostly because I like the stars. That's not really a good enough reason, like kids who want to become vets because animals are cute.

I leaned back in my chair. We should wait a little longer, but then we could leave.

"If Dr. Oliver isn't coming, we might as well go over the work ourselves." Pip pulled a folder out of her bag. Her problem sheets were neatly stacked, with careful pencil work in a notebook.

"I didn't do the exercises."

She pursed her lips. "Lucky no one's come, then. Why not do them now? Do you have any questions?"

"You're not the teacher, Pip."

"We can learn from each other, can't we?" I think it's a trick of makeup that made her eyes look so wide open, but it gave an impression of earnestness that made her forgivable. And she did know the work better than I did.

We were looking at Markov chains. They're series where each new action is unrelated to the past, springing only from its immediate present, not making any kind of deliberate or cumulative pattern. They call it a "drunkard's walk," meaning every step is truly random. My friend Katja lives like that. She doesn't feel constrained by expectations, and picks every new job based on its own possibilities, not to make any kind of climb or progress.

She got me a Christmas job, in the same place where she's working. *Thank God.* The alternative would be to stay with Aunt Clara in Iceland. It's dead boring there, and she acts like I'm still ten. She painted the guest room with rainbows and bought a unicorn lamp for the bedside years ago, and nothing's changed. She invites me to go feed the ducks, and promises me pudding if I help set the table. I can't bear it.

"Oh!" Pip got down on one knee and picked a bright spark up off the floor. One of the earrings had fallen out of my pocket. "I've been looking for this!" she announced. "It was my mother's, from before she met my dad. She used to wear them for dates." She put a hand on her cheek in mock shock. Her mother's pre-marriage romantic life was apparently blushworthy. "Help me find the other one."

I got down on the floor, too. She babbled on about how it could have got there, and that she hadn't worn them to any supervisions. Maybe, she wondered, she put them in a pocket and they fell out.

"That's stupid," I said quickly. Too close to the truth.

"Well, how else would it get in here?"

I crawled over to a corner and pretended to look under a chair. I figured I could pull the second earring out of my jacket and make it look like I'd found it.

Except it wasn't there.

I started really looking.

"Any luck?" she asked. Then, "How could the cleaners have missed it?" She's not dim. She'd found the first one between our two chairs. It's not like it had been sitting there for a week since she'd lost it. The room had been hoovered. She tapped her chin.

"Pip, I—"

"Maybe it had been caught in my skirt?" she suggested.

"Maybe," I cautiously agreed.

"I washed it yesterday. Maybe they were in a pocket, and then got mixed up with the rest of the clothes!"

And what? Nipped onto the skirt?

"It's been twenty minutes. He's not coming." She straightened her paper pile by tapping it on the table and inserted it back into her neat rectangular bag. "Let's go to the laundry room and look there."

I followed along, looking on the way. The missing earring might be on the stairs or the path outside. She'd think it fell off her on the way to supervision.

She turned left out of the building. I forgot that Pip comes this way, closer to her staircase. She paused to peer into the cluster of branchy bushes near the wall.

"Oh!" she said, bounding over to the path near the rubbish bins. She plucked the sparkle up and gave it a little kiss.

"Wow, isn't that lucky!" I said.

"So weird. I never come this way."

"Me neither. The rubbish bins are disgusting."

"Maybe a magpie tried to carry it off and it was too heavy!" she joked, I think.

Gran used to call me "Magpie."

"This is going to sound stupid, but I thought someone took them. I'm glad that's not what happened."

I breathed out and smiled. I think she really meant it. "Me, too."

I pulled my curtains. I know the camera never faces me, but it's there just the same.

I dumped handfuls from out of my bottom drawer onto the bed: pens, gloves, a hairbrush, a scarf, a bag of sweets, books. Surely every one of these has been replaced by now. The earrings were an aberration. I'd assumed they were cheap accessories, not family heirlooms. I'd be more careful.

No, I'd stop.

I'd try.

I checked each item for value and personalisation. Fur lining poked out of the gloves' wrist holes. They were expensive, maybe a gift. The books all appeared haggard from use. One of them, the only hardback, had an autograph inside.

The gloves and the hardback, then. I'd return them.

The rest, including the paperbacks, I dumped into a sack for the nearest charity shop. I didn't have to go far, and one shop in particular caught my eye. In the window, someone had put a book back the wrong way, with the back of it faced out to me.

I knew that face. I knew that book. It was what the girl I watch from the kitchen had been reading.

I gave the woman behind the counter my donation and 50p for the book. It was called *The Timpanist,* by Stephen Casey. I opened it right there in the shop.

It's about the members of an orchestra implicated in an unspecified crime. Well, that's the frame of it, just an excuse, really. The musicians talk to one another while they wait, and answer police questions at their turns. Everything keeps coming back to the timpanist, who wasn't onstage the whole time. Timpani, those big great kettledrums, are only for exclamation marks. Composers use them sparingly, so the percussionist has a lot of free time. One of the violinists is in love with him. That's what I got from the jacket flap.

The kitchen girl had left the book facedown about two-thirds through. I flipped pages to try to find what might have been her place. It opened straight to a sex scene, as if the person who originally owned this copy had cracked the spine at that place.

I snapped it shut. That's not the kind of thing to read in public.

I took it home and read it from the start, in my room. The scene I'd glimpsed in the shop wasn't a sex scene after all. Rape isn't sex, not really. I don't know how any reader could stop at this point; this was something to get beyond, something to escape or avenge. I kept going.

I stayed up late to finish. When I was ready to go to sleep, I still had maths to do.

CHAPTER 15

MORRIS KEENE

I let out a low whistle: two cautions for shoplifting in Milton Keynes. If it made it that far twice for Grace Rhys, it must have been a way of life for her. Nothing to kill over, but interesting. I stretch my arms overhead and look at the clock on the wall. Half an hour since Chloe had gone. Forty more minutes till my bus. What else to ask the database?

Using just my left-hand index finger, I type in "Mathilde Oliver." Nothing. "Stephen Casey." Nothing. They're both clear. I Google Stephen Casey—good reviews, the new paperback, used copies of the hardback going for 4 pence.

Who else? "George Hart-Fraser," Mathilde's father's colleague and Grace's supervisor. His surname is easy to remember; it's the reverse of the name of a jewellery store chain. I'm always looking for memory tricks, now that I can't write. It's not just having the notes as a reference that matters. Chloe does a good job with that, and in this case Louis the porter had done it for me. But I hadn't realised how much the act of writing clarifies one's thoughts. The decisions and sorting that go into putting something on paper do a trick in the head. I cling to other tricks now.

George Hart-Fraser: originally from Bristol. Suspicion of murder, questioned, released.

Murder.

I scramble to print his record and Google for news stories. This happened ten years ago; there isn't much online about it. His University page doesn't have many links, just a photo showing dark hair and a bland expression, and a list of his journal publications. He apparently focuses on "high redshift galaxies" at the Institute of Astronomy.

I sprint to the bus station. The wall of Emmanuel College stretches down towards my stop. I flat-out run its whole length as the bus at the corner pulls away and out of sight.

I pant and swear. I flick open my phone to call Richard, but his mobile is off again. I try his home, but the line is engaged.

I walk back to Parkside station, no hurry. My desk is at the Godmanchester office, not here, but I can stretch out on the sauna bench for the night. I can't justify the cost of a taxi.

But in the station car park, a young officer fresh off shift heads for his Mini. I can't bring his name to mind, but I remember he lives in Cambourne, too. I jog to catch up.

"Sir?" he says, bright-eyed. He's my height, but his chin tilts up at me.

I ask if I can catch a lift, as we live in the same town. He's all kindness, even fulsome. I dodge his name by using "mate." The seatbelt takes only two tries to click in, two quick tugs, then a satisfying *tunk* into its buckle, while he shifts into gear and lunges out onto East Road.

"How long have you lived in Fulbourn, sir?"

"I . . ." My mouth dries up. Fulbourn. "I live in Cambourne." Twenty miles' difference, on the opposite side of the city. This, this is the memory on which I now rely, and on quirkily abbreviated notes in Chloe's tight, slanted printing. I want my own written words back, my emphases, my priorities. I try to make a fist, but my fingers can only hang in the attitude of a weak slap. "I live in Cambourne," I repeat.

"No worries," he says cheerfully, looking straight out.

A jolt, and streetlights streak by in a stripe. I squeeze a quick blink. "Sorry. No, let me out at the corner. . . ."

"I said no worries!" And he faces me with a huge smile. I wonder at what Chloe has said, that I'm golden here.

"You're very kind. Thank you." I swallow. I want to ask his name, but I can't now, not when I've already pretended to know him. "Thank you," I say again. I force my mouth shut. Panting only makes things worse. The lap belt tightens across that part of my belly that had taken the knife. There's only a scar now, with no lasting damage behind it. But that was the cut that, at the time, had scared me. The cut across my hand had seemed like nothing then.

"You said, sir?"

"No. Nothing. What?" Had I said something?

"You said it was all right."

"What's all right?"

"I don't know, sir."

I lean back against the headrest. "Have you ever been in hospital, Harris?" His name made the leap from memory to mouth with no conscious effort. "Harris?" I try again, worrying I'd got it wrong.

"No, sir. Have you?"

I swallow a laugh. "No!" I announce. "Never."

I deny it all. He has no idea.

Chloe has it all wrong. I'm not golden. Harris isn't driving me home out of reverence for the sacrifices of a superior officer. He might have been cowed by my rank, or politic enough to play up to me, or genuinely kind. But my name is nothing to him. I'm nothing to him. My right arm starts to quiver the way that it does at the end of a long day. I tuck my hand inside my coat.

"Cold, sir?" He reaches for the heating dial.

What would be next? A flask of whisky and a homemade scone?

"It's April, Harris."

"Snow earlier," he reminds me.

Snow. Yes. On a slippery trackside.

"Melted now," he goes on, perhaps to justify his speed. "Like it never happened. Sweet?"

Between the seats, a tin of travel sweets tilts my way. They rattle, and the rattle echoes.

"No, thanks."

His hand knocks the tin between the console and the seat. He grimaces, probing with his fingers. "Get me one?" he asks.

I stiffen my posture. I won't be able to open it, not without the ridiculousness of securing the tin between my stomach and elbow while my left thumb tries to pop the top.

"They're bad for your teeth," I say, all on one note, each syllable as dull as the next. As with his name, that sentence comes out on its own, without giving me a chance to second-guess it, which I would have.

But a laugh busts out of him. "You're my dentist now? You don't look like my dentist. . . ." He keeps laughing.

And he doesn't ask again.

———

Richard is taller than I am. I'd thought I'd catch up in a burst by eighteen, but that chance came and went more than twenty years ago. And the lever for moving the driver's seat is on the right side.

He'd left me the car at last, in the drive when Harris dropped me home last night, keys through the front door mail slot.

Now I only need to fit into it.

I try pulling the lever while standing outside the car, but then don't have any heft in the appropriate place to get the seat forward. In fact, it automatically slides back even farther. I curse Richard for not leaving it in a better position, but if he'd tried, he would have trapped his knees under the wheel and still be here.

I put my shoulder behind the seat back, which puts most of my left arm back there, too. I bend at the elbow and can just skim the lever with my left fingers. So I pull out, pull the lever hard, and then thrust my shoulder behind the seat, shoving it forward. Too far. But I've found the way that works, and, enacting it three more times, make it right.

Once in, I lean back on the headrest, right foot resting on the brake pedal. I have to squash the ridiculous burst of victory that makes me want to pump my fist. I can't let myself get off on this stuff. I can't sink my ambitions so low as merely getting into a car. I put it in drive. I press down on the accelerator. I take off for Deeping House.

———

Wanted boys, did they? The mother must have noticed my smirk. She explains that Drew is spelled Dru, short for Drusilla. Max is, of course, short for Maxine. I'd caught the girls and their mum in the parking area in front of Deeping House, buckling in to leave for the day. Just the two daughters, newly teenaged; this wouldn't have been the family Katja had nannied for.

"Who?" asks the mum through the open car door, one leg still out. She seems flustered by my profession, and whispers when she gives me her name: Hillary Bennet. Dru reminds her of the time. Mrs. Bennet blinks rapidly but doesn't close the car door. Chloe isn't here yet.

"Is this a bad time?" I ask.

"I'm sorry. Why are you here? Is something wrong?"

"I just need to talk to Katja. She nannied over the Christmas holiday."

"For the Finleys, Mum," says Max. "Katja worked for the Finleys," she repeats, to me. "They live in the top-front flat." She points towards the house. I count sixteen chimney pots, four each on four chimney towers. Sixteen fireplaces. "How many flats altogether?" I ask.

"Five," says Max, at the same time her mum says, "We really must go. We have lots to do today, don't we, girls?" Her voice is suddenly hearty and loud, and she gazes, specifically, at Max. Max is thinner and paler than her sister. They both have long, fair hair. Dru's is flat; Max's seems to erupt from her head and fall in lavalike undulations over her shoulders. I think it's a wig.

I smile my kindly uncle smile. "Did either of you girls know Katja? When was the last time you saw her?"

The mum takes over. "She worked for the Finleys over Christmas. Then she was let go. We went into London on the day that it snowed, and when we returned she was gone."

Dru kicks the back of her mother's seat. Not hard, just rhythmically, *bash-bash-bash.* "I *know,* Dru," the mum says, pulling in her leg, and then to me, "I'm sorry, we don't socialise with the Finleys as much as we'd like. But we really do have to go. Dru is heading back to school and we're having a special day *together*." She adds with forced cheer, "Aren't we, girls!"

Max smiles. Dru stares up at the car ceiling. Chloe's car passes them coming in as they pull out.

CHAPTER 16

GRACE RHYS

Each free-standing shelf in the new Taylor Library has an individual light at its top that's triggered by a motion sensor. On late, quiet nights, the emptiness lets the room get all dark—until you startle the first light in front of you, then the next, and leave a kind of comet tail behind you as you go. Sometimes I made an S path between the shelves, watching over my shoulder, drawing snakes and paths in the dark, then letting the darkness catch up with me as each light timed out and winked off. I made a game of it, running, trying to light up the whole room at once; or sitting completely still, until the light over my head goes out, too, and seeing how long I can sit without tripping it.

"Look," someone said. I flinched. I'd fallen asleep on an open book; as I moved to lift my head, a page rose with my cheek. I slowed to avoid tearing it and realised the light above the desk had turned off from my stillness. I let my head press the book again slowly, to keep the dark. I chose to stay still and unseen.

Dr. Oliver and another man were in front of a tall shelf, lit from above. Their path from the entrance was illuminated. It was direct; they had walked straight to the maths section, where Dr. Oliver ran his hands over the spines on the second shelf from the top, tilting his head up to read them. "No, no . . . it's supposed to be here." He tapped the side of the shelf with his fist, then ran one finger along the books on the shelf just below it. "Maybe someone . . . no." He splayed his hand flat against the books at his eye-line and rested his forehead on it.

"It's checked out," said the other man, reasonably.

"Obviously, Richard." Dr. Oliver straightened, and whipped off his glasses to clean them with the tail of his shirt. He didn't even push the shirt back into his trousers. "I come here sometimes just to . . ." The light by the door winked off; both men popped their heads up in acknowledgement. The next light in the trail darkened. They startled new lights on in a path to the steps down to this level. Dr. Oliver surprised me by sitting on the bottom step, about fifteen feet from my face.

"What book is it?" Richard asked.

"*Sets and Supersets.*" I recognised that. It was a first-year book. The girl I watched from the kitchen had read it, too.

"I brought it home—oh, I think six years ago. Mathilde was twelve. I was using it to prepare new problem sheets, and left it by my chair in the lounge. When I returned to it, days later, it was *on* the chair, not next to it. She'd been looking through it. I didn't mind. Then I found . . ." He sucked in a breath. "She'd written in the margin, worked out one of the problems. It wasn't brilliant, just a standard undergraduate equation. But she was twelve! And I hadn't taught her.

"I come here sometimes, just to look at it. She takes to it naturally, Richard. I began to hope that there was something for her, something she could do that made her *happy*. . . . I started to hope for her, and for me. I started to hope for me."

Dr. Oliver's voice cracked the word "me" in two. My arm, bent around my book, prickled from lack of circulation. But I kept still.

"She chose Corpus. I didn't ask her to; I wouldn't have. Trinity or Christ's, I would have said. But she applied to Corpus. Familiarity, I suppose. She doesn't like surprises."

"Her choosing Corpus is a good thing, isn't it? Lots of parents would be—"

"But she changed her mind. I don't know—she didn't tell me. I said I'd help her practise for the interview. She doesn't like surprises, so I could prepare her. She said she'd changed her mind. Why? Why? She wouldn't budge."

His friend commiserated: "Not everyone wants to compete. Is she applying to other universities as well? That can take the pressure off the—"

Dr. Oliver cut him off. "I saw him, Richard. Today. I saw him, and I thought I knew. That boy. I recognised his face." The word hardened. "I was convinced, in an instant. It was all I could do to hold back from . . . from putting my hands around his neck. Everything, everything I wanted then, and now . . ."

The bigger man reached across Dr. Oliver's knees, gripping the far one. "Steady," Richard said, and Dr. Oliver complied with a slow exhalation.

"I walked out of the lecture. I've never done that before."

"I'll tell Tom that you need to take leave, just for a few—"

"No," Dr. Oliver said. "No, I don't need to be coddled. It took me by surprise, but I understand now. I understand clearly for perhaps the first time in my life." He cleared his throat with a literal *ahem*. "First, I looked up his name. I was right. It was him. He's at St. John's. It was tempting to storm his Director of Studies and demand his removal. If he was the reason she didn't feel safe applying to Cambridge . . . but I had no proof. I couldn't do it without Mathilde."

I kept my breathing shallow.

"I didn't make it home. I collapsed on the towpath. At the hospital, they prodded and tested and gave me this bottle of pills." He rattled his jacket pocket. "The doctor asked me to reduce the stress in my life. Have you considered that yourself, Richard? Reducing your stress? Why not be happier, Richard? Why not wake up in an easier life? That would certainly help avoid heart troubles." His voice shot up an octave. The doctor, however glib, seemed to have a point.

"But I'm glad I went to the hospital, Richard, because it made things perfectly clear. I remembered when Mathilde had been born. Francine had had a difficult labour. Forceps eventually dragged Mathilde out. She screamed from the start, which in the first moment was reassuring proof of life, but as the minutes went on it became distressing. She resisted comfort. She struggled. Mathilde was strong, that's what one of the nurses said. She had to reach to find a compli-ment: *strong*. It's not always a compliment, not when it's so extreme."

"Even strong people need others. They just don't show it."

Dr. Oliver's laugh was dry and raspy. "You misunderstand me, Richard. You misunderstand me entirely. Mathilde isn't strong. She's just weak in places I didn't perceive. She's strange. And she's a stranger. I took a taxi home today and she was there, eating tinned soup from a plastic bowl. All my planned conversation was a jumble in my mind. I only wanted to assure her. I touched her shoulder; she flinched. *'Don't touch me.'* Automatically, without turning her head."

Dr. Oliver had girled his voice for that "Don't touch me." The con-trast jolted me.

"I knew in that instant, Richard. I knew. I'd sacrificed to protect her from something that had never happened. Amy's son, that boy. He'd never done anything. Perhaps he'd pushed past her or brushed her hand in the bowl of popcorn. 'He touched me.' It hadn't meant what I'd taken it to mean. It hadn't meant . . ."

"You did the best you could."

"I've never been a good father. I tried to be. I threw away my chance at fresh happiness; I threw away a wonderful woman with a terrible accusation. I did it for Mathilde, to protect her. I put her interests above my own, except in one thing: I wouldn't accept her for who she is. I blamed others for making her that way. I assumed—because it was *easier,* because it *reduced my stress,* wouldn't the doctor be proud—that something external and proportionate had caused her upset." He breathed deeply, sucked it in and shuddered it out. "It's hard to fathom a world where it's preferable for one's own child to have been trauma-tised by molestation. But the world in which, as a facet of her basic self, one's child hates human interaction is . . . selfishly, I'll call it worse."

My arm felt dead from the pressure of my head on it. My eyes got those fireworks on the insides of the lids from squeezing together. But I kept still.

"Where does Mathilde, as a fundamental person, start? Where is the line that delineates *who she is* versus an illness or condition that has infected her and needs to be put right? Did something happen in the womb, or between the obstetrician's forceps? Was it school, or grief over her mother, or something on the couch with that boy? Or is it all just *her*? I needed a villain, Richard. I couldn't accept her as she is. I had to blame somebody."

"Was this the . . ." Richard tiptoed through the words. "Was this the son of the woman you went on the narrowboat with? Ann?"

"Amy. Richard, you're an elephant." A memory joke. "I'd thought . . . ever since Mathilde worked out that equation in the margin of that book, I assumed she would go away to university. I assumed she would leave. Now I don't know that she ever will. I want to sell the house, but she clings to it. I can't take it away from her. So I've made a decision.

"She's eighteen. I've applied for a college room. I'll get put on a list. She can keep the house. She can manage by herself now. She can, you know. All these years, I've grown used to being unable to leave her alone. My sister always came to stay when I needed to travel. But since a broken hip last year, she hasn't felt able. I was supposed to go to Chile, but I sent George Hart-Fraser instead. Force of habit. And a faulty assumption: that Mathilde needed me."

Richard said, "A college room sounds like a good idea."

"I thought you'd try to talk me down."

"Do you want me to?"

I hate smug self-help speak. Dr. Oliver apparently doesn't mind it, because he answered seriously: "No. No, Richard, I—I want your help. I want to set things in motion. Next term, in January, may I come stay with you? Just until . . . It's only until a room becomes available. I'll pay. I'll pay," he repeated.

"I'm sorry," said Richard. "It's not money, I—"

"I know. Of course," he backtracked. "Alice would never approve."

"No, I'll ask her. I'll ask."

"It's too much. It was inappropriate for me to think of it."

"I'm still at Magdalene," said Richard, who must have rooms at college himself. "We're not moving in to the house until after the wedding, and then . . ."

"Of course. I'll wait. If, as I claimed, it won't be long, then there's no reason not to simply be patient. It's childish, even. Childish. Do you remember what being young was like, Richard? It seems very far away."

"We're not so old," said Richard.

"Liar. Did you know that my old school is closing to boarders? I lived there seven years, the seven formative years of my life. Boys have been living in those rooms since the first Queen Elizabeth. Now it's done, because it's not fashionable anymore. No more blue coats and yellow socks, either. That's a relief for the next generation, I suppose." He allowed a chuckle but blunted it against a sigh. "I don't know why I grieve for it; I had my experience. I suppose it's because that experience will no longer be shared. That's a kind of death, isn't it?"

Dr. Oliver's next thought stuttered: "I . . . I want to write to Amy. It's hopeless, I know. But I want to . . . at least to apologise . . . and to say that I won't make any trouble for Luke here. And to ask . . . or imply . . . I want to imply that I would like to see her again."

Richard interrupted. "You don't know what she—"

"My doctor has insisted I reduce my stress. Allow me my illusions, Richard; they comfort me."

In the silence that followed, the beat of the new Taylor clock on the other side of the wall asserted itself. Impossible; the wall had been soundproofed. But I felt a pulse.

"Mortality," Dr. Oliver said, tapping along.

The other man shook his head.

"It's a monster, that grasshopper clock. Have you seen it, Richard?" His shoulders shivered. "It's . . . horrible." His voice sounded hollowed out. I shivered in sympathy, then stiffened myself. The sensors ignored my reaction, too small for their notice.

"It's made of metal," his friend said. "It's only metal."

"Aren't you going to try to evangelise me?"

"Do you want me to?"

"No," Dr. Oliver said. "I'm not so worried about the next life. It's this one. I fear waste. I think I've wasted—" His voice caught and shifted register, like a teenage boy's. "Time is a monster. Taylor's an old man like me; he understands. Time is a monster."

I flinched. The light above me fluttered on the way fluorescents do. I quickly faked a yawn and stretch. "Excuse me," I said, forcing my mouth into a smile. "I fell asleep on my book." I wiped my cheek, as if the numbers and letters had stuck to it.

Dr. Oliver looked horrified, caught. I wanted to comfort him. "How long have you been here?" I asked cheerfully.

I gathered up my books and papers. It's not like he needed to answer. But I think I heard, in passing: "Too long."

———

Dr. Oliver acted fine about seeing me in his office the next day, so I don't think he guessed that I'd overheard. He jumped up that way men of a certain age do, rising when a woman enters the room.

He moved a packing box from the tabletop onto the floor underneath. The contents rustled and clattered, as if it were a toy chest. A colourful school scarf, black-and-white photographs bound with elastic bands, and thickly filled A4 envelopes were visible inside it.

"Grace? Excellent. Let's begin."

He'd rescheduled supervisions with me and Pip to make up for skipping. Pip and I couldn't make the same time, so he agreed to meet with us separately. It was quiet without Pip's chatter to carry things. I sat down.

I handed him the problem sheets I'd finally finished this morning. George usually looks at the papers, not at me, which is fine. Between that and Pip being so talkative, I could usually coast through. But Dr. Oliver looked right at me.

"Grace, are you all right?"

"Of course." My hand fluttered over my knee, my lap, my face, checking everything. I was fine.

"Dr. Hart-Fraser's notes indicate a lack of interest in the subject."

Dr. Hart-Fraser? It took me a moment to translate that to George. We called only the older academics by their titles.

He took off his glasses. "That can't be so, if you're studying all night, can it? Are you struggling, Grace?"

He kept using my name. Every repetition jabbed me.

"You're here because we have recognised a talent, and we want to help you. If you need extra instruction, we can—"

More *work*? I could barely manage the work I had.

"—and we believe in supporting those we've brought into the college through to graduation."

Graduation was ages away. Five more terms. Two rounds of exams. 100—no, *146*—lectures, and 352 supervisions. I felt sick.

"Grace?"

Again, *jab*.

"My grandmother died this summer," I began. Maybe I could make him understand. It was hard to put it into words, because what kind of person says that her own grandparent was a burden? "She was really good to me." I had to make that clear. He had to understand that I wasn't saying any of this because Gran had been bad to me. She just required a lot of work when she got very old.

"Perhaps you could talk about this with Dr. Hart-Fraser. He lost a brother during his first year at Cambridge. It must have been difficult for him to complete the work, but perhaps he found it helpful to have the work to focus on. His example could be an encouragement. . . ."

"No," I said. "I'm not grieving, I'm—" It was too awful to say: I was celebrating, celebrating my freedom. Our lives had been on such a tight leash for so long. I wanted to run wild, now that I finally could.

"Your tutor can recommend a counsellor."

"I don't want—"

"Unless you feel you need to be with your family, in which case we can hold you a place to retake second year, when you feel ready. We take such concerns seriously, especially after what happened at King's."

"What happened at King's?"

He hesitated. It must have been supposedly common knowledge, though, because he told me: "A first year Maths student attempted suicide earlier this week. Of course the University will hold her place until she feels ready to return."

I gaped. It had to be. The girl I watched from the kitchen, who had always been working. I'd assumed she started sleeping in a boyfriend's room and slagging off her books. "Is she all right?"

"As I said, she's at home with her family."

I opened and closed my mouth a few times. "Do you know why she did it?"

He couldn't answer that. He probably didn't know, and wouldn't be allowed to tell me if he did. But anyone could guess that it was the pressure. That's why students attempt suicide, isn't it? I remember when our exam results had been posted last year. Pip had organised us to join the crowd in front of the Senate House. There had been a proper crush to read them. Everyone had wanted to see, except for me. At the end of the third year, it gets even more dramatic: The results are read aloud and thrown down from the Senate House balcony. My hands shook. "I thought she was staying over with her boyfriend." Tears ran all over my cheeks.

"You knew her?" he asked, opening drawers. He found a ragged box of tissues and passed them to me. "I'm sorry, I— We thought all the students involved had been personally informed."

I shook my head and honked my nose into a tissue. I meant that I didn't know her. He thought I was denying having been told when I should have been.

"Can I get someone for you? Dr. Fisher?"

What did Dr. Fisher have to do with any of this? But she's a woman. I think that's all he could think to flail for.

"I don't want that to happen to me," I whispered. I've never, ever thought about killing myself. But neither could I picture myself on the other side of graduating. There was just nothing there in my mind. That frightened me.

"Articulating your goals can help. Why have you come to Cambridge? What do you want to do after you complete the course? Further study, research, teaching?" He leaned forward over his arms, which were crossed on the table. "What do you want to get out of this?"

The last two words were superfluous. I stuck on the ones just before: *I want to get out.*

"Maybe your daughter doesn't want to interview for Cambridge because being good at something doesn't mean you have to do it forever! Maybe she hates maths! Did you ever think of that? Did you?" I was on my feet. How did I get there? Those words were awfully loud. I covered my mouth.

Dr. Oliver reared back. Then he stood, knocking his chair over.

I didn't apologise. I'd meant it. Why does encouragement always have to take the form of "You can do it!" I'd like some encouragement to tell me that I don't have to do it. Plenty of people don't study maths. Plenty of people don't go to Cambridge. Not everyone goes to uni at all. Why can't I be encouraged that it's all right to give this up and not be ashamed?

He swept past me. The door fell shut behind him, anticlimactically with a soft *whoosh* and eventual tap against the jamb.

My hands itched. That familiar need.

I reached, getting my shoulder under the tabletop and my hand into the box. I scrabbled against the bottom and pulled out the first item my fingers hooked, squeezing it in my fist. I could feel what it was: a watch. Dial face, leather band. A frisson scampered up my back.

I ran. Rounding the corner felt like breaking the tape at a finish line. I'd stop taking things, I would. I have to. But not now. *Not now.* I needed the rush.

I slowed to a saunter and passed through the college gate.

The pin for adjusting the watchband pricked my palm. The gears pulsed a faint tick against my skin.

CHAPTER 17

CHLOE FROHMANN

Some mornings my eyelids stick together, and I think, *Did I go out the night before? Did I fall asleep with glitter and fake lashes on my eyes?* But it's been years. I pat the bedside table until I knock my glasses onto the floor. I struggle them on, and I can see the time; I haven't slept late. And my hair isn't the crispy and crimped version from my teens. It's not even long anymore. The heat of the shower catches me up to myself, and I emerge thirty-four years old, sticky-eyed from ordinary sleep. I pop my contacts in, rub a moisturiser over my face, and check out the bump in my middle.

I think it's age more than pregnancy. I'm not that far along. Yet I'd started dreaming, hard, of college parties and casual dates weeks ago, even before I'd wee'd on that stick.

Dan's in the shower now, scrubbing with whatever bottle I've left in there. Today he'll smell like mangoes and oranges.

Look in my wardrobe; no wonder my dreams are panicked. Black, brown, blue, beige. You wouldn't think I shop, really shop, but I do.

The cream pullover is soft and fitted, with a gentle ruffle in the rounded neck; the black jacket is pinched in the right places. But it has to look like I didn't fuss. It's the same with makeup; Keene would swear I don't wear any. *Ha.* I dab foundation on my chin and cheeks, and pink my mouth. I shake my head. My hair will dry on the way. I have a brush in my bag.

Keene. What a mess.

I rap on the glass shower door, then wave. Dan opens it and sticks his wet head out. "Off to East Deeping?"

"I have to pick up Keene first."

I've never minded driving before. It was a form of power, being the one steering the investigation and making it go. But now that he needs me to do it, not just is *letting* me do it, Keene is being a bastard about it.

My face must have tightened up. "Play the game, Coco," Dan reminds me.

I back up, away from the growing puddle on the tile. Wet stretches across the bottoms of my black socks.

We blow kisses.

My leather boots are at the door. Bag, keys, wallet, mobile, energy bar.

I dart into the kitchen. I grab a bagel, two more bars, and a smoothie, and cram them into my bag. I've been getting light-headed if I don't eat every two hours. Dan won't hear the drawers and cabinet doors from the bathroom. I don't want him to notice before I tell him.

Shit. I told Keene last night. Right? Or had that been a dream, too?

No, I told him. I haven't even told my mum.

I lean against the kitchen arch. *Aw, hell.* He won't let on to Cole, will he?

Never mind that Superintendent Cole has asked me to report on Keene.

Mangoes and oranges. "You still here?" Dan teases, wearing a towel, heading for the kettle.

"I couldn't find my keys," I improvise.

He reaches into the still-open bread bin for a white loaf. "What were they doing in here?" he jokes, not waiting for an answer. "I'll make you up a coffee."

"No!" I bark.

"Still?"

I've been "under the weather" for too long. I freeze, feeling pinned by ultrasound eyes. But it's not a coded question. He doesn't have any idea. "This case . . ." I say. That's always handy. A case can excuse anything.

He holds both my shoulders. "Somebody killed that woman. He smashed her face and dumped her in the flood. You fuck him up, Detective Inspector. You find that animal and you *fuck him up.*"

We'll have to stop swearing when the baby comes.

"You're sweet," I say, both arms around his neck. I hold tight.

————

The drive gives me that transition time I need. I play music, loud, knowing that once I get Keene in the car it's conversation or nothing. Driving while nodding and shouting along with the refrain is a solitary pleasure. The iteration of vast rectangular fields on either side of the road plays on a loop.

I'm almost to Cambourne when the call comes through, and by the time I perceive it through the thumping bass and wailing singer it's gone to voicemail. I pull off the road to phone back, relieved that it's not the Abingtons again about their runaway daughter. Keene tells me not to come. Richard left him the car; he's already on his way.

On the day we're heading for the same place?

No, I'm happy for him. He deserves his independence, and I can go back to using my passenger seat for rubbish and paperwork. We can split up later, and he can get his own self home. I'm about to forgive him his piss-poor timing when he jokes: "Traffic on the A14 is always a disaster. Coming via Cambourne did you a favour, right?"

My instinct is to swear. My time is not a joke. I'm not his chauffeur.

But the laugh that trails after the comment, the awkward "heh heh" that invites me to join in my own denigration, smacks of panic. The man is down; I refrain from kicking him.

I pull back onto the road and turn up the volume on the CD. My shitty speakers quiver with it, and the treble screams. The blast of sound calms me. I want to move faster, but I'm stuck behind a meandering minivan. It's not that I'm in a hurry to end the drive; it's that speed is, itself, a pleasure.

The minivan exits at the roundabout. I accelerate. Patchwork fields blur into a stripe on either side, the dull green intermittently jolted by the sharp, crazy yellow of rapeseed in bloom.

———

The house has enough land that you can't see it from the road. The length of the driveway creates a kind of suspense that is fulfilled at the curve into what is now the car park. Deeping House is really only an aggrandised box, but the sight of it at last is thrilling for having been withheld and anticipated. Dan thrives on this sort of drama. In his designs he plots an experience to unfold as you walk through a house, rooms leading to rooms, not just existing on their own. He draws people through a space the way that artists drag eyes around a painting.

He would love this. He would hate that it's been chopped into flats, cheap kitchens stuffed in wherever the bathroom pipes allowed, new walls dropped in and old doors blocked up. "It's vandalism!" he lectured when he showed me the old plans online last night. The owner had been obliged to make a record of the original layout before converting it.

Dan knows of Ian Bennet. He bought Deeping House at auction, for what looked like a low price, but the place needed a lot of work. He put money in and he's getting money out. Dan wants to try this sort of thing, but I'm sceptical. He would fall in love with anyplace he does up himself. He wouldn't be able to bear the practicalities required. He'd try to restore its bygone grandeur, and not want to open the gardens to the public or rent bedsits. It's not that he doesn't want to share; he just wants to see a thing employed as designed.

Bennet doesn't seem to have that sensitivity. The lighting in the car park is unapologetically modern, and a colourful plastic-and-tyre-rubber play area abuts the house.

Keene stands by what must be Richard's car. It's comically yellow. He watches me park. The angle makes the scene look like a film poster, house looming. That effect was designed in deliberately; the house is meant to intimidate.

Challenge accepted. I get out of the car.

———

Keene and I approach the grand front door together. An anachronistic keypad and speaker cling to the wall beside it. Each button has a label beside it, which I copy into my notebook:

Holst

Finley

Keene says that's the family the girls in the car said that Katja had worked for. He presses their buzzer. We wait. No response.

Bennet

The owner himself, apparently with teenage daughters on a day out with Mum.

Help

"Help?" I say, as if the house were begging our assistance.

"Servants, maybe?" says Keene. *Sure, maybe there's a gardener or cleaner. But shouldn't such a person have a name?*

*_____

That one was blank. Unlet? That doesn't bode well for Ian Bennet's big project.

Then, *Casey*. Stephen's uncle. Keene presses that buzzer.

"We might be waking people," I caution. "It's Saturday."

He presses the buzzer again, really leans on it with his thumb. I crack a smile.

A window to our right is raised. "What are you on about?" shouts a white-haired, barrel-chested, apparently naked man.

We jog down the steps and stand tiptoe in a flower bed to lift our warrant cards up for his perusal. Rory Casey agrees to throw on a dressing gown and speak with us.

Back up the steps, we wait with friendly smiles for him to let us in. "Richard's car working out?" I finally ask, turning our small talk serious. Keene only grunts, so I persist: "How's Alice holding up? Are they coping?"

"What do you—" he begins. But Rory Casey unlocks the door. He has a mug in hand, topped with steamed milk and a cinnamon flourish we can smell from the step. He's taken his time about it, too.

The wood-panelled hall frames his glower. He looks like a portrait the sitter didn't enjoy posing for. Behind him, a wide stairway sweeps down from the upper floor. Mock-Oriental carpet lolls down it, held in place at the back of each step by a thin brass bar. The newel post is topped by a carved wood globe, its continental outlines worn down to suggestions.

I count seven doors: two up and five down. Mr. Casey reaches for the only door on our right. "Are you done gawping at the hall?" he wants to know. I have Dan's printout of the original design of the house. Casey's flat was once a "parlour."

As Stephen had described, the flat is small. The main room is a lounge, with kitchen units against one wall and a table under a window. It overlooks, as Stephen had said, the climbing frame and swing set. A slightly open door exposes a corner of Mr. Casey's bedroom.

We explain our concerns, and he confirms that Stephen had permission to be there at the time he'd claimed. "And I know he *was* here," he says, "because my cupboards were rearranged. Cups stacked on plates, saucers nested in bowls. He's a savage in the kitchen. His mother coddles him too much; a man isn't a man until he can live by himself with a minimum of fuss. And he was gone when I returned. He'd made the bed, but I didn't trust him. I washed the linens myself."

Outside the window, an attractive young woman pushes a small child on a swing. Stephen had sat here, watching.

"Did you have any reason to wash the sheets, Mr. Casey?" Keene asks.

"When I unpacked I noticed he'd been in my stash of condoms. He's a grown man; I expect he knows what a bed's for, and that he used it as such. There's a utility room across the hall. I washed the sheets in hot water. It's all a person can do."

"Who's that out there?" Keene asks, tilting his head towards the window. The young woman who'd been pushing the swing has gone out of range. This older woman now minding the boy isn't having as much fun.

"That's Eleanor Finley and Daniel. He's a lovely lad, all mischief. She's a sour bitch. They're on their fourth au pair, and I can't say I blame the ones that leave."

We haven't even mentioned Katja yet; we'd started off simply confirming Stephen's account. "Do you remember an au pair called Katja, Mr. Casey?" I ask.

"I don't know their names. But I can tell you that the first one was

lazy and ginger-haired. The second one, this was before I left for Tenerife, she seemed better. More alert, in any case, as if she had a brain
in her head and planned on doing what she was being paid for. Now
they've got an Italian—"

"We'd be interested in the one that was here when Stephen was,"
I say.

"Well, if she was here then, she was here when I wasn't!" He
breathes out slowly and sits down. "Has he got the girl into trouble?"
he asks. Meaning pregnant, clearly. *Trouble.*

"Is he usually so careless?" Keene asks. I shoot him a look.

"He's twenty-three," Casey says in answer. As he's made perfectly
clear, Stephen knows what a bed's for.

"Has he got anyone else in 'trouble'?" I ask.

"I wouldn't know. But he's twenty-three," Casey repeats. Keene
waggles his brows at me. I roll my eyes in response. Mr. Casey must
have had a wild year himself, forty-odd years ago.

———

We find small Daniel digging up a patch of garden. Earth sprays up
into the air and settles on my shoes. "I know that Mr. Bennet hates it,"
his mother says. "But it keeps Daniel happy. He gets bored when his
sister is at gymnastics. What am I supposed to do?" She seems to mean
this as a real question: *What possible alternative could there be?* She hovers near him but not close, protecting her white trainers and pink
tracksuit.

A young woman swoops in as if in answer: "Daniel! You know
you're not supposed to dig. Come have a climb." She scoops him up
and places him on the ladder of the climbing frame. He accepts the
sudden change and clambers like a monkey. Her arms stretch up to
protect him as he travels across the top. The bottom of her shirt rises to
expose a thin strip of belly.

Mrs. Finley barks sharply, "Liliana!" The mother marches over
and tugs the au pair's shirt down to overlap her jeans. Then she returns
to us. "No self-respect," she grumbles. "Spoiled, that's what she is. She
expects me to step in when she needs to run off to the loo. A youngest
daughter. That never bodes well. I always say—"

I cut her off. She bristles when we ask about au pairs and Christmas, as if she only then notices that we're strangers. "What do you want to know about Katja for?" she finally says, once we've identified ourselves to her satisfaction. "Good riddance to her."

"Christmas?" I prompt. The three of us drift towards a bench facing the play area. Mrs. Finley glares at the au pair riding the seesaw with her son.

"That girl, Katja," she says. "She was nice enough at first. Eager to please, only mildly grating accent, that sort of thing." She waves her hand to encompass the general nature of foreign young women. "We were happy to have her at the start, I can tell you that. The first one, Leonora, had to be told how to do everything. Every little thing. And she'd never seen a tumble dryer or a dishwasher. It was like teaching a cat to play cards. Katja at least knew how things work. Daniel was happy with her, and Caitlin, too."

"Can you describe her physically?" I ask.

"Smaller than me." She holds her hand up around her ear, for height. Keene and I meet eyes: *too short for the fen body*. "Fair hair, choppy cut. Flat-chested, thank God." I restrain myself from responding.

Mrs. Finley leans towards us. We lean in, too.

"And I'll tell you the truth, because you're police, and that's just how I was raised. One mustn't lie to police."

Keene commends her.

"My husband turned forty last year. It was all very traumatic and whatnot, forty and still not yet manager, forty and still on the worst shifts. I was overwhelmed with Daniel and Caitlin, which is why we'd given in and hired help. Things were not at their best between us. He ended up having an affair with this silly woman he met at work. Blond, recently divorced, the whole stereotype. It lasted a month. Then one night I caught them in the car just outside. Can you imagine? My therapist says he wanted to get caught, though you wouldn't know it from the look on his face when I rapped on the windscreen."

"Forgive me," I interrupt. "I'm not sure how this relates. . . ."

"I'm explaining to you the circumstances that made it impossible for Katja to stay. My husband is a weak, vulnerable man. The day that it snowed . . ." Mrs. Finley rubs her hands. "That day. In January. You know it?" Yes, it had been news. Even a few inches, when they do come, stop everything. "Marcus—my husband, Marcus—somehow managed to tip our car off the edge of the icy drive trying to get to work. It had blocked the way out so there was no leaving the grounds for anyone. Rain bucketed down after the snow, so there wasn't even any getting out of the house. We were all stuck in together, except for Hillary Bennet and her girls off on their pagan escapade, and our Daniel and Caitlin, who were at my mother's—"

"Excuse me? 'Pagan escapade'?" *Maypoles? Stone circles?*

"Hillary Bennet took her two adolescent daughters to London to have their astrological forecasts done. And, as I was saying, our own children were with their grandmother. Therefore there was nothing for Katja to do, so she stayed in her room downstairs, so we thought."

"Your au pairs don't live in your flat?" I clarify.

Mrs. Finley blanches. "Certainly not! The help use the empty flat downstairs. That day, I imagined she would read or otherwise improve herself. Then the noises started. Sexual noises, from Rory Casey's flat below our lounge. I was used to hearing the drone of television down there from time to time but . . . the *sounds* of male enthusiasm and . . . the *rhythm* of it was persistent. In the middle of the day! Apparently she'd decided to give the little writer downstairs a going-away present." The sex had actually happened, then; Stephen wasn't just wishing.

"We knew he had a crush on her. She and that other girl—the Holsts' nanny—had giggled over it, which was what it deserved. I thought she had more sense. Surely you understand that our working relationship couldn't continue."

"You sacked her for sleeping with the writer downstairs?" I can't keep the incredulity out of my voice.

"I sacked her," says Mrs. Finley, rising, "because my husband had already been tempted once, and I didn't need him to have those sounds replay in his head every time he looks at the cute little twenty-two-year-old without stretch marks with whom we share our home. I sacked her that day, and haven't seen her since." A breeze stirs her hair into a Medusa-like tangle to match the vicious expression on her face.

Suddenly he's before us: Marcus Finley, forty and not yet a manager. His grey suit, beige tie, and defeated posture identify him instantly.

"Marcus," Mrs. Finley says, surprised but not abashed, "this is the police. They're asking about Katja."

"I imagine my wife has told you everything," he says. "Forgive me, the store opens at ten."

"Mr. Finley—" Keene begins, but he waves us off.

"As I'm sure Eleanor has explained to you, I'm not in a position to choose my working hours. Please excuse me." He heads for the car park.

I collect all the factual details: the agency through which they'd hired Katja, and the sources of her recommendations. Mrs. Finley suggests we try the Holsts, who live in the other upstairs flat. Katja had been friends with their holiday nanny. "I'd have hired her away from them if she'd been willing. She dressed sensibly." She shoots a glance at Liliana, who is pretending to be a horse for Daniel the cowboy. It makes her shirt ride up. Mrs. Finley narrows her eyes.

Liliana bucks him off. "I need to move the wash into the tumble dryer," she announces.

"Well, take him with you!" Mrs. Finley flaps her hands, shooing them off. Liliana sighs, and Daniel skips after her. "I've been trying to exercise for the past hour," Mrs. Finley complains, glaring at the both of us.

"If this other nanny was friends with Katja, we'd like to speak with her. What was her name?"

"Grace," she says.

Grace.

CHAPTER 18

GRACE RHYS

Katja elbowed me in the chest as she ran past, chasing the children. Her wellied foot stamped on my white trainers.

I stood stunned for about four seconds. I know it was four because Caitlin was chanting a hide-and-seek countdown. Caitlin is six. She has long hair and sucks on it whenever she isn't talking or eating. She and Danny are Katja's responsibility, but I'm the one who combs that hair.

Caitlin finished the countdown and pounded the pathway paving stones with her running. The garden was vast enough for the other kids to hide effectively, so I had a few minutes to lean against the lip of the dry fountain. The nose of a stone dolphin chilled my cheek.

"Grace!" Katja called.

I turned my head away. She called again, striding back across the frosted lawn. She'd helped them get well hidden and wanted a break.

"You didn't answer," she accused me.

"I was . . ." There was no ready end for that sentence. I used to say to Gran, *Sorry, I was studying.*

Katja stabbed a cigarette between her lips and cupped her hands to light a match. The kids had gone round the house, but we could still hear them. Caitlin found Brent and Lizzy, the toddler twins I look after, quickly. Too quickly. They must have given themselves away. Running. Laughing. Squealing. *Screaming.*

"Katja!" Caitlin bellowed. *"Katja!"* Someone was crying. Danny.

"You go," Katja said. That happened a lot. "I'll finish this." She inhaled deeply, then blew a line of white smoke that curled around the edges.

I didn't respond at first, but Caitlin yelled for Katja again. I pushed off from the edge of the fountain and took off around the house.

"Katja! Danny fell!" His quiet crying became more evident as I ran across the lawn.

He was under the climbing frame, shocked but unhurt. I bent to get under it with him. His sister and the twins crowded around. A dark patch spread across the front of his corduroy trousers. The smell wafted up to my face.

Mum had cleaned Gran whenever she wasn't at work, but after school was my time. I'd got used to the smell as a cue for action, ignoring the sourness of it. But since Gran had died I'd regained my sensitivity. I reared my head back to get away from it, and banged into the underside of the slide.

Katja sidled up, close enough to see the wet spot. "Daniel!" She'd thought she got the better part when I ended up with the littler ones, but Danny was the one with repeatedly wet trousers.

He started to cry again. "I'll get him fresh clothes," I said. Katja scowled. Getting the part of a job that didn't involve the children themselves was always the win. Funny, I'd thought I liked kids, just like I'd thought I liked maths. Now I didn't know what I liked.

I went inside and up the stairs. *Knock-knock.* "Mrs. Finley . . . ?"

I only got the door cracked open. Her footsteps thudded then the door was shoved shut. "I told you, Katja, I'm wrapping presents!" Mrs. Finley shouted, breathing heavily.

I rapped again. "I know, Mrs. Finley. I haven't got the children with me."

She opened the door two inches, looking beyond me to confirm that that was true. "Oh," she said. "It's you." She allowed the door to flop open.

"The kids are cold," I lied, gathering up sweaters for both of them, to hide the pants and corduroys for Danny. She gets angry when he wets himself.

"Would you like a coffee?" she offered. She treats Katja like a servant, but she's nice to me, because of Cambridge. I haven't yet told anyone at Deeping House that I've degraded. They all think I'm starting back up in January.

"I hope Danny's been good," Mrs. Finley said, eyeing the clothes in my arms.

"He's been a treat, Mrs. Finley." A roll of wrapping paper slid off one of the couches, unspooling until it hit a neat stack of boxes. "He'll like that," I said. The bottom box was a Lego Atlantis set.

"I should hope so. It cost forty pounds." Cuttings of paper, some of them crumpled, filled the space up to the fireplace. They rustled as she stepped forward and put her hand casually on the side of her head. "Are you good at wrapping presents?"

"No," I said firmly, gripping the doorknob. "I have to get back to the kids." That was the thing: She couldn't ask Katja to wrap the presents without having to watch Caitlin and Danny herself. I had to be vigilant to avoid getting bullied into doing her extra work.

I popped next door to grab mittens for Lizzy and Brent. They weren't complaining yet, but it was getting chilly. We couldn't really come inside. We didn't have the option of disturbing the present-wrapping apocalypse or the book editing we'd been hired to preserve. We'd have no place to take them but into our own tiny bedsit downstairs if the weather got bad.

I knocked on the Holsts' door but went ahead and opened it while I did so. It was just a courtesy knock; Mrs. Holst wasn't bonkers like Mrs. Finley. They weren't there. The manuscript pages were in piles. Their research books were open on the table. I grabbed four mittens and two hats from the basket by the door and just breathed deeply for a moment. "Dr. Holst?" I said, which I did whenever I meant either of them. I used Mr. or Mrs. when I wanted to specify.

An echoey laugh bounced around in the bathroom. It was made of two voices. *Ha!* They were taking a bath together.

I got out and quickly closed the door. That was really nice, when grown-ups were happy. Mum was worried I would be scarred when Shep started sleeping over, but I thought it was nice for her. I stayed out of their bedroom. They were both always fully dressed for breakfast, so it's not like I had to see his skinny legs sticking out from under his dressing gown or Mum in some kind of lacy thing. Once I saw him put his hand on her bum while they were washing dishes together. They jumped apart when they realised I was there. I never caught that again, and I felt like I'd taken something away from her.

Back outside, the sounds of children arguing, that high-pitched indignation they favour, wafted from the play area. Danny was whining, and Katja told him to "shut up." She shouldn't talk to him like that. I've told her that, but she doesn't listen. She even swore at him once. She swore at me sometimes, too. She was a lot more fun before we lived together.

I shivered and pushed forward. Danny needed his fresh clothes, so I jogged around to the side of the house. Mr. Bennet had planted winter shrubs around all the edge of the building, thin-branched bushes that snagged my clothes as I jogged past towards the climbing frame. They didn't flower but were bright themselves: red, yellow, and orange. Together they gave the effect that the house was being cooked over a fire.

Mr. Bennet worked hard. He was always hammering, painting, sweating.

He emerged from the woods behind the house. The rest of us were buttoned and zipped up to our necks, but he, hot from exertion, wore his flannel shirt open at the neck over a round T-shirt collar. The sleeves bunched at his elbows, baring his arms. He dragged a tree behind him, an irregular fir shaggy with green needles. In his other hand he carried an axe, reflecting sharp sunlight.

He pitched the tree at our feet, grinning like a hunter who's hauled in a carcass for dinner. "Think you girls can put this up?"

Katja laughed and clapped her hands.

Mr. Bennet picked up the rough trunk at the bottom, and Katja lifted the pointy tip. I ran ahead to get the door. Katja entered first, pulling towards the obvious place in the crook of the stairs. Mr. Bennet paused to stamp his boots on the mat, and Katja tugged playfully. He pulled back, almost knocking her off balance.

Together they lifted the tree into the mouth of the stand. Mr. Bennet held it up while Katja crawled underneath to tighten the bolts. The children and I hung back, judging the position, calling out contradictory instructions: *Left! Right!* Sharp twigs caught in Katja's hair; she barked an obvious swear in Finnish.

At last the tree was even. Katja backed out from under it on hands and knees.

Mr. Bennet rapped on his door. "Hill!" he called, for Hillary, I guess. They were a one-syllable-nickname family.

She answered something from inside. I don't know how he understood it, but he did and opened the door for her. She backed through it with a tray of star-shaped biscuits. The kids swarmed her. The shortbread was still warm, studded with silver ball sprinkles and dark gold underneath.

"Dru!" she called through the still-open door. I know that voice. Mums call that way when they want to sound cheerful but actually they're annoyed.

"Dru!" she called again, more annoyed, less cheerful.

"I'll get her," said Mr. Bennet, disappearing into their place, *knock-knock-knock* distantly inside.

"She has her iPod on," Mrs. Bennet called after him.

I was never allowed to have earbuds in when I was at home, in case Gran called for me.

"Her door's locked," he called back from inside the flat, accompanied by a rattling sound. I could tell, just by hearing, the difference between the house's solid, original doors and the ones Mr. Bennet had put in when he added extra walls and Frankensteined the place into flats. This was one of the flimsy new doors.

"Since when does . . ." Mrs. Bennet put the tray down. Caitlin and Dan fought over the last shortbreads while she stormed in after her teenager.

Mrs. Bennet's pounding was profound. The door *thwapped.* "Drusilla! Open this door!"

I tried to distract the kids. "How shall we decorate the tree?" I asked, thinking we could make chains from paper strips or thread popcorn. But Mr. Bennet came out with a box labelled "Xmas ornaments." Katja pulled out a snake of garland and wrapped it around herself. She wiggled, and the kids laughed.

"Where did you get this?" Mrs. Bennet demanded, loud. The kids' giggling trailed off into an audible ellipsis.

Mr. Bennet ducked back into the flat. "I have lots of chain locks," we overheard. "She's welcome to one."

"Did you take it from Ian's supplies? Don't you know that his hard work pays for everything? For that iPod, and your television, and *this house?*"

"It's all right. I don't mind if she took one," Mr. Bennet insisted.

"I mind. *I* mind!"

Dru finally spoke loud enough for us to hear. "I just wanted some privacy!"

They back-and-forthed over taking the lock off the door. Mrs. Bennet wanted Dru to do it. Mr. Bennet said he would do it later. Mrs. Bennet had an agenda: "No, no. I want *her* to do it. What do you need? A screwdriver?" There was a sudden clattering sound. I think Mrs. Bennet kicked a toolbox.

"Hillary, this isn't *necessary.*" He hit that last word hard, and no one said anything for a few seconds.

Mrs. Bennet said, "Dru, it's almost Christmas. Please."

Some kind of mime or exchange of expressions must have resolved things, because they came out together. Mr. Bennet had his hand on Mrs. Bennet's shoulder, and she had her hands on both of Dru's shoulders. "Who wants to decorate the tree?" Mrs. Bennet asked cheerfully. They held that pose, Mrs. Bennet pinching Dru's shoulders, until Dru gave in and mouthed "me."

Her long hair hung in front of her. I'd worn my hair like that, too, the year I got a chest. Two big hanks, one on each side, covering up.

But that left the telltale bra line across my back, which got snapped a couple times a week. She wore a baggy sweatshirt. Teenage boys are bastards.

Mrs. Bennet asked her husband to invite the other residents down for hot chocolate and ornament hanging. I warned him that the Holsts were occupied, and Mrs. Finley told him off herself. That left the writer.

They didn't refer to him by name. They said "Rory's nephew" or "the writer." He was using the flat while his uncle was on a trip.

Mrs. Bennet knocked, mug of chocolate in hand. He answered, wearing pyjama bottoms and a sweater. Maybe he'd been deep in work; maybe he'd been sleeping. He looked around, blinking, then looked down when he saw Katja next to me. "No, thanks," he said, but accepted the hot mug.

There had been this brief thing between them. He'd slid a letter under the door of our flat. A proper letter! He'd written:

Dear Katja—

Sometimes I'm lazy with my work and I look out the window instead. It's a treat when you come out. You're fun. You're sporty. You're pretty.

But I worry that just watching makes me a creep. I'd like to meet you. I'm only here for a few more weeks.

I write books. Well, I've written one book, and I'm writing another. I'm trying to write another, but I'm easily distracted. I would consider it a privilege to be distracted by you.

Stephen

That was when I'd figured out who he was: the face from the book. Katja answered his note with a note of her own, and all on papers slipped under doors they agreed to go out to dinner using his uncle's car. I was only a little jealous of the romantic side of things and a lot jealous of Katja getting away from Deeping House to somewhere that didn't have inflatable play equipment or paper placemats with crayons.

She came back too soon. They couldn't have even got to the restaurant. She called him something ugly in Finnish, sounding really upset. I wanted her to tell me, but she wouldn't. I remembered the rape scene from his book when the conductor forced himself on a woman in his car. He'd specified every thud and rub of their too-big bodies against the car's tight interior as she struggled and he pushed. I shuddered.

I don't think it went as far as that, but, whatever he did to make Katja feel hurt and sad, I was glad he didn't join in the tree trimming now. I was glad he felt guilty.

"Nothing wrong with an intimate crowd," said Mrs. Bennet. "More biscuits for each of us!" she added, and the kids cheered. "Second batch after the ornaments," she promised.

She handed out the pretty objects one at a time: a sleigh, a snow-flake, a donkey. The kids hung them as high as they could, which wasn't high at all. The tree was going to look like it was wearing a skirt and no top.

Then she got to what were clearly the "good ones." They were wrapped in tissue paper. It was a matched set: dozens of brass stars, a moon, and a full zodiac. She removed each piece reverently, making a stack of the tissue, which she smoothed flat with firm caresses. She directed the kids to sit for what turned out to be a reverent cere-mony.

She handled each brass sign delicately, explaining what it was, showing Sagittarius's bow and arrow, and Pisces's intricate scales. She asked the children their birthdays, and lifted them to hang their own signs up high. Caitlin was Aquarius. Katja volunteered that she was, too, so they shared slipping the thread loop around a prickly branch.

"Cancer!" I announced, getting into the spirit of things. I wanted to hang the crab. I'd always liked that my sign was a beach creature. When my dad was alive we went to the seaside every August.

Mrs. Bennet's smile stuck. It was the same smile it had been a sec-ond ago, but the sameness, the unmovingness, made it strange. Mr. Bennet was stuck, too, with his arm half-extended to swag the garland. Dan and Brent had some kind of squabble going on; Caitlin shushed them.

"We don't have Cancer," Mrs. Bennet said quietly. "We don't hang that one," she amended.

Open-mouthed, I looked to Katja. She glared at me as if I were an idiot, and mouthed "Max." I knew there was another daughter. I didn't know she was sick. Mrs. Holst had mentioned them both to me, and I saw Dru around sometimes, outside reading. I just thought that Max stayed inside, or had football practice or a club or a class.

A sharp crescent was thrust into my hand. "You can hang the moon," said Mrs. Bennet. My dad used to say that I "hung the moon." I don't know why that means "I love you," but that's how he used it: "You hung the moon, Grace Genevieve."

I said I had to go to the toilet. I ducked into the flat I shared with Katja, kicking through her yesterday clothes that were still on the floor. I closed the door and sat. If I were ever rich, I would design my house to have a huge bathroom, with a massive tub and a TV. Sometimes a bathroom is the only place you can be where no one will try to talk to you. Dad used to read the morning paper in there, because he couldn't bear conversation until he'd been up for at least half an hour. I never thought about Dad. This was stupid. He's been dead a long time.

I'd expected to return to the promised carol singing, but Dru was shouting: "If Max were home from hospital, you wouldn't care if I sang or not!"

Danny started crying. The box wasn't empty, but the tree was covered well enough. I'd seen in the TV schedule that *The Snowman* was going to be on this afternoon, the one with the pastel drawings and the boy soprano and no words. "Who wants to watch cartoons?" I said.

On the screen in our little flat, the snowman sailed across the sky, little boy in tow. The kids ate fistfuls of sugar cereal from the box. On the other side of our wall, the washing machine *slosh*ed and *thunk*ed. Katja had been supposed to do the washing this morning, but she always puts it off. She hates that the Holsts don't make me do theirs. She says it's because of Cambridge that they don't ask, but what does that have to do with it? And even if that is the reason, Katja studied literature for two years at a uni in Finland. If she doesn't act like it, whose fault is that?

The crescent moon ornament worked a small hole in my jeans pocket. I hadn't said a thing while the Bennets tidied away the ornament wrappings, just kept my hand on it as if its outline would have shown through the denim. I felt that outline through the thin cotton pocket, against my leg. The familiar rush spread out from there, a quick high that distracted and comforted me.

CHAPTER 19

CHLOE FROHMANN

D r. Holst laughs. "Oh, that sounds grand, doesn't it?" she says. "A 'nanny.' No, Grace was just temporary help for over the Christmas holidays. Not even an au pair, strictly. The agency clarified that. In official terms, she was a 'mother's helper,' though I find that rather sexist, don't you? She was as great a help to my husband as to me. We had a deadline coming, and a round of editing to work on."

The Holsts are academics. Journals and papers are piled everywhere. Dr. Holst clears a chair by adding its stack to one on the coffee table. Neither Keene nor I move to take the seat, so Dr. Holst takes it herself. Her hands clutch each other in her lap primly, and she tilts her head up to us. Her curly halo is wound into a bun stabbed through by a red pencil.

The two upstairs flats each get fully half the footprint of the house. The division between the Finleys and the Holsts runs lengthwise, creating two long flats, rooms railroading into rooms. This lounge overlooks the back. Between and under the windows' pastoral views, bookshelves fill the Holsts' walls. Their contents age up: obvious children's books on the bottom, working up to fiction, reference, and journals literally over their heads. One topmost shelf holds a varied selection of sex manuals. *Well, the kids have to get here somehow.*

"She was a help while we were getting the final edits done, but having someone else underfoot at home . . . This is a spacious flat, but, you can see, it is only a flat. Even with her sleeping downstairs, with Katja . . ."

"Have you kept in touch with Grace?" I ask.

"No," Dr. Holst says. "No, why would I? The children liked her, but it's not like they would bond over a month."

"Under what circumstances did she leave, Dr. Holst?" Keene says.

It comes together for her. She gets up to pace. "Oh, dear. Oh—no, you don't think? The body in the fens?"

"Had you considered it might be her?" I ask.

"No! Of course not. I would have contacted the police if I'd had any . . . She's not blond, for one thing. Katja was. Oh! Oh, you don't think it's Katja, do you? I thought she wasn't tall enough to match the description!"

"That's the case. When did you last see both of them?"

"It was all perfectly ordinary. Grace was only to be here another day or two, then back to Cambridge. Term was soon to start." So Grace had kept up the fiction of returning to Cambridge. No wonder Stephen Casey wrote to her there. "But I'd hit a block with the chapter I was editing, and I thought I'd spend some time with the kids. . . . I told her she didn't have to work the rest of the time. She could stay, but she didn't have to work. I even paid her early."

"And?" Keene had to prompt her. She'd stopped walking, stopped talking.

"The day after the snow, she was gone. I wasn't really surprised. She was young, she had adventures ahead of her. . . . I assumed she and Katja had left together, with Rory's nephew. Stephen, the writer. He seemed nice. He looked like a student still, that long hair . . . but he'd had some actual success. That had to be attractive."

"Were Grace and Stephen friends?" I say it casually but deliberately leave Katja out.

"They were all three young people, more likely to be friends than anyone else in the house."

Interesting. So she didn't see any particular spark between Stephen and Grace.

"Did any of them seem sexually interested in one another?" It can pay to be direct.

Dr. Holst blinks, then sighs. "This is about Katja, isn't it? Eleanor told you. It's such a ridiculous . . . It's not as if it happened in the next room while the children were napping."

"So you heard it, too?" Keene asks.

"We were home that day. We all were. But we didn't hear a thing. It's not as if these walls insulate us from sound; we regularly hear Rory Casey sing in the shower. In fact, I wondered at first if Eleanor had been exaggerating."

"Really? Does Mrs. Finley do that often?" Keene asks.

She looks sternly at us. "This isn't the sort of thing I would pass on, but I know that she will have done already: the incident with Marcus and the blond woman. He knows he did wrong, and there was an emotional affair of sorts that ought not to have been. Then the evening she found them in the car, they kissed. It was, according to Marcus, the first time that had happened. The way Eleanor described it, you'd think the car had been rocking."

"You're close with him, then. He tells you a lot of things," I prompt.

"He needs someone to talk to sometimes."

"You believe him about the supposedly first kiss? It sounds convenient, is all." That was Keene, elbowing in.

"You can believe him or not, as you like. But I know the two of them, Eleanor and Marcus, and I know what I think. He knows he did wrong, and feels terrible about those things. But he can't be sorry for all the things Eleanor accuses and that he *didn't* do. The point, though, is what happened on the snowy day. Marcus confirmed Eleanor's account. He said it really was mortifying, and he would have been embarrassed to look Katja in the face after that."

"Did he?" Keene asks.

"Did he what?"

"Look her in the face after that."

Mrs. Holst gazes out over the back lawn. "I don't know," she says. "He would have avoided it if he could. I assumed they got a lift with the writer. Stephen drove Rory's car to the train station and left it there for Rory's return."

"Did you see either of them get into Stephen's car?" Keene asks. But we already knew she couldn't have. Their flat runs along the back of the manor. They have a view of cars moving along the drive but not of the car park, not of people getting in and out.

"No," she says. "No, it's just what I assumed."

Keene looks at me. Stephen said he'd left Deeping House alone.

"Anyone else go by car that day?" Getting a lift from someone known to them was the most likely option; a taxi would have been exorbitant, all the way from Peterborough.

"The Finleys' car slid partly off the drive and blocked it. No one could get in or out. That's partly why I felt sorry for Katja. It's not that big of a house when we're all in it at the same time. She's young, Stephen's young. . . ." Dr. Holst shrugs. "A neighbour with a tractor pulled the car out maybe late afternoon? After that, Ian—that's Ian Bennet, the owner," she stresses to me, supervising my note-taking. "Ian took the Christmas greenery to the recycling centre in Whittlesey. And—oh, yes! Marcus—Marcus Finley—had to pick up their kids from Grandmother's house. Shame they missed sharing the snowfall together."

Maybe Katja and Grace got a lift with Mr. Finley or Mr. Bennet, to a friend's house or to catch a bus or train. Or maybe one of those two saw Katja and Grace get into the car of someone who's already lied to us. We had to ask them.

Or maybe Katja and Grace didn't leave.

"Dr. Holst, one more thing . . ."

What's Keene after now?

"Did you ever see this man with Katja?" He holds out a printout of an academic Web page.

" 'George Hart-Fraser'?" she reads. "No."

"Did Grace ever mention him? Did she mention any boyfriend, or problems at Cambridge?"

Boyfriend? George Hart-Fraser was her supervisor. . . .

"No, I'm sorry, I— We didn't talk very much." She shakes her head.

I pull Keene aside on the landing, after the door has closed behind us. "Boyfriend? What haven't you told me?"

"Nothing. I'm speculating." He counts off the coincidences: "He was attached to both her and to Mathilde. He was late to the memorial. He wore a dark suit. . . ."

"You're wearing a dark suit," I point out.

"I didn't get to tell you yet. There was a suspicious death in his family. He was questioned in the matter."

"What? When?"

"Ten years ago," he admits, deflating a bit. "In Bristol."

"Tell me it involved a train or a hammer."

He shrugs and tilts his head. "Possible arson."

I hold out my hands, begging for something better than that. "Keene, really? There's nothing like that here. . . ."

That's when we smell smoke.

We bolt downstairs; five closed doors confront us. I sniff, but it's a subtle tinge to the air, nothing we can follow. What we can follow is the angry shouting coming from behind the middle door on our right, which turns out to be the communal laundry room.

Liliana is yelling at the tumble dryer. The smoky smell is more evident in here, and she tells us that the dryer has broken. She's in tears, and Daniel is hugging her legs. "Now I'll have to *hang* all the clothes," she says, looking aghast at the full bags of clothes and sheets she has yet to wash.

"I'll help you, Lili," says Daniel, and she scoops him up just like she did on the playground.

Over Daniel's shoulder, she asks us, "Why were you asking about the girl who used to work here?" She looks . . . worried, it must be. But her expression reads to me more like *guilty*.

"We just need to talk to her," I non-answer.

"Someone called here for her," she says. "I said I didn't know where she was, but I gave the name of the au pair agency before Mrs. Finley took the phone. I thought later that I shouldn't have said anything." She was bouncing Daniel this whole time, bouncing and patting his back.

"Can you describe the caller?" I ask.

"She was quiet, almost—"

"'She'?" I repeat. I was expecting an ex-boyfriend or stalker.

"Yes, she. I think she said her name was Tilda. She—"

Now Keene interrupts: "*Ma*-thilde?" asks Keene, emphasising the first syllable.

"I don't know. Maybe. She was quiet." Liliana got quiet herself. "If something has happened to Katja, it's my fault."

I assure her it wouldn't be her fault, and that in any case we have no reason to believe that Katja has come to harm. That's actually true; she's the wrong height for the fen body, which, if Stephen's reference to the sweater is to be believed, is very likely Grace.

We leave her and Daniel unloading wet socks onto a long row of drying racks. Keene saves his enthusiasm for after the door closes them in, leaving us alone in the main hall. "This is it," he says. "Mathilde called here. Whoever killed Grace knew someone was on to him. Well, at least on to her—about to identify her." His energy was nearly manic.

"Slow down, Keene. That doesn't make sense. Mathilde—if it was her, and I for one believe it was some Tilda, of which there are many in the world—called for information about *Katja*. Our body is most likely Grace. It doesn't make sense."

He presses his lips together. I'm convinced he does this to stop himself from saying something he shouldn't, like telling me off when he knows I'm right. "Well," he finally says, "if she called the Finley flat, she may have called other places, too. We should get her phone records. The point is, she was stirring things up."

"Fine," I concede. I make a note to request a list of Mathilde's recent calls.

He wants the cases to be linked. I'm not yet convinced Mathilde's death is a case at all. Her grief and the slippery snow give us two better explanations than murder. And if she was pushed? We'll never be able to attach that to a specific person. No, the only way that someone would end up punished is if we get them for something else. Like for Grace, so that's where we should focus.

"Come on," I say.

"All these doors . . . Take a look at your map?"

I unfold my sketch and hand it to him. He stands in the middle and turns, pointing. "Stephen—Help—Laundry . . . What are these other two?"

"The Bennet teenagers you met earlier. You know, the owner's family. Probably this one." I rest my hand on the one most likely to lead to all the space on the east side of the house that Mr. Casey's small flat doesn't use.

We knock. I want to ask Mr. Bennet if he knows how Grace and Katja left on the snowy day. No answer.

"And this one?" Keene wonders. Between the laundry and the Bennets. He knocks.

Just then, Liliana and Daniel emerge from the utility room. Daniel is wearing Spider-Man underpants on his head. Liliana says to us, "Don't bother. If he were in there, you'd know."

"Who?" I ask.

"Mr. Bennet," she says. "He's always working. The hammering is the worst, but the drill is loud, too."

"What's in there?" Keene asks.

She shrugs. "Nothing yet. He's renovating." Daniel spins in a circle, knocking into Liliana's legs.

Keene had said it was just the mum and the girls in the car. I ask Liliana if Mr. Bennet's car is still here. We all step outside onto the stone steps; she points out his Land Rover, in the spot closest to the house. "See, I saw him earlier," she said. "I told him you were here."

"You what? When?"

"While you were talking to Mrs. Finley."

Keene and I go back inside to rap on his door again. No answer, again. "Maybe he wants to dodge a charge of substandard workmanship," I joke.

"He's probably on the grounds," Liliana calls from the doorway, zipping Daniel into a jacket.

"Is he the gardener, too?" I ask sarcastically.

Now she's the one giggling. "He does *everything*!" She pinkens to her ears. I haven't seen Mr. Bennet for myself yet, but her reactions are giving me the hint that he's not bad to look at. "Come on, sweetheart, we have to pick up your sister," she says to Daniel, bending over to Velcro his shoes. The top of her thong peeks over her belt. Mrs. Finley would be livid.

Keene is anxious to get out of Deeping House. He wants to take a look at the likely dump spots along the B1040, now that the floods are receding back towards January levels, and now that we have Deeping House as a starting point.

"I just want to get this box ticked," I say, about Mr. Bennet. I don't want to have to come back. I need to get out myself, to the offices of Happy Mums au pair service. It's in a PE postcode, so close to here. The woman in charge refused to give me Katja's or Grace's info over the phone; she wants to see my warrant card.

Keene again raps on the door to the flat under construction. Again, no answer. "He must be outside," says Keene.

Stephen's uncle crosses the hall towards the utility room with a plastic hamper full of dingy whites: socks and shirts and probably underwear in there. "Mr. Casey," I call after him. "Do you know when Mr. Bennet will be back?"

He swears when he sees the washer in use, and we follow him back into his place. "Don't know. Maybe he's driving the daughter to her school. Term starts next week." But we know that he isn't. Keene said the mother is driving them. Casey starts up the machine for another coffee. Outside, Daniel is chasing Liliana. No wonder Stephen was distracted by Grace. What else was there to look at?

I look around. "Do you have a television?" I ask. I don't see one. The door to his bedroom hangs open. "Maybe in there?"

"Don't be daft," he chides me.

Fair enough. But Mrs. Finley—here I checked my notes to be sure—had said she sometimes heard television from in here.

No sense being coy about it. "Do you sing in the shower, Mr. Casey?"

He pops his mouth open so wide I fear he's about to let loose an aria. Instead, he laughs. "Yes!" he says. "Yes, I do!"

"You hear that?" I say to Keene. "We're on the wrong track." The Holsts, in the back of the house, hear him sing in the shower. The Finleys, in the front of the house, hear someone's television. Rory Casey's place is also at the front, so the Finleys were right to assume they hear it, but: "The Finleys don't hear this flat. They think they do, because they're above it, but . . ." I look up.

"May I?" I ask, indicating the bedroom. Mr. Casey waggles his eyebrows. I stand inside it, gauging its size. I exit into the hall; the stairs curve up next to the room, and the landing tops it entirely. None of that bedroom is underneath an upstairs flat. The bath is under the Holsts' entry hall. The Finleys' lounge is L-shaped. It covers Mr. Casey's main room, yes, but then it turns and covers . . .

I send Keene back to Mrs. Finley. He resists. "I don't know," I say. "Make something up. Ask her for her husband's work number, or about the Bennets." Why not? I just need him up there for a good five minutes.

Back to Mr. Casey's bedroom. I cast about for something to make noise with, the appropriate kind of noise. Bashing pots and pans from the kitchen wouldn't really be equivalent. "All right, Mr. Casey," I sigh, "this is your cue."

His voice is better than I thought it would be. I don't understand the Italian, but his face and gestures indicate a melodramatic deathbed scene. He hits the high note sprawled across my feet, one hand reaching up to me, his *"amore."*

He's getting back to his feet when Keene returns. "She says Mr. Bennet is stingy with the heating and that Mrs. Bennet overindulges her daughters. 'Even the cancer one'—that is an exact quote. She also says that if we call her husband at work we should remind him that tonight is date night and he had better not be late." He shudders. "I'm more inclined to tell him to escape while he can. Why did you want me up there?"

"Did you hear it?"

"Hear what?"

Mr. Casey grins. He exits to get his coffee.

"The Finleys didn't hear Grace and Stephen. They can't. And there's no television in here. They overhear the Bennets' flat." On the other side of this wall.

I mentally list the occupants of Deeping House, stuck in by the weather on the snowy day: The Bennet girls were out with their mum. The Finley children were at Grandma's. Everyone else was trapped in. I jot the remaining names into my little map, showing where each claims to have gone after the weather started. There are only two people we haven't accounted for yet.

I'm no longer indignant for Katja. We know from Stephen that she didn't have sex with him, as Mrs. Finley had accused. But this was more damning: She'd had sex with the married dad next door.

"What if Grace realised it?" I suggest. "What if she threatened to tell?"

"Stephen didn't mention anything like that," Keene reminds me.

"Stephen was off doing a load of laundry," I remind him right back. I want to get into the Bennet place, to test what can be heard between these two bedrooms, the Bennets' and Stephen's.

No point knocking again, though.

"Where's the recycling centre?" I call out to Mr. Casey. Dr. Holst had said Mr. Bennet drove there on the snowy day to get rid of the Christmas greenery. What a strange job to finish in bad weather instead of waiting.

"Whittlesey," he says. Yes, that's what Dr. Holst had said. Whittlesey. I think that's— "Down the B1040," he finishes for me. "When it's open, of course . . ."

Of course. The B1040 is closed now, but on the snowy day, it crossed over the Nene, right where Grace's body likely went in.

CHAPTER 20

GRACE RHYS

I woke up cold.

I curled my knees up to my chest. It was still darkish, which at this time of year meant about seven-thirty? Roughly? The clock was facing away from me. Sunday was a day off for both of us, so we hadn't set our mobiles to wake us. Every day was about to become a day off for me.

Mrs. Holst had got tired of me. She said I could leave early if I wanted, or stay on and do my own thing; either way, they'd pay me for the week. She said it cheerfully, like it was a favour. If I had someplace to go, it would have been. As it was, it hurried up what I'd been avoiding: that I wasn't going back to Cambridge the week after next.

Mum was in Jordan now, hot and dry in the desert with Shep. Our house had tenants in it. Someone was sleeping in my room, and all my things were in boxes in the garage. The quilt my grandmother had made was folded up in there, and the afghan I wove in a textiles summer course, and my slippers shaped like two of Santa's reindeer.

I was really cold.

There was no staying asleep, so I made myself sit up. Katja's bed was empty. I considered adding her duvet to mine and curling back up, but then I turned my head to the window.

The glow of oncoming morning light behind the curtain was splotched and . . . *undulating,* it seemed. I pushed the curtain to one side.

Falling snow.

I jumped into a kneeling position and clutched the duvet up to my chin. *Snow!* Great thick hunks of it, not a sprinkle or powder. All my winters had been cold, but not to the point of ice—just persistent with the bone-reaching chill of damp and almost-frozen rain. An occasional flurry got my hopes up as a child, but there had never been enough for snowmen or even snowballs.

This was thick stuff, dumping from the sky. The grey garden walls and green yew hedge were topped inches high already. A dark coat flashed past the window, followed by an abrupt wallop against the glass.

I pulled on a second pair of socks, and jeans over my leggings. At the door, I stepped into my wellies and buttoned up my Paddington-Bear-style coat over the college sweatshirt I'd slept in.

Even the hallway felt different. Colder, of course, and the radiator hissed more viciously. The Christmas tree was gone; the stand was there, empty, and the ornament boxes, mostly packed except for a flash of silver garland springing out of the top. There was a weight on the house, an enveloping quietness. Then, suddenly, shrill laughter, and another *whap* against an outside wall.

I opened the front door. Frigid air hit the back of my throat. Snow stung my tongue. The Christmas tree and the dry, browning wreath from the door leaned up one side of the steps, so there was only a narrow path down.

Katja scooped up another snowball, patting it round. She flung it overhand, towards the hedge, where it crashed and shook snow loose from the branches. From behind there, a figure rose, retaliating with three quick balls in succession, then ducking again. Katja was hit, on the shoulder and knee. She squealed and ran around the other side of the hedge. He kept low and came around the front, where I could see him. He lifted a finger to his lips. It was Mr. Bennet. Katja leapfrogged over the hedge and grabbed off his hat. She ran, and he tackled her.

Katja squealed again, but this time it sounded painful. I ran to them. He got off her. "Are you all right?" he asked. She was breathing heavily but sat up. "Bastard," she said, then something vicious-sounding in Finnish. He laughed.

Mr. Bennet's dark hair was wild and he hadn't shaved. Katja stared at him, still breathing hard.

I wondered where his family was, but then I remembered. Mrs. Bennet had talked up her Christmas gift to the girls: appointments with an astrologer in London. It was the perfect way, she said, to begin a new school term and a new year. Max, the sick daughter, had come home for Christmas just like the doctors said she would, and seemed nice, if quiet. She had a lot of wigs. Christmas day, she wore a bright red bob.

I glanced over at the car park. Their car was gone.

"Ow," Katja said, grabbing her neck.

"Are you all right?" I asked, at the same time that Mr. Bennet leaned over.

With her other hand, she smashed him in the face with snow. He roared and shook his head, while she scuttled backwards then got up and ran again. "Get him, Grace!" she called.

"Grace!" called a littler voice from the steps. Lizzy and Brent ran to me. They wore proper snowsuits, all quilted and waterproof. Their outfits were so puffed and shiny that they almost appeared to be inflated. Lizzy took a tumble, and for a moment I thought she'd pop or bounce.

The sun was fully up now, its light bouncing off the white everywhere. The snow was still coming down, piling up on my shoulders, my hair, my lashes, my chest, anywhere there was any kind of shelf. I turned around to see what Katja was laughing at, and a ball of snow as big as my head smacked me full on the face.

Bitch, I thought. How dare she? And how dare she flirt like that with a dad while his family is out for the day? She said once that she wished Mr. Finley had had a full-blown affair with the woman from work. She said Mrs. Finley deserved to be cheated on. Did she think the same of Mrs. Bennet?

Once I'd caught her staring at him. "That's not funny," I'd told her. "His kid is in hospital."

"He's their stepfather, not their real father. Stop being so serious."

If anyone ever said it was okay for someone to sleep with Shep because he's not my real father, only my mum's second husband, I wouldn't take it. But this was Katja. She liked to get a rise out of people.

With my hands I started sweeping together the mother of all snowballs.

Mr. Finley, dressed for work, skirted the war zone on the way to his car. He wiped his windscreen with a handkerchief, then looked back at Mrs. Finley watching from their window. He waved with the handkerchief hand. It looked like a surrender. This weekend they'd sent the kids to Grandma's, Katja thinks so they can have loud sex to make up for his almost-affair. We worked out that we sleep underneath them. So far we haven't heard anything.

Mr. Finley's wheels spun in the snow, then the car lurched back out of his place. We all watched him. He backed far enough to turn and fishtailed a bit. The whole group of us flinched.

He coasted in a perfect gentle curve to the mouth of the exit.

The drive bends, so we didn't see it happen. The snow softened sound, so the impact was muffled; it sounded like a box falling off a shelf. But he hit the horn on impact, so we ran after him.

He hadn't veered far off. Most of his car was still on the drive—across it, actually. The front tyres had dipped into the ditch on the side, and the bumper had come to rest against a birch.

Mr. Bennet and Mr. Holst joined Mr. Finley around the vehicle, discussing options. They decided it wasn't worth it to try to pull it out with one of the other cars, given the chances of a worse accident resulting. Mr. Bennet knew a farmer nearby who could do it with a tractor. "I'll ring him," he offered, and a few minutes later reported that he'd try to come before the end of the day.

Behind me, Mrs. Holst explained to the kids that they couldn't go to a friend's birthday party. There was no way anyone could get a car out around Mr. Finley's. We turned to trudge back towards the house.

The wafting flakes turned to slushy globs, then sloppy, wet lashings. Rain spots stippled the white expanse covering the garden. By the time we reached the footpath to the house, it was spilling on us. We huddled on the steps and around the front door, as Mr. Bennet reached for the handle. It rattled, but he hadn't touched it yet. He froze, hand hovering. The handle turned perpendicular, and the door fell in. We all leaned forward. Stephen, the writer, blinked at us from inside. "Did I sleep through it?"

———

We all dripped in the hallway. Mr. Bennet unfolded a wool blanket to make it wide enough for all our boots and trainers. We hung coats from the bannister and door handles and from the corners of the pigeonhole shelving that divided the mail. Gloves and hats were laid on the radiator. We stood around in wet socks, damp sweaters and jeans, looking to politely unbond. Mr. Finley's accident had blocked any escape by car, and the rain put the garden out of the running. We were all in for the rest of the day. With halfhearted waves and some awkward handshakes, the Holst family and the Finleys as a couple retreated upstairs to their flats. Katja pulled off the sweater she had on over a purple T-shirt and shook out her hair, smiling at Mr. Bennet. He pretended not to notice and apologised to the rest of us that he'd get the Christmas detritus to the recycling centre another day. Their individual doors closed behind them. Ten seconds later, music pulsed from our room.

My heart thudded. It took me a moment to figure out that it was in anger. She knows I hate that CD; she treats our room like it's hers and I'm just there for sleepovers; she pretends to be Dru's and Max's friend and then shimmies her chest at their stepdad; she laughs at Mr. Finley's almost-affair and wishes he would "get some" because Mrs. Finley is a bitch. She is, but she's not the only one.

"Katja," said Stephen.

I flinched and shivered. I hadn't realised he was still there.

"I'm sorry I missed it," he said, half turned towards his door and half towards me. Except his face, which looked straight at the shiny wood floor and his blue socks. "Must have been a good time out there." He tilted his head up just a bit and smiled at me.

"It was," I said coolly. "Why didn't you come outside?"

"I just woke up. Late night. I was finishing a chapter."

My sweatshirt was wet through. My feet were frozen.

"Katja," he said again. This time I twigged that he meant me. "Would you like a cup of tea?"

"I hate tea," I said automatically, because I do hate it. Inside, I was thinking, *That bitch.*

He'd meant me. Katja was always sending me to do her work; the kids must have called for her and got me instead a dozen times. He worked behind that window right in front of the climbing frame every day. He'd written a note for Katja—thinking me—and made a date for dinner—with me—and when she showed up? He must have asked her where I was, and I bet she thought fast. Said that I'd sent her to say I wasn't coming, then told *me* that he had "offended" her. My imagination had filled in the blanks, and held it against him.

"I like coffee," I added.

We went into his flat and closed the door.

He'd been tidying and packing. He'd arranged that he'd drive to the Peterborough station and leave the car for his uncle to pick up on his return train from Heathrow. Stephen himself was catching a train down to Cornwall, to crash at a friend's farm and write. It was a dairy farm, with a guesthouse and seventy-five cows.

Outside, the rain just kept coming. I think he was nervous around me. Figuring out the equipment for grinding the beans and frothing the milk gave him something else to focus on. "Are you cold?" he suddenly asked, over his shoulder. "Would you like a dry sweater?"

None of the fireplaces at Deeping House worked. That was just too much trouble, I guess, but it would have been nice today.

"Yes, please." I pulled off my Corpus sweatshirt and laid it over the back of a chair. My T-shirt underneath was dry but thin. He went into the bedroom, where his suitcase was open on the neatly made bed. I followed. "Here," he said, holding out a red sweater.

His hair hadn't been cut in ages but was clearly the grow-out of a once shorter cut, not deliberately long. He had thick eyelashes and clean fingernails. He was slim, long-legged. Hadn't shaved today but probably yesterday. He was offering me a sweater and had made me a coffee and stayed up late to do work he loved.

I pulled my T-shirt off over my head. He goggled and turned his back; that hand with the sweater still reached out to me. I took it and threw it back into the suitcase. "Would a different one . . ." he said, turning towards the suitcase, full of sweaters, sweaters on sweaters like kittens in a basket. I was in his peripheral vision. I unhooked my bra.

"Katja," he said, glancing at me.

I wriggled the bra down my arms and dropped it. I got close, which rubbed my nipples up against his rough sweater. "Get it off," I said, and he did. Then the buttoned shirt, which caught for a moment at the cuffs, inside-out sleeves dangling from his wrists; then the T-shirt over his head. He put his hands on my bare waist and we grazed lips, tapped tongues. His caution turned into confidence, our standing embrace into a tangle across the pillows.

"Do you have a condom?" I asked. I had some in the help flat, in my bathroom bag. I asked out of convenience, out of don't-kill-the-mood-by-making-me-go-get-them, but he must have thought I was depending on him. He ransacked all three dresser drawers, shoving their contents around. In the bottom one he found a box and he held it up, breathing hard, triumphant.

We got the rest of the way naked, dumped the suitcase, and got under the duvet. We hugged to warm up, rubbing each other's backs with our fronts pressed together. My hair was all over his face; his mouth kissed up and down my neck. He tickled my ear with his tongue, which makes me crazy, and loud.

I got on top. The duvet slipped from my shoulders to my hips. I rocked. "Do you like it?" I said.

"Yes."

"Should I stop?"

"No!"

"Say how much you want me to keep fucking you."

"I want it. I want you to do it. Please don't stop."

"Beg me."

"Fuck me. Please, fuck me." He chanted it while I rolled my hips back and forth, back and forth, until he reached up and pinched my tits and made me come. "Oh!" I yelled. "Oh!" I flopped, and my thighs spasmed. I lay on his chest.

He rolled me over and thrust three times to come, too. We breathed hard together for a few minutes. Finally, "Blimey," he said, and smiled.

He had a crooked canine tooth and pink cheeks. I kissed his mouth. "Blimey," I said in return.

We hugged and petted a little, until the clock reminded him of his uncle's train. "Shit," he said. "I'm going to have to wash the sheets again."

"I'll take a shower," I offered, vacating the linens.

Under the hot water, I considered my options. I couldn't cope with Katja anymore. She'd lied to me about Stephen. She must have felt humiliated when she showed up to see him and he asked where I was. *Good,* I thought. *Fuck Katja.*

Mrs. Holst had said I could leave. Maybe Stephen could give me a lift. Pip's family lives in Peterborough.

Nostalgia for uni knocked me hard: my room, the courtyards, King's Parade, Pip and her crowd. She used to annoy the shit out of me. I can't even remember why. She was never anything but enthusiastic. *Well, maybe* that's *why.* . . . I smiled. She always had her work done. She always had her hair done. I'd been jealous. I was as bad as Katja.

A rap on the door. "Soap?" Stephen offered. He'd unpacked his body wash for me. I said thanks, and he handed it past the shower curtain. "I have to visit London in a few months," he said. "That's not so far from Cambridge. . . ."

I flinched. How did he even know? Did everyone know that I'm a "Cambridge girl"?

Then I remembered my sweatshirt. Mum had been so proud. She'd bought us all Corpus sweatshirts. I bet she and Shep took them on their trip, for cold shipboard evenings, and bragged about me. I'd worn it because I was cold, but accidentally I'd been flashing the college crest everywhere.

"We don't really need to do that," I said. I didn't want to explain why I wouldn't be there, at least not the rest of this year.

"You're right, of course. Sorry," he said. "I'll be in the laundry room."

He was nice. Maybe explaining wouldn't be so bad. *His publisher will have some address, or his website will have something,* I thought. *Maybe, once I've made some decisions and figured things out, I'll write to him.*

There were towels on the rack, but he would have washed and hung them this morning for his uncle. I made wet little footprints into the bedroom.

The duvet made a heap on the bare mattress. Stephen's clothes were gone, presumably on him or in the wash with the sheets. My clothes, which I'd tossed to the floor, were on the bed, with the red sweater he'd intended to loan me. I used my T-shirt to dry off.

While I rubbed it on my legs, I heard a worrying moan. "Stephen?" I said. But it wasn't coming from the direction of the rest of the flat.

It came again: *Uuhn.* And again: *Uh, uh, uuuh . . .* from the wall.

Oh, shit. If I could hear them, they'd heard us. I didn't usually dirty-talk. I didn't usually make a man beg. I guess they'd liked the show. I covered my laugh with my hand. I didn't want them to realise I was hearing them.

He got growlier as the rhythm sped up, and louder.

Mr. Bennet! I thought. *Who knew you had it in you like that?*

Then I remembered: The rest of the Bennets were in London; Mr. Bennet was home alone. And with the Finley kids at Grandma's, Katja had nothing to do.

I thought she'd been joking, just posturing. A married man, maybe . . . but Dru and Max's dad? These were people we knew. Max was sick. Dru was lonely. How could she do that? And in their *home*?

Maybe, like me, she'd got a little competitive, and a little spiteful, if she figured out I was in Stephen's flat. Where else would I be, if I wasn't in with her? It was pouring outside. Mr. Finley's car blocked the drive. She knew the Holsts were sick of me. I had to be somewhere.

The grunting got faster. She made noise, too, a continuous keening that wobbled every time he pushed it in. It went on like that. I got into my clothes. The last big groan sounded like all N's and G's with an exclamation mark at the end: *Nnnnnnnnnggggg!* Quiet; then he said something I couldn't understand; then a door shut.

I put the sweater on last, Stephen's red sweater. My Corpus sweat-shirt was still damp. I left it on the chair to dry. Stephen would be back shortly. I'd ask him about a lift then.

I opened the door to the front hall. The outside door just clicked shut, and through the mullioned window I saw Mr. Bennet head out into the rain. He rubbed his face with his hands. *At least he knows he's guilty,* I thought.

I walked around the stairs to the Bennets' door. She was still in there. Every cruel compliment she'd ever thrown me, every time she'd shoved her responsibilities off on me, every chance she took to make herself the A to my B, coalesced into a hot anger.

I knocked by hitting the door with my fist.

CHAPTER 21

MORRIS KEENE

We're near the tail of the fens' annual swell, and January would have been at the head. So the water levels would have looked much as they do now.

The area where the body had been found, and the flooded areas along the road where it might have gone in, had both been searched and given nothing. The water was wide, and there were too many ditches and conduits feeding it. But now, with Deeping House as a starting point, and the waters receding to January's levels, perhaps the source of the body dump could be narrowed down.

The B1040 is still closed. I park at the defunct Dog in a Doublet pub and walk down the road until it slips under the risen river. This is the road Marcus Finley drove to pick up his children from his in-laws'. This is the road Ian Bennet drove to dump the Christmas tree at the recycling centre. This is a road back to Cambridge. To have got where it ended up, the body likely went in somewhere along here. Divers had searched. Nothing additional had been found.

I stare out over the water. Chloe prefers action. But we've split up; she's visiting the au pair agency that booked both Katja and Grace. I can think as long as I like.

Where are Grace's things? They had to have been got rid of. They could have gone in with the body, and floated or decomposed differently. But if her shared room had been occupied at the time of the murder, they may have been gathered after.

There are side roads between here and Deeping House, leading to ditches that, at higher water, would connect with the river and floodplains. They all seem too wide-open, though. Next to a farmhouse, or commuter road. Then I start coming across tracks, running along more wet ditches, more secluded ones. I follow two, noting their locations for possible future forensic search. They're long; it will be a slog. Halfway along the second one, something catches my eye. It turns out to be a crushed beer can reflecting sunlight off its facets. And a toothbrush next to it.

Maybe someone dumped their rubbish here.

There, a ChapStick. And a plastic hairbrush. This is a very specific kind of rubbish, and, looking at the brush, not actually rubbish at all.

I think about the body, how it had sunk at first, and then filled with the various gases of decomposition and rose with the spring heat. I wonder what else might happen underwater. I wonder what might happen to a suitcase or duffel bag, weighted with personal objects. Maybe it took this long for a fastener to deteriorate, or for a creature to gnaw a hole through, freeing floatable objects. There, bobbing on the surface: a clear plastic bottle. Not a drink. Maybe shampoo.

I crack a thin branch off a tree. It's not long enough.

I roll up my trousers, choose ruining my shoes over maybe cutting my feet, and step in up to my knees. I sweep the bottle to me with the branch's twig fingers.

It's a nearly empty bottle of cheap purple shampoo. Someone had written, in permanent marker, two small letters on the side, like one might write if sharing a bathroom, in the help flat at Deeping House, or in a college residence. "G.R." Grace Rhys.

I wade out, pulling the bottle behind me with the stick. I don't want to touch it without gloves. I bump it up the bank onto the grass verge. I need to call for a forensics team.

The phone resists at first, rubbing up against my keys also nestled in there. So I grip hard and jerk it out. It pops out from between my fingers and makes an arc towards the water. I reach with my other hand to catch it, my right hand. But, without me being able to close my fingers round it, it bounces, making a second, greater arc.

It sails. It plops. It sinks.

I take off my coat, to keep it dry, along with my suit jacket. I step in, pushing down hard to avoid slipping on the slime underfoot. I can't use a stick for this; I'll have to get right to the centre where it fell. I force myself to breathe slowly, making a whistling sound exhaling between my compressed lips. I hesitate.

Turns out the water in which Grace Rhys's belongings bobbed isn't more than three feet deep. I get wet up to mid-thigh, then up to my left shoulder bending to retrieve a hard little object I've stepped on. It's not my phone. It's a watch face without a band; probably that was leather. It's tangled with a thin gold necklace and a single earring shaped like a crescent moon.

The watch has an engraving on its back: a year, a city, school initials, and a surname: Hart-Fraser.

Hart-Fraser? That's George, from Corpus. I swirl my feet farther around the bottom until I kick into my phone. I pluck it up and wade out, dropping down on the grass. I squeeze out my trousers and wrap my coat over my shoulders. I wipe my mobile and shake it and press its dead buttons, over and over and over, my teeth clacking together from cold.

——————

Back at Deeping House, I use Rory Casey's landline while he plugs an electric fire in next to me to dry me off. I need to call a forensics team to the site, which I'd marked by tying my scarf to a branch. I have the shampoo bottle with the initials, the necklace and earring, the hairbrush, and the engraved watch with me; I didn't dare leave them.

But I don't know the number. I don't know even Chloe's number. Why would I? They're in my phone, my now-dead phone. I shiver. *Wait*—Chloe had handed her business cards out to witnesses like they were little prizes. Mr. Casey has one. I phone the number.

"Detective Inspector Chloe Frohmann," she answers. I realise that with me calling from this phone, of course she doesn't know who I am.

"Chloe, it's me. I'm—"

"Keene?" Her voice transitions from clipped and formal to exasperated. "What are you doing? Where's your phone?"

"I've got something."

"Bad timing, Keene. I'm in the thick of it. Just tell me."

She gets angry when I don't phone with new developments right away, but she doesn't want to be interrupted? I could do without the parental inflection. "I found Grace's belongings. They were dumped in a wet ditch. Can you call forensics for me?"

"I'll call CSI," she says, correcting me. "Where's your phone? Where are you?"

No need to answer that tone of voice. "I think George Hart-Fraser is the man we're looking for. His watch is tangled up with her things. It could have fallen off him while he hauled the body about or packed up her belongings. Maybe she called him when she wanted to leave, and he picked her up at the road." I hadn't thought it through yet, but it sounded good as it came out of me. When was the heat going to reach the inside of my body? The bone chill shivered inside me even as the heat from the electric fire grazed the hairs on my leg.

"Keene, what's going on?"

"I went in the water. I'm cold. But it was worth it. Don't fuss; I've got a heater blasting me now. Thirty-five centimetre, dark brown hairs. Sound familiar?"

It takes her a moment. "The hammer?"

Yes! The hammer and bloody shirt from Trumpington Road. The hairs wrapped round its claw seem consistent with the hairs from Grace's hairbrush, at least in my eyeballing of them.

Chloe gets it.

"George's address should have bit me harder," I say. It's close to where the hammer and shirt had been found—too close. Chloe admits she's in Cambridge. I ask her to feel him out about the watch, just the watch, because she's near. And to call forensics for me, to meet me at Deeping House.

"Keene, what happened to your phone?"

I'm really cold. Just shivers at first, but with my voice added it sounds like laughing. "I dropped it. Going after the watch." It was almost as true as stumbling on the watch after I dropped my phone.

"How cold are you, exactly? Is that your teeth?"

"I'm fine." I am fine. I wish people would stop making me say that. I turn up the dial on the electric fire. I cough. *No,* I lecture myself. *Now is not the time to fall ill.* "You sound like my brother."

"Richard? Bloody hell, Keene, what's wrong with you?" Her indignant tone chills me further. It's like we're having two different conversations.

"What are you talking about?" I ask meekly.

She sighs, exasperated. "Richard brought you his car. He must have told you."

"No, see, he left it for me. He left me the car. We haven't spoken."

She breathes a few times—in, out, in, out—without saying anything. Then, "Alice near miscarried on Tuesday. That's why Richard had the car when it was supposed to be waiting for you. He'd driven to the hospital. She's home on bed rest now."

Alice is pregnant? "How do you know that?" I ask. It's like there's some pregnant-women secret society.

"Shit, Morris, I knew something had to be wrong when Richard hadn't come through with the car. I called and asked."

No, no, no, no, no. This is not the way things work. Chloe is work. Richard and Alice are family. Not just family, a certain kind of family. My old family, my childhood family. Gwen and Dora are my family-family. And anything that goes between those different groups is supposed to go through me. That's how it works. "Why do you even have their phone number?"

She doesn't have to answer. The hospital waiting rooms. They'd all mixed together there, worried for me. Nervous laughter, comforting hugs. It was my fault, too. I call her Chloe now, instead of by her last name. I'd got used to Gwen calling her that. It just came out. Now the clear boundaries in my life were rubbed away.

I think, *I don't want you talking behind my back to my family.* Before I actually say it out loud, I hang up.

I have to phone Richard. Maybe he'll accept my apology for hounding him about the car, and maybe he won't. Maybe he'll spew a whole lot of words that I pretty much deserve. I don't know if I can manage saying anything right, but I could be a target for him. Sometimes a person has a right to be angry at life, and no one to pummel. I could give him that, at least.

But I don't know Richard's new number off by heart. His wedding and move weren't so long ago, and, with the number in my mobile, it wasn't necessary to memorise it. At least, it hadn't seemed so.

I breathe out. Chloe will know it. Will she give it up to me without a lecture?

I reach for Mr. Casey's phone one more time. I almost lift the receiver.

Instead, "Cheers, mate," I say to Mr. Casey, standing up.

I kick each of my legs. The trousers are mostly dry.

If I want Chloe to stay out of my family affairs, that has to start with me.

No, not "Chloe." *Frohmann.* It's important to address her like the co-officer she is, and insist on the same in return. I have to get things back to the way they were when things worked.

"Do you know where Mr. Bennet is?" I ask Mr. Casey. If I expect Frohmann to go after George in Cambridge for me, it's only fair I pursue her interests here.

"I saw him head to work an hour ago. He won't finish until late. But he works nearby."

I ask for an address. I don't need Chloe to write it down. It's "across the hall."

I knock at the flat under renovation. No sound of power tools or hammering inside, but there's a lot else a person can call work. I try the door, only to check if it's locked, but it pops open an inch, as if the latch hadn't been lined up with its catch exactly right.

"Mr. Bennet?" I call out. I don't enter. I don't have permission.

Behind me, Mr. Casey barks, "Inspector! Telephone call for you."

It has to be Chloe. I try to close the door, but it doesn't hit the frame right. If this is the kind of work he'd overseen or himself performed elsewhere in the building, it's no wonder people were hearing one another through the floors.

I pull up roughly, to bring the hardware in line, but my grip slips. The door swings all the way inward, with a whoosh that ruffles the sawdust on the floor.

The room is all skeleton, no skin. Posts and beams are exposed; wiring runs up and down the walls like veins.

The man, however, is fully clothed: A thick buttoned shirt tucked into belted jeans. White socks and trainers, one of them untied and hanging off from the toes.

A jostle from the door is enough. The shoe drops.

"Inspector! Telephone!" Rory Casey near brays.

"I'm here," I say, not turning.

He comes up behind me, then with a swear charges in. He gets up on a stool, pulling the body up to take the pressure off the neck. "For Christ's sake, man!" he calls at me.

I get on a crate. I pull the rope off, up around the face, catching on the nose. The head falls back and its hair tickles my neck. A suck of breath.

Casey has the legs and I get my arms under the shoulders and around the chest, my left hand clutching my right wrist tight. We lower him to the dirty floor, where the head flops. Casey leans over his face to listen for another breath.

But it was Liliana who'd gasped, the Finleys' au pair, on the stairs with the little boy. He stares at us through the bars of the bannister.

Casey tilts the head back. He pinches the nose and blows air into the grey-lipped mouth.

On the stairs, the au pair pulls on the little boy, and he elbows her. Daniel. His name is Daniel. He's what, three? "I want to see," he insists.

I lunge to close the door. The latch refuses to catch, so I lean back on it, to hold it shut. Through it I hear something like a quick shriek and a tussle and the boy crying. Pounding footsteps on the stairs.

She'll call 999, I assure myself. We need the pathologist, and the forensics team. And Chloe. We'll need her here.

Casey pumps on the chest. I swear I hear a rib crack, just crunch under the pressure. "Please stop," I say to Casey. But he's wild-eyed. He keeps on; he keeps pushing. And the body jolts and wiggles, rubberlike, every time.

PART III

CHAPTER 22

GEORGE HART-FRASER

TEN YEARS AGO

I had to wear my school uniform. Nothing else I had was suitable. The other applicants I saw wore personal clothes that had been pressed and well matched. Mine didn't need pressing. I was sheathed in a cheap, unwrinkleable acrylic.

Stephen had interviewed wearing borrowed cashmere and good shoes. He'd driven with a group of friends. His was the sort of school full of Oxbridge applicants. I took the bus.

Stephen Hart-Fraser was my brother. He was charming, and took tests well. He followed instructions with seeming alacrity, then mocked the teachers later with his friends. He was a bully. He was popular. He had a gift for gleaning from any question what the asker wanted the answer to be.

That's why we attended different schools. He was plucked out and granted a "scholarship for fatherless boys" to the school on the hill. The day-boys, such as he, wore practical, plain clothes: a jacket with crest and orange-striped tie over white shirt and dark trousers. The boarders still wore the old Elizabethan pattern of uniform, and he was merciless towards those blue-belted coats that looked like dresses, the white collars, the canary-yellow knee socks.

Stephen did very well there. He'll never know if he came first or third in the exams. The school names the top three, and identifies only which of them was in second place. First and third are left to forever wonder, and no one is able to claim to be the best.

I remained in the state school, struggling with handwriting and peers, the two things the teachers seemed to most concern themselves with. The only subject that inspired me was maths. It was a revelation. I wasn't dependent on lessons or books for the answers. Everything that had ever been learned from numbers had come from the numbers themselves, and could be discovered and proved anew. No special knowledge or trust or interpretation was required. It was a safe place.

A girl from my school got in the year before me to read history at Oxford. It wasn't unheard of to reach.

I thought the interviews would be like tests, but they were conversations. Conversations about maths, to be precise, but not questions and answers. I wasn't expected to bark solutions. The teachers mused with me. Tobias Oliver was one of those teachers. We talked about Bristol; he had gone to Stephen's school and had happy memories.

I stilled inside when he said the name of it. Tobias—I called him Dr. Oliver, then, of course—didn't notice the change. He carried on the conversation, but my gears had stopped turning. When he asked the next question, I had no context. I opened my mouth but said nothing. He repeated the question.

I shook my head. What if I did make it? Stephen would be here, too. Not at this college—he had applied to Trinity—but in the lectures. We would sit the same exams. He would get a first and mock anyone I called a friend and fuck women I wouldn't even be able to talk to. He belonged here.

"George, why do you want to come here?"

I didn't anymore. Wouldn't I be better off somewhere Stephen wasn't? It wasn't enough to leave home if the worst part of home came with me. I shook my head again.

He tried a different tack: "Why maths?"

Because it's perfect. Because it's certain. Because I can work it out for myself and not be dependent on others' subjective judgements. Because it's vast. It's a road that doesn't peter out. "It makes me happy," I said.

Dr. Oliver leaned forward. "I feel the same way." He smiled at me. "Shall we have some fun?"

We played. Numbers are the perfect toys. He let me overrun my appointment time. Eventually he flicked a glance at his watch. I stopped; I apologised.

"Thank you, George. I hope we may continue our conversation," he said.

Did he mean that he would recommend me? Are they allowed to say that?

"Yes, sir," I said. I wanted it again. Stephen was irrelevant. Stephen was outside of this room. So long as I could be inside this room, and rooms like it, and carry on the rest of my life as this last half hour had been, Stephen could do what he liked. It didn't matter that Stephen would do better. So long as I could do *this*.

I didn't have money for a café; I bought a sandwich to eat on the bus. The person in the seat next to me played his music so loud that it leaked through his headphones. I curled my posture away from him. As we neared Bristol, my stomach tensed. Traffic crowded around us. I felt squeezed by it. Squeezed, and shrunken. By the time I was home, I was small again.

———

Stephen was pooled. That means his college of choice had declined to admit him, but his application had been opened to the other colleges, who could consider him to fill leftover spaces. None did.

It was wondered in our family what would have happened if he hadn't been so ambitious in aiming for Trinity. Trinity was Isaac Newton's college, and remained the top for maths. Perhaps if he had applied to . . . "Newnham," I teased him. Newnham is all-girl. He poured his breakfast glass of milk on my head. I wiped my school clothes as best I could; I didn't have another set clean. I stank of sourness the rest of the day.

I received a conditional offer from Corpus Christi, contingent on my exam results. Our mother called to confirm that this was correct, assuming there had been a mix-up with our names. But Stephen hadn't applied to Corpus.

My arrival for the interview had been meek. The bus was dirty. The architecture had seemed too grand, and the saints and founders in the niches to look down on me.

As a student, I arrived by car. My maths teacher from school, Mr. Avery, had driven me there. I was his first Oxbridge acceptance. He shook my hand.

CHAPTER 23

CHLOE FROHMANN

The address of Happy Mums au pair service is an ordinary home, not a business address. As I'd been instructed over the phone, I walk behind the house to a large garden shed, one of those expensive "spare room" options garden centres are pushing now, with a porch and windows.

Inside it, Mrs. Heatherly, CEO of Happy Mums, is at work. She looks up from her laptop and comes to the door. I show her my warrant card and get to the point. "Have you spoken with Katja Koskinen since she left the employ of the Finleys at Deeping House?" Maybe Katja knows what happened to Grace. Maybe something has also happened to Katja.

"No. She's being childish. She's not taking my calls."

Or she can't take your calls, I think. I take the seat Mrs. Heatherly offers me.

"Mrs. Finley was most disappointed by the whole situation. We're lucky she continued to hire through us. Do you know how Liliana is getting on?"

"She's fine. About Katja—"

"I have work for Katja, but I suppose she thinks she's too good for it. It's mostly cleaning," Mrs. Heatherly concedes. She removes her glasses. "Really, what did she expect? After the Finley incident, my hands were tied. I couldn't *lie* about it."

I wonder if Mrs. Heatherly has had sex this week. I wonder how Mrs. Heatherly would feel about spending life as a permanent guest. I wonder how Mrs. Heatherly would like it if she were stuck being an adult to the children, but a child to the parent employers. "Do you know where she's working now?" I ask evenly.

She answers the frostiness in my voice instead of the question. "It's not just the sex," she says. "There was stealing."

"Stealing?" That seems more Grace's purview. According to Keene, Grace had a shoplifting past.

"Mrs. Finley reported a digital clock missing from the flat she'd provided. Oh, and a cup. A 'decorated mug.'" She looks up from the page.

"She shared the room. How do you know it wasn't Grace Rhys?" I ask. Maybe Grace threw those things into her suitcase on top of all her own. No—that didn't feel right. Shoplifters get a rush from their crimes. Sweeping things up while packing doesn't seem deliberate enough. But if she'd been killed before she left the house, those are the kind of things the killer, covering for her absence, might accidentally remove along with her things. Yes, it was reading more like Grace had been killed before she left Deeping House.

"Oh, Grace!" Mrs. Heatherly says, face full of smile. "She was just temporary, for a holiday lark. She must be back at Cambridge now. If I had more girls like her . . ."

"In what way?"

She purses her lips. "Some parents don't want to take the time to help with English, even though that's the point of it for a lot of the girls. A British girl takes that out. And parents like the idea of a Cambridge student teaching their toddlers to read and add." She lifts her shoulders then lets them drop. Her head tilts to the side, as if the snobbery of doting parents were an acceptable mystery, one she's apparently willing to go on and on about. I interrupt.

"And do you know where Katja is working now?"

She thumbs the paper-clipped corners of several paper stacks, sliding one out from between the rest. "We can play a little trick," she whispers, touching a pink fingertip to her lips.

She slides the top paper towards me. It has a photo of Katja clipped to it, and her contact information neatly typed. This is the first I've seen of her. She looks young. She *is* young. It says "Age: 22."

Mrs. Heatherly instructs: "*You* call. She's avoiding me, but she won't recognise your number."

I dial the number. It rings and rings. It diverts to voicemail. I shake my head.

"Well, it doesn't surprise me. Who knows what she's up to?" Mrs. Heatherly rolls her eyes. What does she mean to imply? Laziness? Still asleep, past noon? Or more sex in the afternoon, as vilified by Mrs. Finley? Imagine what she would think if she suspected what I did: that Katja had slept with married Mr. Bennet on the snowy day. She would probably think she deserves to be dead. Maybe she is. Maybe Grace found out about them, maybe she went looking for Katja and found her. Mr. Bennet might have silenced her. And what about Katja, then? Might he have silenced her, too?

"It's a funny thing," Mrs. Heatherly muses, having no idea how much I despise her. "You're not the first person to come looking for her."

"What? Someone came here? When?"

"No, no. Not in person. A woman phoned. Just like you, she wanted to know where Katja was. Of course, I didn't tell her anything. You can understand why I insisted on seeing your warrant card."

"This person claimed to be from the police?"

Mrs. Heatherly rolls her eyes again, this time at me. It doesn't take much to get on her shit list. "No, she didn't claim anything of the sort. But she wanted information. I respect my clients' privacy. It's only right."

"So who was it?" I cut in, interrupting her preening.

"I have the name here." She shuffles papers. "Mrs. Finley called afterward, complaining that this woman had called her at home. She thought I'd sent someone to ask for a reference. As if I would do that without permission. Aha! Here it is. Mathilde Oliver."

I suppress my incredulity. That was the first thing I learned on the job: Don't react. I hold my breath for a moment. Everywhere we've been, Mathilde's been there first. Makes me wonder where we're headed.

"About Liliana," Mrs. Heatherly prattles on. "Do you think Mrs. Finley is looking for a change? She'd previously requested an older, less . . . less *fit* au pair, and I think I've found one for her. Matching girls with families is a bit like being a detective." She smirks.

I see myself out through the side gate. I lift my foot to step off the property, but the house hangs on to me. I look back.

Dan hates houses like this. They're bland and expedient. They iterate down the street, likely to have been carpeted and papered in the seventies. The doors are chipboard. But the contents are a symptom, not the problem. The problem is that they're fundamentally ugly, and allowed to flourish because they're cheap. They are architectural weeds.

Dan and I won't be able to stay in the ex-almshouse. It's too small. I don't even know what local schools are like. He wouldn't even look at houses like this when we decided to buy together four years ago. I don't think he cares about a garden. Do *I* care about a garden? I think a mother is supposed to care about space outside to play. . . .

Breathe, Chloe. I lean against my car.

My phone rings. "Who are you? Why are you phoning me?" a woman berates me.

"I—You phoned *me,*" I stammer.

"You called me before. What do you want?" she demands.

I almost ring off, but I figure it out. "Katja?" I say.

"Who are you? Who gave you this number?"

"Katja, I'm Detective Inspector Chloe Frohmann. I need to speak with you."

No answer. Has she put the phone down? Then: "Is this a joke?"

It's not a joke, but I almost laugh. Sometimes that's how relief bubbles up. Katja's alive. Alive, and scared.

Columns hold a pediment up over me as I enter. The place still has the feel of the university "gentlemen's club" it started out as. Now it's a pizza chain.

As soon as I walk in, the smell of cheese gets me. I step back, seriously reconsidering. "Would you like a table?" chirps a cheerful waitress in a long white apron. It wraps around her from breasts to knees, the strings winding twice around her waist before they meet in a little bow at the front. She's like a column herself. I ask for Katja.

"Katja!" she calls. Potted palm trees waft as she brushes past, her heels clicking on the shiny checkerboard floor. I hold on to the back of a leather club chair and breathe through my mouth.

I must look awful. When they come back, Katja asks me if I'm all right before she asks me who I am. I show her my warrant card and ask if we can talk outside.

We sit on the steps, and she lights up a cigarette. The smoke is bitter and almost overwhelmingly strong. I lean away from her. In any social situation I would ask her to stop, but I don't want to antagonise her when I need her to talk.

"Tell me about the person who's been harassing you," I say. That much had been easy to guess from her reaction to my call. Once I gleaned that it wasn't someone connected to Deeping House, I let her think I was following up on her complaint, to get her to tell me where she works. I *am* going to prod the officer she originally spoke to, so it's not a complete lie.

"Ugh, I met him at a club. I told him to get lost, but one of my girlfriends told him where I work. He calls here a couple times a week. When you rang me, I thought he'd got my number."

I take down the basic information. I add, "Did anyone called Mathilde try to get in touch with you?"

She looks at me like I'm crazy. Maybe I am. I'd let myself get superstitious that Mathilde was leading us by the nose around this investigation. *Don't get sucked in,* I remind myself. No, Mathilde had just followed the same clues, and at this juncture didn't have the authority to wring Katja's mobile number out of the au pair service. That's all. Back to our fen body.

Katja scrunches her nose in disgust when I mention Grace Rhys. "Yeah." She blows a line of grey smoke straight out towards the street.

"You like her?" I say, deliberately present tense. I turn away to breathe in, then look back at her for the answer.

"We were friends," she answers cautiously. *Were*. "Did she say something about me?"

"You know Grace," I commiserate, hoping that might prompt a reaction.

"You're trying to trick me. If I didn't want a smoke so bad I wouldn't talk to you at all." She sucks on the cigarette. "Ask me more! I have a whole box, and I hate pizza."

I belly-laugh. "I hate pizza, too." I used to like it, but now? I shudder.

"You want a cigarette?" she offers.

I shake my head and swallow down the bile that comes up at the thought of it. "I jog," I lie.

"I hate sweating. The only good reason to sweat is sex."

"Mrs. Finley says you had sex with Stephen Casey."

"That bitch. It was Grace. But it doesn't cross her mind that a *Cambridge girl* would have sex in the middle of the day. That's what she said! That it was wrong to have sex in the middle of the day. That it was wrong to have sex in the same house as children. She pays a therapist to tell her why she's unhappy. That's why. *That's* why. Stupid bitch."

"I know it was Grace with Stephen."

Katja smiles, which plumps up her cheeks. Her teeth are a pale yellow from the cigarettes, and her lipstick clashes with it. "Grace is the bad guy. That's a nice change."

"Were you always the—"

"Stop fishing! I'll tell you." She adds something exasperated and probably profane in Finnish, then: "I lost my job because of her. Not just my job, but with the Finleys' complaint I've had a hard time getting another one. So now I'm a waitress, which pays better but doesn't give me somewhere to live. I'm lucky I have friends, but the couch is shit on my back. Why do you want her? What's she done?"

I remain oblique. "Mrs. Finley says a couple of things were missing from the help flat. Grace take them?"

"What was in there to take? Mrs. Finley is a crazy person." The cigarette's finished. She stubs it onto the stone step and slides out another.

"Did you talk to Grace after you were fired?"

"No. Her things were still there, but I didn't see her again."

"How did you leave?" I assume she caught a lift with Mr. Bennet on his way to the recycling centre.

She chuckles. "With Mr. Finley! On his way to pick up the kids. His wife would murder him if she knew." She smiles placidly. "He felt sad for me," she adds. "Not sad enough to stand up to her, but he took me to my friend's house."

"Friend have a name?"

She gives it; I write it down.

"How do you think Grace left?" I ask.

"I assume the writer. . . ."

"What colour nail varnish did Grace have on last time you saw her?" That's one of the descriptors we've been holding back.

Her eyes narrow. "Why are you asking?" The ash end of her cigarette spreads long. When at last it drops off, Katja shakes herself and answers. "The girl in the . . . ? No. Grace wasn't blond." She shakes her own fair hair. "Grace had dark hair. The newspapers say the girl in the fens was blond." Her hand shakes. She sucks on her cigarette.

"Did you notice the colour of her nails?" I persist.

There's a 5p coin on the ground. She touches it with her toe. I think she says "silver," but my phone is ringing. "We painted each other's nails silver," she says, forcefully. That's the right—or wrong, if you wanted to be hopeful—answer. There were traces of silver colour left.

I hold up one finger and look at the number on my mobile. It's not a number I know, but the area code is Peterborough. *Shit*. Terrible timing, but a call from the vicinity of Deeping House isn't something I can ignore. I say I'll be a minute. Katja hunches over her cigarette and stares at the pavement.

It's Keene. His voice is strained, but it's him.

"Keene? What are you doing? Where's your phone?"

"I've got something," he says. It's that gloat he gets when he's made a break. He wants me to ask for it.

"Bad timing, Keene. I'm in the thick of it. Just tell me."

He'd found Grace's suitcase, and a further connection with George Hart-Fraser: an engraved watch from a Bristol school. "And her hairbrush," he crows. "Guess the colour and length of the hairs. Go on—guess!"

He's giddy. And . . . shaky?

"Keene, what's going on?"

"I went in the water. I'm cold. But it was worth it. Don't fuss; I've got a heater blasting me now. Thirty-five centimetre, dark brown hairs. Sound familiar?"

"No, should it?" I look back at Katja. She's rocking. I want to get him off the phone but then it grabs hold of me. "The hammer?"

He nearly cheers. "The hammer and shirt! From Trumpington Road!"

"Grace Rhys's hairbrush hairs match the hairs stuck to the hammer? Is that what you're telling me?"

"And George lives there, on Brookside. George Hart-Fraser."

I shake my head. "That doesn't make sense. Why dump something incriminating near himself? And why dump it separately at all? Why not with the body?" Again: *Don't get sucked in.* "Look, I've got to go."

"Where are you?"

I slide a look at Katja. She's hunched over and looks ready to go through the whole box. Fine; she'll hold a minute. I give in to Keene. "Cambridge," I say.

"Perfect. Just do me this favour," he asks. "Check George out. Nothing about the body or hammer or Mathilde Oliver. Just say a concerned citizen turned in the watch. See how he reacts. I have to stay here for forensics. Listen, can you call them?"

"Keene, what happened to your phone?"

"I dropped it." Is that a laugh? "Going after the watch." Yes, he's laughing.

"Are you daft?" All his numbers, lost. And now I can't reach him when I need to. "I think I'm supposed to be flattered that you had my number memorised." Something rattles. "How cold are you, exactly? Is that your teeth?"

He says he's fine. He tries to sidetrack into a discussion about Richard and Alice. I give him the minimum and ring off. Katja is quivering. "Is Grace dead?" she asks. "Is Grace that body in the fens?"

"Nothing is sure at this time. We're investigating a number of leads."

She coughs into the crook of her elbow, then sucks on the cigarette again. "I was so angry. I looked for her. I wanted to tell her off. We'd thought he liked *me*. Before Christmas he left me a note. We made a date. But when I showed up, he looked confused. I understood that he wanted Grace. I never told her that. I told her I didn't like him."

"Wait . . . who?"

"Stephen Casey." She looks at me like I'm stupid. "He mixed up our names. Can you believe that? I expect that from Mrs. Finley—she called me Marta sometimes—who's Marta, right? But a man should do better if he wants a yes. At least get the name right. I guess Grace didn't care about that. It was like we were trapped at that house. Mrs. Bitch hated me to use the car. He was the only man there. What else were we supposed to do?"

"What about Ian Bennet?"

Her mouth makes an oval of surprise. Then she laughs. "The landlord?"

"On the snowy day, when Grace went with Stephen, were you jealous? Is that why you had sex with Ian Bennet?"

"That's stupid. Because it's gross! Why would you think that? I was on the phone with my mother."

"Phone calls don't take that long." Sex doesn't always take long, either.

"It was about my sister's wedding. We talked for an hour. More than an hour! I told Mrs. Finley, but she didn't believe me. I told her my mother would send the records. She didn't care."

"Really? You could produce those records?"

"My mother could." Her eyebrows pinch together. "Why? It isn't a crime. If you want to know what Mr. Bennet was doing that day, ask him. Ask his daughter."

"His family were in London."

"Not Dru."

"No, that's not true. They had an appointment in London."

"Yes, with an astrologer. We *all* knew about it. Mrs. Bennet thought it was a good gift." She raises her sharply plucked eyebrows. "On their way out that morning, they had an argument. It was ugly."

"What about?"

"Nothing! Dru and her mother fight. It's how they communicate. Mrs. Bennet said if she was going to be that way, she could stay home. Dru apologised, but it wasn't good enough. So she stomped her feet"— Katja acts this out—"and Mrs. Bennet and the other one—the sick one—they left. I can't believe you'd believe such made-up shit. I'm done." She rubs her cigarette into the ground. She stomps up the steps.

I call Rory Casey's number back. Keene's not there.

Dru was home. Dru was in the flat with Mr. Bennet on the snowy day. The Finleys could have overheard him having sex while she was in another room; parents do that all the time. But everyone was accounted for. If it wasn't Katja . . .

I flip through my notes. Dru is being dropped at her boarding school today.

I push the heavy glass door in. Katja is rubbing a cloth over a table. She says, without looking up, "If I'd been with Stephen, I would have told Mrs. Finley so. I don't think I need to hide anything. I didn't do anything wrong. If I'd been with Mr. Bennet, I would tell you that, too. What do I care? But I wasn't."

I ask her where Dru goes to school.

She looks up, startled by the apparent non sequitur. "The Leys," she says.

In Cambridge. Here.

CHAPTER 24

GEORGE HART-FRASER

I went home to Bristol for Christmas. It was always Stephen's and my job to cook the dinner. Mother had to have a turkey. She liked us to cook recipes from television programmes, so we spread mincemeat onto puff pastry and rolled it like a Swiss roll and sliced it into ovals. We made a vile curried stuffing. Ridiculous.

Stephen had not started university. He'd moved out to live with a new girlfriend, whose parents paid the rent on her own house. Mother didn't like her. She said the girl was a tart. I said that's why Stephen liked her.

I braced for a hard shove or cruel riposte. But he laughed. It was real laughter, great *hah-hah-hah* laughter, with a fully open mouth. He put a hand on my shoulder and shook me back and forth the way friends do.

"Where'd you get her?" I asked. He said the pub. It was a lucky pick-up, then, because what are the odds the girl you meet out having a drink also has the means to take you in? She even dressed him in good clothes. He wore an apron to protect his crisp cotton shirt and wool trousers.

"She's asked me to join her family for Christmas lunch tomorrow," Stephen announced.

Mother's lips pressed together. "That was kind. I presume you refused. Bring her here if you must."

Mother had cleaned, which meant she'd hoovered. But that did nothing for the dust that coated every small item—every ceramic animal and small brass bell that she'd collected and filled shelves with. The glass bottles of after-meal liqueurs were thickly furred. They had last been touched exactly a year ago.

"I already agreed, but she'll come by here in the morning first. She has a present for you."

Another bell? A family of porcelain geese? I'd got her a Cambridge teapot.

Mother put on the television. That was how she sulked. It was a game show. Three symbols were on the screen: a Gemini, a triple-lined equals sign, and a Chinese symbol. "Identicality," I said. You were meant to say what the items had in common.

"We've got a right scholar in this family," Stephen joked.

I wasn't sure where this was going. I knew he'd be jealous. I'd hoped, though, that perhaps we'd be peers now.

"If you want to try again, I can help you," I offered. He didn't have the A-level grades to get in. When he didn't get an offer, he stopped trying. But he could resit the exams if that was important to him.

"It's not for me. I'd only done it as a lark with my mates. It takes a special mind to enjoy that shit." He used "special" the way schools do, to politely label the developmentally disabled. Mother turned up the volume on the television. "If anyone needs a hand, it's you," Stephen said. "Have you even got any friends?"

Dr. Oliver had taken me in, in a way. He had me round for an occasional meal with his strange daughter at his cramped house. He showed me his work with galaxy clusters. The uses I wanted to put my maths to were becoming fixed.

"That's what I thought. Look, I didn't get you a prezzie." That was usual. "So let me do this for you: Friday night. Give it a go. See what it's like to be normal. Have a beer, throw some darts. Pub quiz."

"You want to take me out with your friends?"

"Oh, *that* would work. You'd hunch over your drink refusing to talk, and everyone would ignore you. It's not enough to drag you out. You need a whole new way of looking at the world."

The timer buzzed for the potatoes. Stephen dropped the topic. We chopped and basted and sliced and served, and ate with the telly playing a Dickens adaptation.

Three days later, Stephen kept his word. He brought me tan trousers and a blue buttoned shirt. He put me in his straight, knee-length grey wool coat, and his school scarf: long stripes of orange and dark blue.

Why did I believe him? He'd only ever been cruel. But I believed, I think, that Cambridge had earned me something. That Cambridge had changed me, that I'd become deserving of different treatment. I expected new respect, so I saw it, even from him.

He unclasped his watch. It had been a prize for high achievement at his school. He always wore it, except to shower. He put it on my wrist.

"Now smile," he said. We looked in the mirror. We were just alike, split from the same egg. But my posture was different. "Pull your shoulders back," he said. "Stand like you mean it. Look, spread your feet."

I tried it.

"Don't duck your head. That's an apology."

It was uncanny. That wasn't a mirror. I was looking at my brother.

"That's it. I told them I'd be along to the Duck and Feathers at nine. Go on."

"Do you want my coat?" I said.

He laughed. "Don't be daft." He sneered at my short jacket that gripped at the hips with elastic.

I shrugged. *Let him be cold.*

"You don't get it. This is your turn. Go out, have a good time. They'll treat you like you belong. It's the only way you'll learn to act like it."

Warnings screamed in my head. "They won't be happy to see me."

"They'll be happy to see *me,*" he said.

I got it.

"Merry Christmas," he said. He shoved me out the door.

———

The Duck and Feathers was smoky and crammed full. I wasn't sure I would recognise his crowd, but I did. Two of them had hung about our house in the summer, smoking in the garden. I'd forgotten their names. They clapped me on the shoulders.

They had girls with them. They were called Heather and Molly, and wore lots of bracelets and brightly coloured hair. Molly, the red-haired one, wore a pendant that hung right between her breasts, in the V of her sweater. Heather, the yellow-blonde, wore a black see-through blouse and lacy bra. There was a football match on the telly, and when Heather jumped to cheer she bounced.

They bought me a pint. I sucked it down to avoid joining the conversation. I was terrified to speak an error and reveal the joke. When I finished I was given another. "Daisy can buy a round when she comes," Mark said. Mark and Rob. I had to get the names right.

Molly plucked darts out of the board. "Who wants to play?" she asked.

Nobody did. I just wanted to watch her pull her arm back to throw, making her sweater taut around her chest.

"Stephen!" she begged, stretching out the name and pulling both my hands.

I demurred. "I'm terrible at darts," I said, then froze.

Was Stephen good at darts? Had I just contradicted the illusion?

"I *know*!" she said, grinning. "I want to win."

I was on my third pint, and rarely had more than one at a sitting. I'd be lucky if I could hit the board.

"Stee-*ven,* Stee-*ven,*" chanted Mark and Rob.

I carefully watched her have a go, so I could mimic her technique. You hold it back by your ear to start. She got seventeen points, then twenty-six, and twenty-five.

I threw. The dart lodged into the wall, between panelling. Molly cackled. Heather laughed so hard she had to lean against the bar.

"I told you I'm not good at this," I said. I was next to a radiator, and sweating.

"Don't pout, big baby boy," said Heather. She stuck out her lips. She looked like a duck.

These were his friends? I excused myself to the toilets.

I pissed away three pints of beer and splashed water on my face. What was the point? I could get an eyeful of bouncing tits on the computer if that's all I was here for.

"George?"

A boy from school was washing his hands in the sink next to me. His name was Andy . . . something. We'd had a couple of classes together.

Before I could answer, Mark shoved the door open and unzipped his trousers at the urinal. "No," I said to Andy. "George is my brother." I pushed back my shoulders and widened the gap between my feet.

Andy didn't look convinced. "Oh. Tell him I said 'hello,' then." He left. Mark followed him without washing his hands.

When I came out, karaoke had started. I got another beer.

Molly was singing a Mariah Carey declaration of love to Rob. When she squeaked out the high bits at the end, Rob barked. After she gave up the mike, she walloped him on the chest. "Are you saying I'm a dog?"

"I'm saying you're a dog *whistle,* fuckwit," he said. "Luckily, brains isn't what I'm after." He pulled her head back by her hair and stuck his tongue in her mouth.

I finished the pint. "I think I'm going to go," I shouted to Mark. Two girls were attempting drunken harmony over the thumping amp.

"Daisy isn't here yet," he shouted back.

That was the point. This was stupid. She'd know me for a fraud. *Breathe.* There was time. Extricate, exit. I had to get out. "Tell Daisy I'll see her at home," I improvised. Stephen *would* see her at home, so that was all right.

The crowd had got thick. I had to walk sideways and shoulder-first to make a way. I got almost to the doorway when she walked in through it.

I'd seen Daisy, briefly, Christmas morning. She'd brought a bathrobe for Mother, and stayed for an instant coffee. Then she and Stephen had gone off to her parents'. I'd seen enough of her then to recognise her now: pretty, slim, and blond-haloed. Tonight she had on white jeans and a tight white pullover under a wide-open fake-fur jacket. She had small breasts and no bra and cold tits. I forced myself to look at her face.

"You complete arsehole!" she said cheerfully, linking an arm in one of mine. "Were you going to leave without waiting for me?" I let my-self be pulled into the group as if I belonged, as if I were Stephen. She thought I was. She believed it.

She bought a round for the gang, and started up a group sing of "We Are the Champions." Her breath hit my face. My lungs filled.

I belted out along with the chorus. This was *it,* this was fucking *it.* It's like my blood was pumping for the first time. Rob slung an arm around my shoulder and we rocked, the whole room rocked. Daisy cheered at the end, holding the mike over her head and clapping her hands up there.

"You're just, you're just so beautiful," I slurred at her after.

"How much have you had?" she asked. Without waiting for an answer she added, "I'd better catch up!" She tossed back a shot, then she and Heather danced.

I shouted, "We are the champions! Whooo!" I held my hands up over my head.

"Shut up, arsehole," a woman behind me said. But Daisy smiled. She put her hands in her hair and turned to wiggle her hips at me. I licked my lips.

———

The walk home was almost all uphill. All that tilted ground made it that much harder to figure out exactly what angle "upright" was. I overcorrected and lurched backwards. We put our arms around each other to hold each other up.

"You're so, so beautiful," I said again. My mouth mashed up against her ear.

She giggled.

I almost dragged her past the house because, of course, I'd never seen it before. It was in the middle of a terraced row, slanting up. She stopped, and my head pitched back. The sky was clear, freckled with stars. Daisy had freckles. I bumped my mouth onto her nose.

"Ow, Stephen!" she said, still laughing.

We stumbled up the steps. I pressed her against the front door. I pushed against her.

"We can do it inside. Just let me find my key," she said. It was at the very bottom of her purse. Finally she opened the door. I pushed her through after. The narrow stairs up were right there, and we fell forward onto them. I got my knees between hers. "Ow, my back!" she said, pushing me up. "I need a coffee first, if you don't want me to fall asleep!" She yawned elaborately, showing the inside of her mouth as a tease.

The house was once-grand, embellished by chipped plaster mouldings and an elaborate but listing bannister. The carpet had been rubbed away in paths starting from the bottom of the stairs: to the kitchen, to the lounge, to the door. She walked the one to the kitchen, kicking off her shoes. She flicked on a fan heater as she passed it. The house was otherwise frigid.

She put on the kettle. I got my arms around her from behind and pushed her against the counter. "Oh, all *right*," she agreed.

I nuzzled her neck and rocked my hips against her. Her jeans were tight; I didn't know how to get them off her. "Please," I said, still pushing.

The kettle screamed. A slow clapping beat from the hallway. Stephen laughed and applauded. I went soft.

"I can't believe it!" he said, laughing so hard he bent forward. "You dog! I can't believe you pulled it off!"

Daisy had got away into the corner, clutching her furry jacket around her chest. She looked at both of us, me to him and back. Her eyes got big when she got the joke. She ran at him, fists swinging. "You bastard!" she said.

He grabbed her wrists and held her easily. "You'd do it to anybody," he sneered.

She picked up one of her shoes and threw it at me, then stomped upstairs.

"Seriously, congratulations," he said. "I didn't think you had it in you."

He went upstairs after her. Their arguing rattled through the whole house. Then their doing it rattled the house. I knelt in front of the toilet and was sick into the unwashed bowl.

I flushed. I wiped my face on a cheerfully red-and-white-striped towel, which I dropped as I stumbled out. I kicked the fan heater, wishing it was Stephen's face.

———

I don't remember the walk. I suppose the downhill journey just rolled me home. I woke up in my bed in my boxers. Stephen's clothes were on the floor. Mother was screaming in the lounge.

I wrapped a dressing gown around my body and ran.

Every step sparked a pain behind my eyes. Movement hurt. Light hurt. I stalled in the doorway.

She stood in front of the telephone table, tethered receiver in hand. She held it out in front, facing her, and she howled incoherently towards it.

I slammed it back into the cradle and shook her shoulders to make her stop.

"A fire!" she said. "A fire on Windmill Hill!"

"What?" I swear I was surprised. None of it had been real, of course. None of it had actually happened. It was stupid. I wouldn't have done any of it.

"Katherine Ward says that girl's house is in the thick of it. That Daisy. Three fire engines. There was an evacuation of the whole street. At least one house is gutted and the two beside it damaged. There were ambulances there. She said she saw two bodies come out covered. She hasn't been able to raise Stephen on the phone. Two bodies covered!" It turned into screaming again.

"Stop it!" I shook her again, until her chin hit her chest and snapped back up. "You have to stop that sound." I squeezed my eyes until all I could see were white sparks on dark. Stars like freckles. Daisy's freckled nose.

She grabbed on to my wrist. I wrenched my arm away, but she reached again with her other hand. I still had the watch on.

Everything stopped. She put her finger on it, tapped it, then stroked the band. Her face crumpled up, and she threw her arms around me. "You!" she said. "It's you!" She shook. Her face had never been so close to mine.

"No," I said. The watch didn't change who I was.

"You didn't know I overheard, did you?" She picked at and patted my dressing gown. "I knew what you were up to last night. I thought you were only going to embarrass him, give him a taste of what he did to you."

"What?" I hadn't planned anything. Stephen had planned it all. Realisation smacked me hard.

"No," I repeated. "It wasn't like that."

She pressed her face into my chest. "He should never have accepted a place he didn't deserve," she said. "It was rightly yours. You only did what you had to do to correct that. It's the University's fault, getting it wrong. It's their fault."

"No, Mother, I— I'm George. I'm at Cambridge. Stephen's . . ." *Dead.* Stephen was dead.

Had I done it? Had I started the fire? Not on purpose. No, I wouldn't. I hadn't known the towel would catch. Where had I dropped it? How close to the heater? There wasn't a way to know that, was there? Not when I'd had so much to drink. Not when I was so angry.

Angry enough to start a fire?

No. No, of course not. Who would do that? It was impossible. Easy to be careless; impossible to be so malicious. Killing, over a joke? Over a stunt? Who would do that?

"You never would have done it if you didn't have to," she said.

Did I have to do it? Did I? Maybe I did. . . .

Then I understood. She meant Stephen had had to kill me. "No."

She released me, and stepped back with a sweet smile, nodding. "I'll never tell." She put a finger to her lips. Snail-trails of tears striped each cheek.

"I'm George," I said. "Stephen's . . ." *He's moved out. He doesn't live here anymore. He doesn't go to university. He didn't get into Cambridge.* "Stephen's dead," I said. And Daisy. Two bodies covered. The stripes from the hand towel flashed behind my closed eyes.

"We'll say that," she said, patting my arm.

The doorbell chimed. The top of a police cap loomed in the glass window at the top of the door.

She clawed at the watch. "Give it to me," she said. "I'll hide it."

I let her get at it. She ran upstairs with it and sent me to answer the door.

———

Stephen's prize watch was not among the inventory of objects in the house or on his body. Stephen's friends agreed that he always wore it. It wasn't one of them, though, who stirred things up around the fact. It was Andy, who'd seen me in the gents' at the pub and known me for me.

It was enough to spark as rumour the same story our mother had formed. Daisy's parents ran with it. They weren't content with the verdict of accident; they wanted blame to be laid. Where better than on a living person who could be punished? They felt that the fire had been purposely set, and there was little satisfaction in blaming the dead.

They persuaded the police to talk with me about it, though I didn't think they believed in the convoluted story of Stephen's revenge. They asked me to prove I was George, which was surprisingly hard to do. Neither of us had had surgery. We each had a filling in the same tooth. Twins are not truly alike; we had our own fingerprints. But to what to compare them? We'd both been at home for Christmas. My room at Cambridge had been cleaned. Stephen's house with Daisy was . . .

That was ten years ago. I returned to Cambridge and revelled in the work. At graduation, I gripped the Praelector's third finger, knelt before the Vice-Chancellor, and basked in the Latin. The students who tick-box the option for generic words rather than the standard Christian formula are ignorant of the point of ceremony.

Mother guarded the watch and kept it secret. It was her treasure, supposedly proving that it was her favourite son who was alive. I let her think it; I needed her on my side. Dozens of people had seen the watch on "Stephen's" arm that night. If it was found to have not been lost in the fire, the theory that George had died, not Stephen, would be given more weight. Along with the assumption that I, supposedly Stephen, had arranged it.

I began doctoral study at the Institute of Astronomy. I excelled. Back home, news of my achievement restarted the rumour that I was Stephen, having killed to take back my proper place in the order of things. My success was proof that I couldn't really be me.

CHAPTER 25

CHLOE FROHMANN

The car park and grounds of the Leys school are thick with parents dropping off their teenagers for term. Suitcases, musical instruments, tennis racquets, and quick, intense hugs abound. I intercept an adult without children in the hope that she works there. She does, and she's not happy to have that work interrupted.

Her glare flicks back and forth between my warrant-card photo and my face. Once satisfied, she demands, "Quickly, please. Today is not a good day."

I ask if Drusilla Bennet has arrived. She knows her. "We have only one Drusilla. Perhaps you mean Dru Rodgers?"

That's right; Ian Bennet's her stepfather. "Yes, please," I say.

She lifts her hand to her head like a showy prophet calling on second sight rather than plain old memory. "Yes. She dropped her bags in her room. She was here with her mother and sister." She snaps out of it to editorialise: "Poor thing. Leukaemia, I think."

"Where are they now?"

"I don't eavesdrop. But it was impossible to refrain from hearing that they intended to visit the Botanic Garden." She points with a pen. "Across the road." Off I go.

Keene had told me something of what they look like. The girls are fifteen and thirteen, Dru with long fair hair, and Max in a similar wig. The mum has that "mum look." That's not how he said it. He said: conservative clothes, shoulder-length hair in a clip, harried. I did the translation to "typical mum" all by myself.

I swear at the tangle of paths through the garden; how am I to guess which way they'd gone? But the long views across lake, lawn, and beds allow me to cover more than one area at once. I'm looking for three women together; that's distinct enough. My eyes skip anyone with toddlers, anyone alone, and every man.

I climb atop a rocky mound that hosts tenacious, colourful shrubs and mosses. I shade my eyes from the sun and scan the lawns. I spy them quickly from there.

Max's shiny blond waves puddle on the ground where she sits. It's thicker than real hair, or perhaps she's just so thin it seems that way. Her mother crouches behind, winding hanks of it into thin, decorative plaits.

Dru leans back on her elbows, legs stretched. Her loose jeans and rugby shirt bunch up around her body. I don't blame her for making the most of comfort; school uniform starts this week.

The clouds shift. Sunshine falls hard on them, as sudden and dense as a cloudburst. For a moment, they glow gold. Dru closes her eyes.

I put on my talking-to-minors voice for the girls, and hand my warrant card to Mrs. Bennet. "Hi, I'm from the police. I need to ask you a few questions about Grace Rhys."

"Who?" Mrs. Bennet is flustered. "I thought you people were looking for . . . the nanny? Katja?" Yes, Keene had asked them in their car park this morning.

"Mum, *Grace*!" Max reminds her, twirling a slim braid and stabbing at it with a small daisy. It's already fraught with little wildflowers and bits of grass.

"Oh! The other one. The Cambridge girl. Well, why don't you go and talk to her?" She lifts her open palms to indicate Cambridge all around us. "She doesn't live at the house anymore."

"Yes, I'm keen to know more about the day she left. That was the day it snowed."

You might think it snows on us right now. The three of them freeze still for a moment.

"We weren't home that day. We were in London," says Mrs. Bennet.

Funny use of "we." "All of you?"

Max says, "Me and Mum."

Dru is digging a little hole in the grass with a stick. Mrs. Bennet snatches it. "Stop it, Dru. How do you think the gardener will feel?" She tosses the stick away towards the base of a tree.

"Dru, did you go into London that day?"

She shakes her head. Max strokes Dru's hair, loosely plaiting it.

Mrs. Bennet's voice rises. "Dru, use words! You're not a toddler!" To me she says, "Do you have teenagers?" in commiseration.

"No," I say, wondering how old she thinks I am. And what does it say about my upcoming motherhood that I identify much more with the surly daughter?

"We had a fight that day. We fight almost every day that we're together, despite giving Dru *everything she ever asks for.*" She thrusts her face forward for each of those last five words, and finally gets the rise she's looking for:

"We fight because you don't listen! We fight because when I give you a real answer instead of a fake one, you get mad! We fight because you don't *like* me!"

"Shhhh . . ." says Max, resting her head on Dru's shoulder.

"Do you see what you do to your sister? Do you see?"

"I'm all right, Mum," insists Max. She sounds tired.

This could go round for hours. "Dru, you stayed behind on the snowy day? Did you see Grace at all?"

"No."

"Did you play outside, make snowmen, throw snowballs?" I try to sound upbeat.

"No."

"You stayed in your flat?" This was key. If that's the place the Finleys overheard, it's essential to clarify who was in it.

Dru nods, which triggers Mrs. Bennet again. "What a waste! This is exactly what I'm talking about! Do you see, Dru, that your behaviour is a bigger problem than you and me not getting along? You have issues, Dru. It's bad enough you shut out your own mother—but you shut out *life*!"

Dan had woken me up the day it snowed. We didn't play outside, either. We watched it from bed, drinking hot chocolate, until we had to shovel around the car to get me to work. "Sometimes I don't care for the cold myself, Mrs. Bennet." I smile at Dru, but she looks at the ground, pulls up grass.

Mrs. Bennet grabs her hand. "I should think Ian's hard work in the house and garden would give you more respect for what effort goes into maintenance."

Speaking of . . . "Your stepfather was home that day as well? What was he doing?"

"Working," says Mrs. Bennet. "He's always working. The upkeep on the property requires constant attention."

"Dru?" I say, as if the target of my question hadn't been clear enough the first time.

"Working," she agrees.

"Working on what? Something inside?"

"I thought this was about Grace," says Mrs. Bennet.

Good catch, Mum. I dial back the emphasis on her husband. "Yes, I'm trying to ascertain who interacted with her that day."

"Well, apparently my daughter did not. Apparently my daughter holed up in her room and interacted with no one. As for my husband, you'll have to ask him if he was shovelling, or cleaning, or renovating the new flat. Probably all three in turns." She stands up and brushes loose grass off her tan trousers. "We're not wealthy, you know. Ian sacrifices so that I don't have to work. Before Ian, I barely had the time to be with . . ." She swallows. "Now I can look after my girls. Even if one doesn't want me to."

"Mum . . ." says Max, in the elongated whine of embarrassed teenagers.

Dru doesn't say anything.

"Are you married, Inspector?" Mrs. Bennet asks me.

I say yes, even though Dan and I haven't had the wedding yet.

Her lips split, showing me all the front teeth. Her cheeks squeeze her eyes. It has all the right ingredients but isn't quite a smile. "Aren't we *lucky,*" she says.

———

I follow them to the exit of the Botanic Garden. They stop to use the toilets, which gives me a chance to get ahead of them and position myself around the corner. Dru and Max link arms, while Mum leads them down Trumpington Street. They turn off into Brown's.

This could take a while. Brown's is for lingering. It's a university-town chain that started in Oxford and became the go-to restaurant for parents visiting their little scholars. It's a place for drinks, and multiple courses, and coffee after.

I lean against a brick wall and unwrap an energy bar.

I'm not sure how Grace fits into the family drama I'm getting into, but when something is this explosive, anyone near can get hurt.

I feel sick. Walking helps. I retrace the path back towards the Botanic Garden, and stop at the thick, octagonal monument to Hobson's Conduit, marking the old path for fresh water into the city.

A spring-fed brook separates the traffic of Trumpington Road and the quiet streets alongside it. The water is subject to winter highs, summer lows, and periodic drain-downs for maintenance. It was during one of these that the bloody shirt and hammer had been found.

A teacher from Perse Girls, disgusted by what appeared to be rubbish, had pulled it out with a stick to throw it away. When she saw the stains, she brought it to the police. Her alarm was justified.

The stand-out discrepancy to me is: *If this came from killing Grace, why not dump it with the body?*

Shirts can be tricky, though. I remember an old case where the killer had wiped every trace of his presence from inside the crime scene, then gone out for a drink with blood on his face. It's easy to see everything yet forget oneself. If this killer only realised the blood on his shirt after the fact, then it makes sense he would want to avoid returning to the initial dump site.

This was the address that had got Keene excited, a three-storey, grey-brick terraced house. It was like all its neighbours: six steps up to the front door, and a dugout front below, to give each basement a sunken patio six feet beneath pavement level. Front windows jutted out, each half a hexagon, stacked three-high to serve basement, ground, and first floors.

George Hart-Fraser. I don't think much of that theory. Why dispose of something so obviously close to home? A dad dropping his stepdaughter off for term, on the other hand, might well feel safe here. . . .

Hillary Bennet and daughters will be a long time eating—if they've even got their food yet—so there's no harm going down this rabbit hole. I can't follow up on Ian Bennet until they're done, and the mum and sister set off home. Dru won't talk with her family present.

I follow through with Keene's suggestion and ring George's shrill bell. He's an academic; he could well be at home at odd hours during the day.

A woman comes to the door. Curly black hair and dangling bead earrings accentuate her round face.

I show my warrant card but put on an unserious expression. "We might have some good news for George Hart-Fraser! Is he in?" Damn, that was *too* jolly. Surely no one falls for that sort of thing anymore, do they?

"What about?" she asks, her body filling the entirety of the cautious slit she's allowed the door to open. She has on a full-sleeved peasant blouse and a sloppy purple skirt. She's barefoot. Artist? Or an academic herself? Perhaps raising kids, with a baby asleep in the background?

"It's about his watch. When will he be in?"

She says they'll both be in this evening, after five. Her name is Juliet, she tells me when I ask. It might have been a sweet name in her teens, but I, personally, wouldn't want to be a doomed heroine into my thirties and beyond.

"Has he missed it?" I ask, no notebook, half-turned, as if in passing.

"Missed what?"

"His watch?"

"You'll have to ask him." She backs up while closing the door, filling the view so that I don't catch even a glimpse inside. The interaction folds closed so gracefully, it brings to mind the shutting of a pop-up book.

———

Dru exits the restaurant first, taking the brunt of pushing the revolving door. Max steps into the section behind her, not touching the glass. She really does seem weak, and probably expert at avoiding germs by not touching anything. Tears spark in my eyes, mother-daughter-cancer-death-babies tears, a pregnancy reflex that has dogged me for weeks. My eyes get wet at television programmes, at sentimental greeting cards, at child-sized mannequins in outfits costing more than my weekly pay in the window of John Lewis. I even cry at that series of BT adverts, will-they-or-won't-they make it as a family and how can their BT phones and Internet service help make that happen? That time they were talking, and the substandard, non-BT phone connection cut short his apology and she thought he'd rung off on her? That one? I *bawled*. I told Dan I'd bit my tongue and it was bleeding.

Mrs. Bennet *en famille* crosses Trumpington Street. They head back towards the school and I follow discreetly. They gather around their car. Goodbyes, hugs, seatbelts, brake lights, reverse. Mum and Max leave Dru standing on the campus grass, waving her arm back and forth from a hinge at the elbow. Her hair gets blown forward and tangles round her face. I hang back until she turns away.

I follow her to a plain brick Victorian. Potted plants cling to the edges of the steps.

"Dru," I say, to make her turn around. "Dru," I repeat. "We have to talk about it. I'm sorry."

"There's nothing to talk about."

"Is there someone here you trust? The housemistress? Do you like her?" I require an "appropriate adult" to witness any interview with a child.

"I don't want to talk to you."

"Dru, we can make him stop. It won't have to happen anymore."

A big-haired woman in jeans opens the door. She carries a shallow cardboard box holding yet more plants. She must have brought them in from the brief flurry yesterday, and is returning them to their outside home. "Hi, I'm Missy Barnes!" She sounds American. She plonks the heavy box down at the bottom landing and shoots out her hand for a shake.

"Are you the housemistress?" I ask. She is. I show her my warrant card. "Is there somewhere the three of us can talk?"

"What's this about?"

"Best to say in private."

"No!" says Dru. "I don't want to be alone with her. I don't have to be alone with her."

"No, you don't," I agree. I can't force her, and it would do her no good if I tried. If we're right about what happened, she's been forced enough. "But if you do, we can make it stop. Don't you want it to stop?"

Missy Barnes holds up one hand. "Stop what? Miss Detective, I think you need to explain yourself."

I almost laugh at such a moniker spoken so indignantly. "We have reason to believe that Dru may have been sexually assaulted. I'm eager to get her the help she needs."

Her blue eyes get big. She bends to Dru's height. "Honey? Did something happen?"

Dru fish-mouths a few times: open, closed. "No! I've never done anything."

"I think someone did something *to* you," I say.

Dru grabs her housemistress's arm. "Ms. Barnes, can you make her go away? Nobody's done anything to me."

"You don't have to talk to me," I admit. "But if I believe that you have been assaulted in your home, I'm obliged to alert Children's Services. They will be required to investigate."

Ms. Barnes takes both Dru's hands in both of hers. "Sweetheart . . ." she says, and tries to pull her in for a hug.

Dru twists her hands out of the grip. "Call my mother," she says. Dru has brown eyes, polished-wood brown. She turns them on me, unblinking. "She'll tell you you're wrong."

I have no doubt she will.

Ms. Barnes already has her phone out, pressing at it with her thumbs to scroll through, I assume, a roster of family contacts.

"You don't have to do that," I say. We can approach this from the side of questioning Mr. Bennet. Maybe we can trip him up. Maybe

someone at Deeping House will have something to say. Not Dru—not
yet, anyway. She's safe here at school, and clearly not interested in
making words out of the memories.

"Mrs. Rodgers? This is Missy Barnes. From the Leys. Your daughter asked me to phone. I hope you'll call back, okay? Okay. Bye!"

The one-time Mrs. Rodgers, now Bennet, isn't picking up the
phone, presumably because she's on the road.

"Dru, I'm going to leave now," I say, "but this is my card. Please
phone if there's anything you want to talk about. I want to help." I try
to say the same to Ms. Barnes, but she's hitting the buttons for another
call.

"Hello? Mr. Rodgers?"

"Bennet," Dru and I both correct. I smile at the lucky simultaneity,
but get in return only the back of Dru's head. A thin braid hangs
straight down with a little daisy woven into the end of it, Max's doing.

"Can I speak to Mr. Bennet, please?"; "I'm calling from his daughter's school."; "When will he be available to speak? Can you ask him to
call me back? Who are you, exactly?"

Dru leans against the iron railing edging the steps. She runs her
fingers over the spindly rails, like plucking at a harp.

"Thank you." Thumb, *beep, click*. Then the Allman Brothers song
from the Barclaycard advert starts up. Ms. Barnes glances at the name
and brings it up to her ear so quickly she smacks herself in the head.
"Hello? Yes? Mrs. Rodgers? Bennet? Mrs. Bennet?"

Missy Barnes flusters easily.

"Some woman who says she's a detective is here and she's said some
things that Dru says aren't true. I really think you should—okay,
thanks. In a few." *Click;* phone into pocket. "Dru, honey, she's on her
way."

Mrs. Bennet will complain. Best to stay and try to smooth it than
run away and leave it to Missy Barnes's potential hyperbole.

I'm invited to wait with them in the common room. A teenage girl
pops popcorn in the kitchen and wants to know if we'd like any. Another one wants to play Wii in here. Ms. Barnes says no, and slides the
pocket door shut. It screeches and rumbles as if it's not used to being
closed.

CHAPTER 26

GEORGE HART-FRASER

A siren keened past the house. Juliet looked up from the stove. She followed the sound with a turn of her head.

That wailing effect is immediately interpreted by our ears in the same way that perspective is interpreted by our eyes. The rising sound is coming; the lowering sound is going. The smaller object is farther away; the larger object is closer. We understand these things without thinking about them.

This effect on the scale of distant space manifests in colour. There's a red tint that increases as objects speed away from Earth. A blue tint means an object is coming towards us. That's rare, because everything is supposed to be rushing away from everything else. That's the way the universe works. It expands.

The galaxies farther from us are also faster. Therefore, detecting greater speed proves greater distance. Greater distance . . . takes us back in time.

Light has a fixed speed. When it has a short distance to travel, what we receive in our eyes is very close in age to the actual age of the object. The farther the light has to travel between object and eye, the bigger the age gap. In the time it takes for me to receive the light-image of a young blue star in a galaxy some tens of millions of light-years away, it will have grown to maturity. I will look right at the red giant and see the infant.

The reddest, fastest galaxies, which are the farthest galaxies, show us the infant universe. Because of the time it takes for light to travel, we could look right at their corpses and see their births.

———

"Do you think that's a fire engine?" she said.

"I don't know."

"It could be an ambulance."

"It could."

"Or the police."

"It's passed. What does it matter?" I clicked the browser window shut and spun in my chair. Juliet pushed eggs around a pan.

"I wish we could see out of that window." The kitchen in this place was on the bottom, at basement level. The bay window swelled out onto a sub-pavement patio. It brought light but no view.

"It would only show us traffic."

She slopped the eggs onto plates, with Ryvita crackers and chives she'd grown in a pot outside. "Enjoying the term so far?"

Talking while eating was the sacrifice the relationship required. If I talked over meals, all else was forgiven. She'd been recently away in the States on a research trip, so at least we had the past few weeks to talk about. "We've lost a student. Second year Maths. She degraded. It doesn't surprise me."

"Wasn't she up for it?"

I shook my head. "Never prepared."

"They're so young. Maybe she'll come back ready."

"I don't think so." Readiness can grow, but that's of little consequence without a passion for the subject; the urge is either there or it isn't. "I don't know why she was admitted."

I hadn't interviewed Grace Rhys. I don't know what she said that made Tobias bring her in. He shows terrible judgement sometimes. In ten years, he'd gradually stepped down from the pedestal I'd put him on. It was a slow thing. As he aged and I matured, he'd grown distracted and I'd grown frustrated with him.

So things were already tense before he brought the watch into it.

"I need the car today," she said, slinging her bag over her shoulder. She works at Addenbrooke's, and normally catches the bus. She must have had errands. She left her plate on the table for me to deal with. That was the exchange; she had cooked.

"That's fine."

She went upstairs. That's why, when the phone rang, she scooped it up. It was right next to her, on the table by the door. I bounded up the steps, but she already had it up to her ear.

"Mrs. Hart-Fraser! How are you?" She lifted her eyebrows at me. She knows I hate these calls. Her head bobbed with what I assume was the cadence of Mother's rambling monologue. Finally, "Well, here he is! Bye!" She passed me the handset; her kiss hit my ear as I turned my head. I waved goodbye over my shoulder.

I wish Mother would have called my mobile. I hate being chained next to the front door, but that's where the jack is, and the range of the handset is abysmal. And this is the number she calls. She won't be persuaded. Juliet closed the door behind her; I sat on the floor with my back against it. "Mother, I've been trying to reach you."

"Yes! I was so pleased to get your messages. You never call enough. Does this mean you're coming home for Easter?"

She still looks at life as half-terms and holidays. Being an academic doesn't make me a schoolboy. "No. I need to know what's going on. Where is it?"

She paused before she said, "What?" She knew full well what I meant.

She'd kept the watch, all these years. It was her talisman. I can't be said to have allowed her to keep it; she kept it hidden even from me. I hated it being in the house, but I was more afraid of its potential vulnerability if it was exposed in some rubbish heap or dropped in the Avon. She promised me it would be safe.

"Have you lost it? Is it gone?" I demanded.

She said nothing. Pouting, preening; I didn't have to see it to know it was there. "You were meant to look after it," I said darkly.

"I *did* look after it. Don't you say I didn't. I was burgled. They broke my back window. I was down the shops. They took the computer and all my jewellery. Your father's wedding ring." Father in biological terms only. "They let Roscoe and Tabitha loose." She'd become a cat lady when the nest emptied. "Roscoe got locked in the neighbour's garage. He suffered. Don't you talk about suffering!"

"It was taken? You're saying it was taken? Why didn't you tell me?"

"And worry you?" Her voice was wide-eyed.

Damn. It was the real thing. Tobias had told me it was, but I had hoped he was mistaken. . . .

"How did you know?" Mother asked.

"It doesn't matter."

"Stephen?" she said, in that sly voice that sounds like a naughty child.

She still believed it, or chose to believe it.

I slammed down the receiver. She couldn't help me now.

It rang. I unplugged it from the jack.

Damn.

My mobile rang from downstairs. *Well, well . . . she had the number after all.*

From my low vantage point, I noticed a box by the stairs.

Juliet had picked up a fan heater from B&Q. I chucked it out with the rubbish. I'd told her I won't have them in the house.

––––––

Tobias said the watch had been sent to him while I was in Chile, collecting data from the VLT. Then the term had ended, then Christmas. It had slipped his mind. "Mathilde needed . . ." he began, and I tuned out.

At first I'd thought he was taunting me, but he was ignorant. He thought it was happy news, that something of my brother's had been lost and then found. Whoever had stolen Mother's jewellery had got rid of it in a pawn shop, and a sharp-eyed "Old Boy" had recognised it as one of the school's annual prize watches. He'd sent it on to Tobias for the close-of-boarding exhibit. Like Tobias, he'd attended decades before Stephen. Before the gentrification of the waterfront and the tourist queues for Brunel's iron ship. He didn't appreciate its meaning.

But others in Bristol could. Daisy's parents were still alive. Alive, and angry. They still checked in from time to time, a reminder that though the police had ruled the fire an accident, they had not. The watch was supposed to have been lost in the fire with Stephen. It had been seen on my wrist at the pub.

Tobias asked if my brother "would have minded" sharing his prize as part of the collection at the close-of-boarding festivities, after which it would be returned to my family. I told him Stephen had been a private person and would have minded very much. I was adamant that he turn the watch over to me.

He "forgot," repeatedly. I gave him every chance.

I caught up with him at the Institute during Easter break. Not many people were around. He was foraging in the small kitchen that, in term time, was the domain of the tea ladies. If we worked during break, we served ourselves.

"Tobias, so good to run into you." I forced my tone to be casual.

"George! Have a biscuit. The doctor says I'm not allowed them anymore, so I live vicariously. What was it you wanted?"

"Can we talk in your office?" It was probably in there.

"Mine's a tip. Yours?"

That's when I knew. He wasn't going to give it up willingly.

He walked ahead of me. Papier-mâché planets hung from strings over our heads. We turned a corner at Earth. Down this corridor, ping-pong balls hung in the pattern of the constellation Orion, but were only recognisable when viewed from standing underneath our home planet. Orion's stars are all different distances from us. As soon as you move from Earth's viewpoint, the illusion of a human figure is broken. If I leave my door open and look from my chair, it looks more like a snake.

"What can I do for you?" Tobias leaned back in my guest chair.

I remained standing. I closed the door. "My brother's watch, Tobias. I want it."

"Oh!" He raised a finger in recognition. "The watch! Yes. It had slipped my mind."

That's what he'd claimed, whenever I'd pressed him. He'd promised to bring it with him to dinner, or drop it in my pigeonhole.

"Confession time: I can't seem to lay my hands on it." He shrugged.

"I told you: as bad as a rubbish tip. I thought I had all the archives in one box, but . . ."

He wasn't meeting my eyes. *Liar.*

"Mattie's been . . . *difficult* lately. Just when I imagine life is going to move forward, it all snaps backwards. I try to be a good father. . . ."

He rambled. I leaned against the door jamb. I pushed my hair up off my forehead.

"Stop it," I whispered.

He didn't hear. ". . . She won't see a doctor. I can't force her. But surely, then, if she defends herself as entirely able she shouldn't be dependent upon . . ."

"Stop it!" I said. I did not shout. I merely spoke firmly.

His head snapped up. "Pardon?"

He'd made his decision; that was clear. That box of alumni donations—including my brother's prize watch, inscribed—was going to go back to Bristol unless I stopped it.

The colour left his face. He pointed a key at me, tip first, arm extended like a fencer. His other hand was splayed over his chest. "George, can you get me my pills?"

All silence except for his breaths. No one else was about.

If it had been term time, the other offices would have been full. There would have been chatter in the common area. But today the quiet was thick around us. In that quiet, a memory stirred:

In Stephen's kitchen, wiping my hands on that striped towel. I could have tossed it onto the countertop, or table or floor. I wanted to throw something, make an impact, but of course a towel would do nothing. A towel can't make a sound or knock something over, but that's all that was in my hand.

I'd dropped it on the heater on purpose. I hadn't known it would make a fire, but I had hoped. I even kicked the heater nearer to a pile of old magazines. That was my impact; that was my noise. A towel and magazines were all I'd had. I'd done with them what could be done.

I plucked the key from Tobias's fingers. I exited, shutting the door behind me, and crossed the hall. From here, Orion looked beaked and ducklike.

I unlocked his office. It was, indeed, a tip. I opened drawers. I

checked his jacket, hanging limp from a hook. I pocketed his pill bottle. Alumni correspondence about the Bristol event made a neat stack
on the guest chair, but the box of memorabilia was absent. That must
have gone elsewhere. Not sent on yet, surely. He was still aggregating
it all.

I searched every corner and folder, even between pages. The watch
was not there.

I sat in his chair, gave the room a silent once-over.

I closed his door behind me. I returned to my office.

It was his own fault. If the watch had been quickly found, I wouldn't
have taken so long. I would have returned with the pills immediately.
As it is, he made himself wait.

He lay diagonally across the chair. He dripped sweat. Nothing of
him moved except for a shallow respiration.

I searched his pockets. Tissues, a pen, and a wallet. Nothing else. I
sighed and fingered the pill bottle in my pocket. When he stopped
breathing I called 999.

———

"Mattie, I was coming to get you," I called, running after her. "It's your
father. He's had another heart attack. He's been taken to hospital. I
should bring you." This was my chance. The box with the memorabilia had to be in his home office. "We'll stop by your house first. We
can pick up some things for him to . . ."

She smacked my hand.

I made fists but held them at my sides. I breathed in and out.

I backed down. I waited. I gave her every chance.

CHAPTER 27

CHLOE FROHMANN

Mrs. Bennet's arrival involves a clatter. I think in her rush she knocked a plant off the steps. She thumps on the pulled-to pocket door, which Ms. Barnes has to struggle to reopen.

"Drusilla! Sweetheart!" says Mrs. Bennet, both hands extended. Dru shrinks back and looks away. Mrs. Bennet lets her hands drop. She turns on me. "What are you saying about my daughter?" she demands.

Ms. Barnes eagerly sets about recapping. Mrs. Bennet stops her with one finger raised.

"I'd like to hear it from you," she insists of me.

I comply, saying only that we fear Dru may have been assaulted.

She sucks in air. "Someone at the house? Was it that writer?" I keep my face blank. "Dru?" But Dru's looking down and there's only hair.

Mrs. Bennet, hands on hips: "On what are you basing this assumption?"

On Mr. Casey not having a TV? Is that really all we have? On it being a good story that explains why someone might want to kill Grace? On the length and colour of hairs in a hairbrush matching those tangled in the claw of a bloody hammer fifty miles away from the scene of the crime?

Mrs. Bennet sneers at my hesitation. She makes a call. It's a number she has programmed, so she's not lodging a complaint about me. Yet.

"Damn." She tries a different number. "Rory? Please tell Ian I need to speak with him immediately."

Max has taken a chair in the corner. It's a leather library chair, much bigger than her. Her legs are tucked underneath her, and her eyes are closed. Her chest rises and falls like the fake breathing of Sleeping Beauty at Madame Tussauds.

"Just tell me. No, I can't come home just now. You tell me what's going on."

The high-pitched wail sounds like a fire alarm. I start to rise to exit the building. But it's Mrs. Bennet, keening into the phone. "Rory Casey, you lie! You're a liar!"

What's going on over there? I itch to get Keene on the phone, but the number I would use is the number Mrs. Bennet's already speaking on.

"No, I have my car. Yes, I can drive. *Of course* I can drive. We'll all come home." Her phone hand drops, and her face falls into the other hand.

"Mum?" says Max, still curled up but eyes open.

Mrs. Bennet calls the girls to her. They join her on the couch, even Dru, one on either side.

"There's been an accident," she says. "Ian needs us. We have to get home right away."

She bends over to retrieve her bag from near her feet. Max asks, "Is it bad, Mum?" Mrs. Bennet stays bent over, and tears drop straight down onto her shoes. Max puts a hand on her back, which bounces from sobs.

I go into the corner and call back the number Keene had dialled me from. Rory Casey answers.

"This is Detective Inspector Frohmann," I whisper with as little voice as I can get away with. "I need DCI Keene."

"He's indisposed."

Bloody hell. "Mr. Casey, what is going on over there?" Fire? Carnage? Had someone got their hands on a gun?

He tells me everything. Mr. Bennet hanged. Keene fainted. Paramedics and CSI on the scene. "He *fainted*?" I repeat incredulously.

Mrs. Bennet jumps up, tipping her daughters back. "Fainted?"

I shake my head. "No, no," I say. *Shit.* "I'm not talking about . . ." She reaches for my phone. I hang up. "Mrs. Bennet, what Rory Casey told you is true. Your husband did not faint." I purposely maintain vagueness for the girls' sake.

"What happened to him?" Max persists. "Did he fall off a ladder?" And into a noose.

Max will not be put off. "Is he at the hospital, Mum? We should go to see him."

Mrs. Bennet doesn't look like she can drive. "I can drive you all home, Mrs. Bennet. Or, if you're not comfortable with me, I can arrange for someone else to do so."

"Mum, is it a bleeding thing? Is he bleeding? That can look worse than it really is."

"Stop it, Max." Mrs. Bennet clutches her stomach and leans forward.

"She said she'd drive us, Mum. Let's get home."

Dru looks at me. "What did he do?"

That is as close as she's got to admitting my suspicion was true. She knows he's "done something," not slipped on a roof or missed a nail with a hammer.

That hammer. I wonder if Dru saw him take it to Grace's face.

"Your mum will tell you at home," I say.

"Is he dead?" Dru's voice is loud.

"Baby . . ." Mrs. Bennet puts her hands over Dru's ears and pulls her into her breasts. It's supposed to be a hug, but has too many angles. Dru's rigid.

"Is he dead?" Dru looks right at me, from her mother's chest.

I beg Mrs. Bennet with my eyes.

"He's gone, baby," she admits.

Max twitches, then starts to shiver. Ms. Barnes pulls an afghan off the back of the couch and puts it over her shoulders.

Dru wriggles out of her mother's arms, but Mum's fingers get caught in her hair. They tussle over it, Dru pulling back so hard that Mrs. Bennet is left with long strands in her hand. Dru turns around and beats the wall, smacking it with the palms of both hands. Then she switches to her head.

Mrs. Bennet grips Dru's shoulders. "I know, baby. He loved us so much."

Dru stills. Her head is stopped against the wall. She rolls from her forehead to turn sideways. "He didn't love you. You wouldn't keep your end up, so I had to do it."

Mrs. Bennet looks honestly baffled. One hand flutters against her neck. "What, baby?"

I say, "Dru, he can't hurt you anymore."

Dru covers her face and slides down the wall. Nobody else moves, except for Ms. Barnes's slight rocking of Max.

The girl who made popcorn taps and pokes her head through. "Ms. Barnes? The shower isn't . . ."

Ms. Barnes waves her hands vigorously. The girl backs out, trying to close the door behind her, but it's stuck.

"This is ridiculous," says Mrs. Bennet to the whole room, then specifically to Dru: "You never liked him. You just want to hurt me." She clutches her stomach.

"Did he do it to himself?" Dru asks me.

I look down. It wouldn't do to override the mother.

"Was it suicide?" Dru demands. "Insurance doesn't pay if it's a suicide, does it?"

"Money?" says Mrs. Bennet. "You're thinking of *money*?"

I remember what Mrs. Bennet had spoken of in the Botanic Garden: how marrying him had allowed her to quit work and care for Max. Money doesn't just buy things; it can buy time.

"Stop it. You're heartless. You're upsetting Max." Mrs. Bennet sits on Max's other side and clutches her hand.

"*You* stop it! Stop saying I'm hurting Max when you mean that I'm hurting you!"

"All right! All right! You're hurting *me*. You hurt *me,* over and over again, you ungrateful—" She stops herself. But we've all filled in the blank in our heads.

"Shut up!" Max covers her ears with both hands.

"Max, sweetheart . . ."

Max cries out, "Please stop shouting. Please stop *talking*. Please, please, please . . ."

Dru stands and reaches out, but Mrs. Bennet pitches herself between them, to embrace Max. Mrs. Bennet's rocking bounces Max's head on her shoulder. The sisters lock eyes, then Max's close. "Daddy," she wails.

Dru's body spasms. I fear she's having a seizure. Then she stills and looks at me.

"Two years ago, my mum and I had a fight at dinner. She thought my clothes were too tight. He stuck up for me."

Too tight? She had on a sweatshirt and baggy jeans.

Dru carries on. "Afterward, Mum went to do the ironing in the bedroom, and I washed the dishes. He stood behind me, and I thought he was going to help with the drying. He reached round and rubbed my chest. 'I like what you wear,' he said. I didn't say anything. I didn't even move. He walked off, and it seemed like it hadn't really happened. It couldn't have, could it? You don't touch someone, and then turn on the football on the telly. I thought I'd misunderstood, or he'd brushed me by accident.

"Everything was mostly normal after that. He said things like that I smelled good, or that I looked nice. He even said them in front of everyone and Mum thought it was normal. So I figured it was. One time I was folding the washing and he picked out my pink knickers and said, 'Wear these tomorrow.' I knew that was wrong. But I didn't think she would believe me.

"That's why I asked to go away to school."

Mrs. Bennet cries quietly, her hand cupped over her mouth. The timeline must be coming together for her: when Dru wore clothes that were too tight, then suddenly everything was gappy and oversized; when Dru asked for boarding school.

Dru has a dreamy look. "I thought I'd managed it. I'd got out. I didn't worry about you. . . ." She turns to face Max. "When you were home, Mum was always with you. He wouldn't have a chance." Max looks uncomprehending. She grew up sheltered. How much does she even know about sex?

"I dodged him at home and packed my bags. But then, on the way to start here in September, he pulled over, down the lane by the big farm? The one before we get to the river?"

She waits for acknowledgement of the location. Mrs. Bennet and I both give her a nod.

"He pulled in, and said I had to be at least as nice to him as I am to the boys at school. I said I didn't know what he was talking about. He put my hand down there, and said I had to rub it. I told him no, but . . ." She shakes her head. "His hand got tight around my wrist, really tight. He said I had to. So I looked out the window, and I did it. I thought I'd hurt him because of the noise he made, and I thought he'd be angry but . . . There was a mess under the steering wheel. He pulled a box of tissues out of the glove box and made me wipe it up."

Dru turns to face her mum straight on. It can go either way: Mrs. Bennet can decide to deny it, or to believe it. Mrs. Bennet's voice squeezes up out of her, an octave too high: "Why didn't you tell me, baby?" Dru throws herself into her mother's arms.

"Because if you didn't believe me you'd hate me! And if you did believe me, we'd end up back to the way things were before. Above that restaurant, and the cockroaches, and rubbish, and Max home alone or in hospital alone." Mrs. Bennet loosens her hold so she can look at Dru. "I don't want to go back there," Dru whimpers.

"Baby, we . . ." But they might well end up back there, unless Ian Bennet has left substantial savings. Is Deeping House mortgaged? "Oh, baby, that's why you insisted on *me* driving you here after that . . ." Reinterpretations of the past two years' events flash in her eyes.

"Tell us what happened on the snowy day, Dru," I say. I hate to press her, but she's likely the only witness.

Her eyes swivel in all directions. "I don't want to talk about it."

"She doesn't want to talk about it," says Mrs. Bennet, stroking Dru's head.

"He killed Grace Rhys, Mrs. Bennet. Because she found out what he was doing to your daughter."

Someone upstairs laughs. We all look up. Only Mrs. Bennet doesn't; she's fixed on Dru's face. "Is that true?"

Dru squeezes her eyes shut and burrows into her mum, nodding. The girls upstairs cheer something. Ms. Barnes slips out and back again. We don't hear anything more from upstairs.

I think hard. It would be kinder to leave them be, let them grieve, and come back to it later with a psychologist and video camera at the station. That is, if she'll be willing to talk. One case, I got told off for having gone easy at the scene when later the victim refused to speak of it.

Even with Mr. Bennet dead, I won't be allowed to close the case without proving it. We need her witness statement. I convince myself: There would be no trial; this would be enough. She wouldn't have to talk about it again.

"We can get this done today, if you want to. We can get this done, and we'll leave you be."

Mrs. Bennet is appalled. "No! No, absolutely not."

But Dru is eager. "I want to, Mum," she says. "What do I have to do?"

She's in shock. I'm manipulating her. But it seems better to get it over than to leave her to worry and practise and watch an appointment on the calendar nearing. And maybe change her mind.

"May I record this?" I ask. I carry a mini-recorder in my bag. "If I record it, then we can refer to that, instead of having to ask you again."

Dru says yes. I need Mrs. Bennet's assent as well. She's under the spell of it all for now, but could demand a stop at any time. ". . . Yes," she cautiously agrees. I put the machine on the table and press RECORD.

"Are you comfortable, Dru?"

She nods.

"I need you to use words. Is that all right?"

She nods again. "Yes," she adds.

Date, location, names, age: *fifteen*. I ask her to talk about the snowy day. She does so in declarative sentences.

"We were all up early to catch the train into London. Mum was excited. Max had a new wig. It was still dark out. Mum and I had a fight." She opens her eyes. "Do I have to say what it was about?"

"Only if you want to," I say.

"Sure, baby," says Mrs. Bennet. "Say whatever you want."

"Mum, I don't even remember!"

Mrs. Bennet's lip twitches into a brief, wan smile. "I don't either, baby."

I prompt Dru to continue.

"It started to snow, and I heard him go outside, so I didn't. I just stayed in my room."

"I'm sorry, you've got to state who 'he' is."

"Ian Bennet. My mum's husband."

Mrs. Bennet's face crumples up.

"Did you see Grace Rhys?" I ask. "Was she out in the snow?"

"I don't know. I didn't look."

"That's fine."

I don't want to lead her, so I just wait. She flails a bit. "Uh . . . It started to rain? So everyone came back in? I heard him come in. I heard Ian Bennet come back in. I put my iPod on." She shrugs. "Then a while later he came into my room and he said, uh, he said I had to take my clothes off. I said no, but . . . I said I would do the thing from the car. Just the thing from the car. But he said, no, I had to take my clothes off. He pulled off my jeans."

Mrs. Bennet covers her face.

"He, uh, he did it, and—"

"I'm sorry, Dru. I need you to be specific. Do you mean sexual intercourse?"

"Yes."

If I were building a rape case, every touch would be catalogued. With Mr. Bennet dead, though, I can spare her that. We only need the fact of the rape as motive. "What happened next?"

"He left."

"He left the apartment?"

"No!" She looks side to side, panicking that I'd taken a wrong turn. "No, my room. He left my room. I stayed in it." She looks at her sister. Her breathing evens.

"What happened then?" We need to get to Grace, but it has to come from her.

"There was a knock? At the door of the flat?"

"You can hear that from your room? Your door was open?" I need to establish that she could hear things clearly.

"Yes," she says. "She was telling him off. She knew Mum wasn't home and she'd heard it."

"She . . . who is 'she'?"

"Grace who worked for the Holsts."

"Grace Rhys? You're certain that was her voice?"

"Yes."

"And what exactly had she heard?"

"When he was . . . when he was doing it. . . . he had made some noises. . . ."

Mrs. Bennet interrupts: "Inspector, is this necessary?"

"Had she heard the rape, Dru?" I compromised. I can't put words in her mouth, but I can ask a question.

"Yes. Yes, she— She said she knew what he'd done and, and she started to call the police."

"She made a call?" This is huge.

"No, she didn't finish the call. Then there was a, a . . . thudding kind of sound. And it, um, like . . ." She mimes with her fist four times. "He hit her with the hammer."

"And you were in your room?"

"Yes."

"You heard this? You heard the tones from her mobile? You heard the hammer?"

"No, I—I saw it was a hammer when I came out of my room. Yes, I heard her phone."

"Why did you come out of your room?"

Her mother interrupts. "Please! She came out of her room to help the poor girl. What do you think?"

"Is that why you came out of your room, Dru?"

"Yes. And he had the hammer and she was . . ."

Mrs. Bennet coos that she doesn't have to say anything more. But I need her to.

"What state was Grace Rhys in when you saw her?"

"She was dead."

Already? Or dying? I'd been told the specific blows she received would likely have left her gurgling and rasping for minutes.

"Are you sure?" I glance at the recorder. Do I really want to go down this road? If Grace had been still living, helping cover up the crime could open Dru up to an accusation of conspiracy from an over-zealous prosecution.

"She . . . her arm stretched out, but then it stopped. She stopped moving. The blood kept coming. I . . . I had to step back because the blood was . . ." Dru kicks her feet, trying to crab away from it.

Mrs. Bennet squishes Dru's face against her shoulder and rocks her. "Inspector, please!"

For Dru's sake, I have to be clear: "You walked into the room and, to the best of your understanding, you saw her die almost immediately? Is that correct?"

"Yes. Then he took her away with the dead Christmas tree. Is that all you need?"

It's like lights on at the end of a movie. Everyone shifts and blinks.

"That's really good, Dru. Thank you." I click off the recorder. "Is there someone I can call for you, Mrs. Bennet? Do you want to go home, or . . . ?"

I don't know where in Deeping House the man hanged himself. If it was in their flat, that would not be a good place to return to. Even if he'd done it out on the grounds . . . I needed to send CSI to look for traces of Grace's blood in their lounge. I had to declare it a crime scene. "Do you have family we can contact for you?" Though from Dru's description of their struggles before the marriage, probably not.

Mrs. Bennet starts to shake. I don't know what to do for them. Ms. Barnes has a plan:

"We have a holiday home, in Florida. You can stay there as long as you like. It's near a beautiful beach. There are sheets and towels in the . . ."

Mrs. Bennet shakes her head. "Max needs her doctors, and I—I have to work."

I suggest various services. It all feels hopeless. I keep it together until we all split up, then I pull the car door shut and cry over the steering wheel. I get it all out, in snot and tears and hot breath. *I hate this. I hate my job.*

I've done no good. Grace is dead. Ian Bennet is dead. Dru was raped and the family is in straits. Connecting the dots hasn't changed any of it. My prize of a recording will close the case and cut another notch in my bedpost. I've proven my promotion. *Cheers.*

CHAPTER 28

GEORGE HART-FRASER

I had every right to call the hospital. Tobias and I worked together. We were close. There was nothing suspicious in my concern. I called. I told them who I am; nothing to hide. They wouldn't let me speak to him. Did that mean he was unconscious? They wouldn't tell me his condition. I called from my office every hour; that seemed a reasonable span. I called his house. Mathilde didn't answer. *That bitch.*

I slammed our door and pounded the stairs with my feet. Our bedroom is up three flights. I flicked on the light. Juliet was home. She filled the bed and the covers were tangled up around her. She shifted and groaned. I turned off the light and backed out. I locked the bathroom door behind me. It was the bathroom on the landing. She would use the en suite. I was safe.

I pulled my mobile out of my coat pocket and called the hospital again.

————

Juliet eventually left for the lab and I was alone.

After I heard the front door, I unclicked the bathroom lock and returned to our bedroom. The covers remained twisted. She hadn't bothered to make the bed up. I could smell her.

I ripped the sheets off and dropped them down the stairs. I stuffed them into the washer in our kitchen, punched them to make them fit. I added soap and turned the temperature as high as it would go.

Tobias was dead. He had died of a heart attack.

I don't drink. I hadn't had alcohol since the last night that Stephen was alive. But Juliet keeps wine. She buys it in boxes so she doesn't feel like she's wasted a bottle by only drinking one glass.

She came home late. I was drunk. Daisy was on my mind, beautiful fucking Daisy. I thought about if Stephen hadn't been home that night, or even had just slept through it. What if I'd fucked Daisy in the kitchen, and laughed at him when he stumbled down the stairs, instead of him laughing at me?

Juliet stomped downstairs. What the fuck was wrong with her? "What happened to the sheets?" she wanted to know. They were still in the washer. Then, "What's wrong with you?"

Me? What was wrong with *me?* It was *her* wine.

She stood over me and kicked the empty box. "Jesus, George."

I pulled myself up on a drawer handle. I closed my eyes. *Daisy.*

I pushed her against the fridge. "Stop it! You're drunk," she whined. I held her hands at her sides and rubbed my face against her neck. She wriggled and pushed. I pushed back.

Her body was wrong. Daisy had been slimmer and taller. I kept my eyes screwed tight and ground our hips together. It wasn't working. *If I could just get it out and do it with my hand for a minute . . .* She got one of her arms unpinned. She shoved my shoulder.

I fell against the kitchen table behind me. I caught on the back of a chair and steadied myself.

She ran up the stairs and slammed the front door.

I blinked. I stumbled up all the stairs, all the way up. I slept on our bare mattress.

———

Juliet forgave me when she found out that Tobias had died. She forgave grief.

There were some awkward moments at night and in the kitchen, but after a fortnight we had refounded our routine. "The police were here a couple of days ago," she said one morning over breakfast.

I forced myself to swallow the unchewed toast and yolk in my mouth. "What did they want?"

"Something in the brook outside. They were in those white space suits, searching it."

Not here. Not at our door. I pushed my plate away.

"Isn't it good?" she asked. She wanted to be praised for her efforts. Everything costs something. I nodded. I apologised. It was babble.

She got up and stood behind me, rubbing my shoulders. "I know how you feel," she said. Her mother died last year. She thinks she knows what that would feel like for everyone. "Tobias was a good friend."

I shook my head. I needed her to stop. The memorial was today. I'd been asked to speak. I'd refused.

Her hands moved down to rub my chest. We hadn't had sex since the night I drank the box wine.

Juliet uses sex as comfort. She fucks when she's upset. She thinks it's the same for everyone. She thinks I can somehow get it up when the police are searching the water outside our house and Mathilde is blackmailing me for my brother's watch. She fucks through disappointment and grief and worry; she holds on and lets sex black it out. Easy for the woman. She just has to spread her legs and say yes.

She backed off when I didn't respond to the chest rubbing.

"Do you want me to come with you to the memorial?" she offered instead.

"Please stop talking about it," I told her. "Please stop." I said it again, to myself, to my brain, to the panic in my gut: *Please stop, please stop, please stop.*

Mathilde swore she'd bring it. I waited outside the church, near the bronze city map. Grieving colleagues and students gathered behind me and were ushered inside. I traced the miniature river with my fingertip, following its pregnant bulge around the west edge. I saw her in the mouth of Senate House Passage. It should have been a straight line to the church door from there.

She saw me. She ran.

I have longer legs. She dodged side to side to avoid other people. It was easy to keep up.

When she turned down Station Road, I burned. Did she think she could just leave? Did she have the watch in her pocket?

The new ticket gates had been left open to allow returning commuters to pass through quickly. She surged through them onto the platform. She didn't buy a ticket. What was that girl up to?

I lost sight of her in the crowd. I looked for the top of her head: fair hair, split down the middle. I got to the end of the main platform and turned. She'd got behind me somehow. She goggled. A sudden flurry confettied between us.

"Stephen?" she said.

The snow stopped. It hung, suspended. *I'm George,* I thought. *I'm George, you bitch.*

I put out my hand. It's a shock how solid a body is, even a small thing like her. But snow got under her feet. That helped.

Her bag slipped off her shoulder. It fell with her, and dumped out onto the tracks beside her: paper, fruit, coins. Her wallet. A watch. A watch!

It lay on the tracks, well out of reach. Police were surely on their way. *Why hadn't she just given it to me?*

I pushed through the crowd. *What now?* They'd find it. They'd know what it meant. I got out of the station and walked quickly away down side streets. I rubbed my eyes.

The image of the watch face hovered in front of me. The twelve numbers shifted and re-formed. Something was wrong. Stephen's watch had used Roman numerals. He used to joke that he couldn't read it. The face of the watch on the tracks—I was certain, the image was burned into my eyes—was made of Arabic numerals. It looked familiar.

It was Tobias's.

She'd tried to trick me.

———

A hymn was audible outside the church.

I smoothed my suit jacket. My chest heaved; I slowed my breathing. The brief snow shower had stopped. A droplet of melt fell out of my hair and slid down my face.

I slipped into a pew at the back. The woman next to me slid over, then tilted her open hymnal towards me. I waved my hand over it to indicate "no." I don't sing. I clasped my hands and looked straight ahead. Organ chords rattled my body. The music crescendoed in grand style, except for the howl of the woman next to me who couldn't reach the note.

Turns were taken to remember Tobias. Generic prayers were half-heartedly murmured. The eulogy recapped his marriage and father-hood, his career achievements and the nurture of those under him. Heads nodded in agreement. That's all the view I had: the backs of bobbing heads atop dark suits and jackets.

"Tobias Oliver treasured every stage of his life. He was an active member of his school's alumni organisation, and it's thanks to their contributions that I can share with you these photos from his boy-hood."

A standing screen had been set up in front of the altar. A slideshow was projected onto it. The first photos were black-and-white, but I knew what colours they represented. The coat was blue; the socks were yellow.

More pictures followed: a succession of graduation photos with ever more elaborate hoods and hats, as his academic career progressed. Wedding pictures. Infant Mathilde. Fewer as she grew older.

Those early photos, from Bristol. They'd come from the alumni donations for the archive. I opened the program. *Eulogy: Richard Keene, Magdalene College.*

I knew who had the box.

CHAPTER 29

CHLOE FROHMANN

I call the CSI team. The Bennet flat needs processing. Had Dru been forced to participate in getting rid of the body? Or cleaning the floor? One of them had had to collect Grace's belongings from the help flat, without Katja or Mum or Max seeing. My stomach hurt.

But CSI had come and gone. They're back at the lab already. The hair from the hammer is indeed a superficial match with the hairs from Grace's brush, just as Keene had eyeballed. The brand of hammer matches a brand popular in Mr. Bennet's admittedly haphazard tool collection. It's suggestive. You can say that with authority if you're a prosecutor, or a sneer if you're the defence.

I'm parked on the grounds of the school, facing across Trumpington Road. I look through the windscreen towards the brook beyond. *Why would he bring it all the way here?* I can understand avoiding the original dump site, and the rain in which he'd dumped the body had kick-started the flooding that closed that road, anyway. But why not with Grace's things, which Keene had found? Why here? On a busy road? Was he even here after dark? He dropped Dru off and then he . . .

Except he hadn't. Mrs. Bennet had said that after September *she* was the one who took Dru to school, at Dru's then-inexplicable insistence.

Maybe Mr. Bennet made Dru take it well away from the scene of the crime? It was only a few days later. But why would he still have it? His bloody shirt he could have missed, perhaps, in the frenzy of the original disposal, but the hammer? Wouldn't he have just tossed it in with the body? Wouldn't dropping it be the first thing you'd want to do when the adrenaline falls and you realise what you've done?

I picture the hammer in my hand. I picture the spattered shirt on my body. Spattered, not soaked. The blood had transferred in the moment of killing, in close proximity to it. Wouldn't I want to get it off me? Wouldn't I drop the hammer down?

Unless I was scared. Unless I was ashamed. Unless staying clothed and continuing to defend myself were my top priority.

Oh, Dru . . .

What if she did it? What if she killed Grace? Grace was going to . . . what? Call the police? Call Children's Services? Ruin everything that Dru had sacrificed herself for. If Mr. Bennet were arrested, he couldn't support Max's care anymore. She'd continue to get NHS treatment, of course, but Mrs. Bennet would go back to work. They'd live hand to mouth again. Maybe she hid the shirt, crumpled in her hamper, then suitcase; maybe she didn't take it off for days, wearing sweaters on top. I looked after a rape victim once who wouldn't give us her semen-stained clothes. She'd been fierce about it. No one was going to make her undress again.

Maybe she'd held the hammer up to Ian Bennet, with the proof of her power bleeding at her feet. Maybe later she kept it in bed with her. Maybe, only when she was safely here, away from him and with a snooping housemistress to worry about, did she let it go.

No, I have to stop thinking like this. There's no proof. Her witness statement is sufficiently coherent. Don't go looking for trouble.

I look towards Dru's campus house with Ms. Barnes. Dru won't be back. Whatever money Mr. Bennet had in hand when he died would be best kept back against necessities, not tuition. They can sell Deeping House, or live off the rents, if they're able to keep it up themselves or hire a handyman. . . .

A sharp rap of knuckles on glass jolts me. It's the teacher I spoke to earlier. "Inspector, is there a problem?"

People don't like it when police linger. I start up the car and ease out between the posts.

I'm pregnant. I'm driving. No drink for me. I think back to my irresponsible youth: What besides getting pissed makes the stress fade to the background?

I twist the steering wheel hard right. I throttle the gear shift and stomp the accelerator. Barton Road leads me to the motorway. It's commuter-free this Saturday evening, and I let the car have its head. Eighty, ninety . . . at ninety the blur is almost enough to extend to my mind.

———

I've come to Milton Keynes and pulled over. I look in my notes for Grace's parents' address, and park in front of their house.

The drive has cleared my head. What did my imagination have to do with anything? Who knows how that shirt and hammer got there, and whether that hair had been pulled from Grace Rhys's head? We have a witness. The suspect has accomplished near-confession and ample punishment with his suicide. Finished. There's only the tidying up left to do.

I flip the mirror on the sunshade open and brush my hair. Formality is key. There's no way to get through these things except as ritual.

My mobile buzzes the way I have it set for callers who aren't in my phone's log. "DI Frohmann," I answer, curious.

It's Keene. He explains that he's bought a cheap pay-as-you-go.

"What the hell happened to you?" I demand.

"We found Ian Bennet hanged."

"So I was told." He doesn't mention passing out. I'd told him I was pregnant; what the hell was he holding back on me for? "I recorded a witness statement from Dru. She saw him commit the murder."

"Dru? The daughter? What about Katja?" The connection crackles. Or his voice is hoarse. We're worlds apart. I have to explain it all to him to catch him up.

"Brookside's a strange place for Ian Bennet to dump the weapon," he says, coming to the same conclusion that I did. "Traffic, daylight. Unless he stayed late or overnight when he brought Dru to school in January. Did you ask her about that?"

I can't remember if it had been before or after I started recording that Mrs. Bennet had mentioned that she was the one to drive Dru into Cambridge in January.

"No," I equivocate. I hadn't, it was true, specifically asked. "The hair evidence is tenuous, Keene. It could well be nothing to do with Deeping House. I'm going to recommend the case to Cole as closed." I've made my decision. There's nothing to be gained by looking deeper.

"That's my decision, isn't it," he says.

Is it? Is it, D-C-I Keene? That one extra letter, c-is-for-chief, makes all the difference, except that one of us is bearing the load and the other is flopping and fainting and crashing the car. He's not ready. Cole is expecting my report, not just on this case but on Keene.

"I have to go," I say. I have a bell to ring.

The woman who answers the door is not Mrs. Rhys. "No, we're just subletting! They're on a trip," she lets me know. She's bright from head to toe: yellow hair, orange blouse, white jeans. She hurts my eyes. She copies a handwritten list of phone numbers that Mrs. Rhys and her new husband have left for emergencies, including various cruise-line offices.

Tomorrow. I can set that in motion tomorrow.

But Cole can't wait. I have to report in before Keene does.

I push all the air out of my lungs. My phone feels slippery in my hand. Cole answers.

I assert the evidence. Cole agrees with my conclusions. There are formal processes to go through, but agreement has been found.

Then, "What's Keene's opinion?" he asks. "I haven't been able to raise him on the phone."

"About Keene . . ." I begin. I tell the truth: His hand is a problem. His frustration with his hand is a problem. His stress levels are at full throttle. He broke his phone. He fainted at the scene of Ian Bennet's suicide.

"Fainted?" That one takes Cole aback. "What do you mean, fainted?"

"I don't know any more than that, sir. Keene's not well."

Keene will raise holy hell when Cole calls him in. He could fling my pregnancy out there, to get back. I have to be prepared for that. And even if he doesn't, it'll come out anyway, soon enough.

"Get him to call me before you set the paperwork in motion. I'd like to hear his take."

"Pardon?" I've missed a transition, surely.

"I want to hear Keene's take on the case."

"I told you, sir, he's not well."

"I'll judge it myself. I appreciate your views." He rings off.

He appreciates my bloody views?

I slam my head back against the headrest. *Damn.* Cole set me up. That's what it is. He set me up to see if I'd throw Keene to the wolves. To show what kind of team player I am.

My heart bangs into my ribs.

This is worse than pregnant. This is Judas.

And if Keene pushes the inquiry about the hammer and shirt . . . If he raises the same questions that had come to my mind . . .

I'd recorded Dru as a witness. I hadn't cautioned her about her right to silence, because, to my mind, she hadn't been a suspect. The tape would not be admissible as evidence. All of it—not just about the murder but the rape and molestations—would need to be regained, if that was even possible. She wouldn't want to say it again, and certainly wouldn't willingly incriminate herself. I'd botched it.

The inside of my belly flip-flops. No, it's not the baby. It's panic.

If she turns out to be the killer, and my cavalier hurry with the interview costs us proving it, I'll deserve to lose my job. If I keep it somehow, I'll never be trusted again.

I drive home, clutching the wheel tight.

Dan is waiting at the door. I smell potatoes and gravy, balsamic from a salad, and washing-up soap. For someone so apparently well-fed, he doesn't look happy.

"What?" I say.

"Your friend Alice. She's been hurt. You have to go."

"Alice?" I'm lost.

"Keene's brother's wife? Alice?"

"Shit. Did she miscarry?"

"Chloe, she was attacked. The police are interviewing her. Richard couldn't reach Morris, so he called here."

What? No, I can't . . . I just want to sleep. "I can't. Dan, I'm not up to this."

"Coco . . ." he says, catching me in a hug. *I love this man's chest. I love his arms.*

I could quit. I could stay home with the baby. Everyone would think I've given the job up out of fascination with motherhood and not because I've ruined the case and betrayed my partner.

"I'm pregnant," I say.

He loosens the hug to lean back and look at me.

"You're what?"

"I'm pregnant. Ten weeks."

He looks up, counting back in his head. But there was no drunken or distracted forgetting of birth control. No birthday or Valentine's romantic abandon. It's just one of those things.

"How do you feel about this?" he asks cautiously.

"So you can just agree with me? No way. You tell me how *you* feel."

"It's awkward timing, but . . . I'd like a baby with you, Coco."

I nod.

"You going to tell me how *you* feel?" he presses.

I shake my head. But I say, "All right."

"You feel all right?" His hands are on my cheeks.

"No. 'All right,' I'll tell you." He waits. I pull his hands off me. I squeeze his fingers. "I don't like sharing my body like this. I don't like what it's doing to me. I like to sleep. I like to work. I'm bad at this already. If I feel this way now, it's only going to get worse."

I'm still outside the door; he's still in. The lamplight behind him puts him into silhouette. I can't read his face.

He says, "You don't want to have this baby?" He's trying to sound neutral. He's not succeeding.

Tears again. I hate this. I push him into the house and stomp past. Who's the child again? I'm throwing a fair tantrum.

"I do want this baby. I do," I say, sucking snot back up my nostrils. "But the me that wants it isn't the me I'm used to. There's another me in here, a me who leans into other people's prams, cooing, and looks up baby names on the Internet. That's what I mean by sharing my body. There's two of me in here, the me I know and always have been, and this baby-crazy mum. I don't know her, I don't know if I'll like her, and when the baby comes out I don't know how much of the old me will be left. I like me, the old me. I don't want her to die. I don't want to die." I fold in the middle, leaning forward, bouncing with sobs. "When I told Keene, I—"

"You told Keene?" Everything up till then he's absorbed, generously, but this he throws back at me, incredulous.

"I didn't tell him like a friend, I told him to fuck off. I told him he wasn't the only one with a, a . . . physical problem."

Dan cringes at the last word. "Our baby is a problem?"

"No, I . . ." But then I rally. "Yes, a baby is a problem. It's not only a problem. It's a gift, too. A beautiful, wonderful, lucky gift. And, dare I say it, a problem. Anyone who doesn't admit that is full of shit. Or the one who isn't pregnant."

I catch my reflection in the dark window. My arms are folded over my breasts. My shape is obvious. Under my elbows is a curve that wasn't there before. I won't be able to hide it much longer.

I lower my arms. My breasts are larger, too; hasn't he noticed? My areolas have darkened. I'm tempted to go on the offensive: *Don't you even look at me?* But that wouldn't be fair. That wouldn't be kind.

"Let's start over," I say. "Dan, we're having a baby." I attempt a smile. "I'm scared I'm going to be a bad mother or a bad cop. Or both. I don't like feeling this way."

Dan hugs me like ribbons round a maypole, in parallel diagonal stripes: one arm up across my shoulder to my hair, the other stretched across my waist to my hip. We rock a little, until my breathing slows down.

When we pull apart he says, "Alice needs you. Richard sounded scared."

"She would hate me if she knew what I've said about being pregnant."

"This isn't about miscarriage. It's police business. She needs you."

I nod. I wipe my face with a tissue. "I'll come home . . ." I mean to say "quickly" or at least "before midnight." But I know I might not. It's not that kind of job. "I'll come home," I repeat.

That will have to be enough.

CHAPTER 30

GEORGE HART-FRASER

Richard had a lecture scheduled the next day. So did I; I cancelled mine. Juliet stayed home to let in the gas man to repair the boiler. I had the car to myself.

My hand quivered. I forced the key into its hole and started the engine. I'd brought a screwdriver. That should help open a door. If that didn't work, it could shatter a window. I supposed. It's not as if I'd done any of this before.

I parked in a pub lot and walked up the road. House numbers were hidden behind hedges or within calligraphic renderings on tile. I finally found it—a white Tudor wigged in thatch.

I didn't have to break anything. The door to the conservatory at the back was merely latched. I pushed and jiggled until the hook jumped off the eye.

Boxes filled the lounge. Either it was a recent move or they hoarded. The boxes were labelled "dining room" and "books" in black marker. I didn't think Tobias's school memorabilia would be there.

The stairs were uneven and turned a sharp corner up to the first floor. One step squealed under my foot. An answering moan came from upstairs.

I held still. No further sound came. Lifting my foot quickly from the step would probably release the noise again. I pulled up from my knee very, very slowly.

I waited in silence, postured like a flamingo. The moan might have been an animal. Or a person, asleep.

I put my foot on the next step, and the next and the next, now keeping to the edges. At the top, three doors bordered a square central landing. I had to choose.

The landing itself was made of apparently original boards that had warped and probably were never well-fitted to begin with. I kept to the edge here as well, to avoid making them whine underneath my weight. I shuffled along the wall.

The first door was slightly ajar. I nudged it, revealing tiles and a white sink. Two doors remained.

I looked for evidence of use. A corner of paper peeped out from under one.

I squeezed the iron handle and eased the door in. It was a cramped study. A laptop lay closed on a desk, and a scanner. Next to them, a box. The photos within showed cricket and rugby and choir and a vast dining hall full of young boys, cups raised. Underneath those pictures: certificates, a small football trophy, a fat knitted scarf in school colours, and two old, faded books. I upended it all onto the desk. Photos slid, books thudded, and the trophy clanged. I rooted around but found no watch.

Through the wall, a springy creak. In one step I pushed the door closed, but not clicked. A door slapped its opposite wall. The landing floorboards did indeed complain, lightly. *A woman?* Water rushed into the sink.

I held still. The floorboards again. The middle stair. *Damn.*

The dining room and lounge downstairs were connected by a wide arch. If she were in either, there would be no getting past.

A gurgle ran through pipes in the wall. The kitchen! I made for the stairs, skimming over the noisy one.

At the bottom, angles were such that I saw her, through the convergence of the wide dining-room arch and the thin kitchen doorway. She stood, back to me, leaning against the counter, next to a white grumbling kettle. She wore a pale nightdress. A shock of red patched the back of it. My disgust must have been audible. She turned.

She reached for the telephone on the wall. I rushed her, slamming her across the room against the fridge. But the spiral cord stretched. Three tones for 999 beeped right in my ear. She released the receiver and it sprang back towards the wall behind me. The low tones of an answering voice came from it. I threw myself at it to hang it up.

Hot shock hit me in the back of the neck. I convulsed backwards. Pain ripped a shriek out of me. She'd poured boiled water down my back.

I wrenched the kettle out of her hand to beat her with it, but she skittered behind a door I didn't realise was there. A lock clicked. I banged the kettle on the door, then threw it down.

Fingerprints everywhere. Police on the way. I ran across the street, hunched over. My shadow looked like a badger's. I huddled in the car, banging my head against the steering wheel in a dull rhythm. I turned the key. The car lunged onto the road.

———

I gave my back to the cold shower spray, each stream hitting me like a blade. I braced myself against both sides of the stall.

Juliet knocked. "Occupied!" I called. She could wait to relieve herself. Or she could piss elsewhere.

"A police-person came while you were out!" she called through the door. "She said they'd found your watch. I didn't know you'd lost a watch."

I needed my passport. I could not stay.

"I haven't," I shouted over the water noise. "I don't know what they're talking about."

The water turned dully warm; I got out. The soft towel scraped my back. I knelt on the bathmat, dripping, quivering.

The door shook from her knocking again. I hadn't locked it, I realised a moment too late.

"You done in there? I need it."

She barged in. She saw the blisters on my back. "Holy shit, George. You have to see somebody."

"No," I said.

"I'll take you to A and E; that looks serious."

If I didn't go, she'd call them to come for me.

"No," I said, pushing myself up.

"What the hell happened to you?"

I grabbed her by the back of the neck and slammed her head against the toilet.

In Bristol, I'd never had to see Stephen's body. Mother did that. To me, Stephen remained fleshy and vital, not stiff and charred. He was gone, not changed.

Juliet bled.

"What the fuck is wrong with you?" I shouted at her. Her head leaked, matting her hair. The blood came at me, drained towards me, chased me out of the room.

———

The door under the stairs hung ajar. That's right; the gas man had come today. That's why it was warm. The heating was working.

I pulled the door open farther.

It took a spanner to loosen the coupling between two pipes until I got a hiss, and a stink. A botched job, creating a gas leak, could explain why Juliet fell and hit her head.

I had my passport. I had cash. I locked the door behind me.

CHAPTER 31

MORRIS KEENE

The cottage is more than four hundred years old but with shiny new thatch on top. It nudges right up against the edge of the road, like so many buildings from the days before cars.

I'm noticing these things because I haven't been here before. Richard and Alice have lived here for four months, since they got back from honeymoon.

I haven't phoned. I should have, to ask if this is a good time, but I didn't want to hear no.

I don't want to hear no in person, either. I wait in the drive.

Gwen miscarried once, after Dora. I never told anyone that. Gwen did; she told her friends and her siblings. I didn't tell anyone. Who would I tell?

I rub my head. Maybe he doesn't want me to know.

Then, just like that, without any fumbling, I'm out of the car. I'd reached across with my left hand, popping the door handle. I reach across the door to press the bell. The window in the door looks straight through into the lounge, and three heads pop up at the noise. Richard, Alice . . . and Chloe. No, *Frohmann.*

For an instant it looks to me like an interview. Frohmann's note-book is on the table. But, *They're friends now, Keene. Get used to it.*

Richard opens the door. I say, "Thank you for the car. Sorry I was a bastard about it. Sorry about . . . Alice."

The apologies are like a password. Richard nods, and steps back to let me in. I follow him through the kitchen to the lounge.

"Hello, Alice," I say. "Is everything . . . ?" I didn't mean to move my hands like that, in the "pregnant belly" motion. Frohmann stops me with a curt head wag. The miscarriage completed, then. "This is a beautiful home," I say instead, with inappropriate heartiness. This is every kind of visit in one. Condolences! Apology! Thanks! And, housewarming! *Dial it down, Keene,* I kick myself.

Richard turns back around to the kitchen. I follow him. "Beer or tea?" he asks. "Tea," I say. I don't need alcohol. I'm making an idiot of myself without it. He fills a mug from the tap and puts it in the micro-wave.

"Gwen miscarried once," I say, like we're peers here. Except mine was a decade ago. And we already had a kid.

"I'm sorry to hear that." The microwave finishes. He drops a teabag in and hands it over. I go for it with my left hand. Smoothly, no last minute mix-up. It's like my hands have figured it out: The right one's stepped aside; the left one's stepped up. I feel cocky. I feel good. I feel like I could juggle one-handed.

"I didn't expect you to come," Richard says.

I hadn't given him any reason to. "I really am sorry," I say. "For everything." My physio says I delude myself that other people have perfect lives and that I'm just playing catch-up. She says imaginarily perfect people make good punching bags. She says I have to accept that nobody's life is perfect. We're all playing catch-up together.

He finishes a second mug in the microwave. This one, he dunks the teabag in and pushes it around with a spoon and scoops it out and drops it in the bin. He adds milk and sugar. I follow him back to the lounge, and he hands the cup to Alice. We sit around the coffee table.

No one says anything. *Where's a board game when you need one, right?* I almost laugh. I think it's almost, but Richard is staring at me. *I didn't laugh, did I?*

"I should have come sooner," I say. I should have come round for a hello weeks ago. Gwen wanted to. I put it off.

"You've had a break in the case. I get that."

Tonight? Did he mean I should have come sooner tonight? "Yes," I say cautiously. "It's been a tough one."

"But I need to know that you'll take this on." He's looking up now. He's looking right at me.

I frown, and shoot my eyes over to Frohmann.

"He doesn't have his phone," she says. "He probably doesn't know," she says.

I look around. Nothing is familiar. "Know what?"

Alice says "Someone broke in—"

But then Richard overrides her: "No. No, you don't have to tell it again."

"I can tell it again."

"You don't have to."

"I want to! I want to say it as many times as I need to! Morris can help."

Richard stands up. He says, louder than Alice: "I don't want to hear it again." He pauses in between every word: "*I*—don't—want—to—hear—it."

He turns on me. "Chloe can take you home. I'm keeping the car. When Alice phoned today, I had to get home on the bus. It stopped everywhere. It took over an hour."

I fish the keys out of my pocket. I put them in his hand.

———

Chloe's parked across the road. I walk right up to the passenger door without the usual swear and swerve away from the driver's side. I open it up. Frohmann's looking at me. "I'm learning," I say. The seatbelt is a struggle again, because I'm thinking about it. Then, it just clicks.

She tells me what happened. The break-in, the attack. Alice nailed him with the boiled kettle, then barricaded herself in the downstairs loo.

"She got him with the kettle?" Bloody amazing. *That's why Richard microwaved the tea,* is the first thing I think. Then, *That's why he married her,* is the second thing. A strong woman. I miss Gwen.

Alice reported it to the local police. They took it seriously, but it's not getting bumped to us at Major Investigations. *Well, now it will be.* We'll see to it.

"Was Alice able to describe him?" I ask. "Did he take anything?" Not that any taking matters in comparison to what he did and could have done, but it would give insight into his motives and, possibly, identity.

"He was in the study. Probably looking for computer equipment. We're guessing he didn't think anyone was home, and was surprised when Alice got out of bed. Nothing is missing, Richard says. There was a mess in the study from an overturned box of school memorabilia."

Why would Richard have school mementoes? Our unremarkable childhood didn't warrant many souvenirs.

"What school?" I ask, which seems to exasperate her.

"Does it matter?"

"I'm asking."

She throws up her hands. "Someplace in Bristol."

"Richard didn't go to . . ." *The watch.*

"What?"

"The watch I found with Grace's things. George Hart-Fraser's watch. It was from a school in Bristol."

"Why would Richard have—?" she says at the same time I ask "What did the man look like?"

"Alice said about the same size as Richard, dark hair, cut short, clean shaven. She said he had thin lips. And thick eyebrows. Black wool coat. Green scarf. Black gloves." She closes her notebook.

"That's George Hart-Fraser," I say, remembering the photo on his departmental Web page. *Well, "consistent with" George Hart-Fraser.*

"And hundreds of other men in Cambridgeshire."

"Did you talk to him?" I'd told Chloe to go see him.

"I talked to his girlfriend. He wasn't home."

"When?"

She refers to her notes. "When Alice was being attacked," she admits.

I smack my side of the dashboard to punctuate the coincidence. I hit so hard the glove box pops open.

"Easy, Keene. Most people aren't at home in the middle of the day, even a weekend day. It doesn't necessarily mean anything."

"What did she say? The girlfriend?"

"I said we may have found his watch. She said George had never mentioned the watch and would be home after five."

"And when you went back?"

"Keene . . ."

"You didn't go back?"

"Morris, it's over. I'd got the witness statement from Dru. There was no reason to go back."

"There's reason now."

She's not starting the car.

"Please, Chloe," I say. Once I sprained both my ankles playing mandatory school rugby. For one humiliating month I rolled around in a wheelchair. It was meant to be propelled by me pushing the wheels with my hands, but my "friends" were always grabbing the handles that stuck out from the back behind my shoulder blades. There was nothing I could do when they did. They rolled me around, snorting with laughs. I want to tell Frohmann to let go and just let me steer.

"No," she says.

It's not the word that surprises me; it's the nothing after. Sure, we contradict and challenge one another, but we don't just say no, full stop. "And . . . ?" I prompt.

"I didn't want to have to say this," she says, "not to Cole or to you."

"What the hell does Cole have to do with anything?"

"Morris," she says. Not "Keene." It sounds motherly. It sounds pitying. It sounds like we're not equals on the job anymore. She wants to get personal.

It's my turn to say no, see how she likes it.

"You're not ready," she says. "You want to be but you're not. Maybe if you took some more time—"

"To do what? What, exactly?" Staying home doesn't exercise what needs to be exercised. "I've apologised for my hand—"

"Nobody wants an apology."

She's making me raise my voice: "It doesn't matter. I've apologised anyway, because I know I've been a drag on you. But that's changing now. I'm changing. It's reaching with my right hand that's been the problem. It's the trying and failing and dropping. But I know that now. I'm letting it go. I'm letting my left hand step up. I'm—"

"It's not your hand."

I sputter. I open the car door and slam it shut behind me, all in one motion, left-handed, smooth. Loud.

I cross the road. Their door's locked. Of course it is, after what happened this afternoon. No one's in the living room. I ring the bell. Richard takes his damn time. He turns the bolt and slides the chain with exaggerated gestures. Chloe catches up.

"Alice is trying to sleep," he hisses.

"I've got to show her something." I have the printout of George Hart-Fraser's University Web page. It's been crammed in my pocket; the fold lines cross, framing his photo in the corner. "Ask her if this is him."

Richard takes it upstairs, leaving us outside. Frohmann and I don't speak. The tumble dryer thuds and whooshes, in its own continuous conversation.

Richard pounds down the uneven stairs, calling as he does. "Yes. It's him." He rushes at the door, catching himself on the jamb. "Go!" he says, breathing hard, listing.

We run across the street. Into the car, onto the road. I lean as Chloe takes a corner. She reads my mind, accelerating even more. I don't recognise the feeling inside me at first; I worry I'm going to be sick. Then it comes back to me: It's that intensity that coils up at the climax of a case, waiting for the moment to spring. It used to be familiar. It used to be my high. It's been a while, but it's back.

CHAPTER 32

CHLOE FROHMANN

I keep my eyes aimed out the windscreen. Hands on the wheel, foot to the pedal. There's no room for any part of me to deal with Keene on a personal level now.

We turn off Trumpington Road into Brookside and park in front of the girls' school near the end. Most of the street is private terraced homes, but they're bookended by four school buildings. Cambridge is made of schools.

I reach for George's doorbell. Keene throws his right hand over my arm, batting it out of the way.

"Stop! Do you smell that?" Keene says. I hold short of the buzzer.

He lifts the flap on the mail slot. A foul odour comes at us. He drops the flap and we scramble backwards. I punch 999 into my phone.

Gas. The house is full of it. Even the click of an electric doorbell could set it off. The flick of a light switch. If someone is sleeping in there, and we rouse them . . .

I request an ambulance, fire fighters, and the Gas Emergency Service. "You take that side," I say, pointing. I run down these steps and mount those on the other flank.

Keene hesitates. He's still at George's door, staring. "Keene!" I call from the steps beside.

He flinches, jumps, really. He shakes his head like a wet dog. Down the steps, up the other side. He pounds on that door. We've got to get the neighbours out.

———

The fire engine comes first, followed by the ambulance. The flashing lights on their tops add a flickering of cinematic unreality. I corral the residents of the attached houses to mill by the monument at the end of the street. They hug themselves against the cold. A paramedic stands on a bench, enumerating gas exposure symptoms: queasiness, dizziness, headache. A similar flu is going around; several people raise their hands and step forward for priority examination.

Two firemen, huge in their coats and with snoutish masks, force in George's door. No explosion, thank God. Windows are unlocked and raised from the inside.

Shouts. A plus-shape fills the doorway: a fireman up and down, and a body in his arms lying across. The hem of a purple skirt hangs off the legs.

The paramedics abandon the neighbours and scrum around her. No compressions are attempted. I stretch to see; there's a head wound. Black curly hair and black matted blood. They discuss her injuries and the scene inside. I'm not immediately needed; the house is still unsafe. I peel off to vomit in the brook.

On the other side of the water, a bench faces the cars circling the roundabout at Fen Causeway. It's missing one long seat slat. Keene's already there, elbows on knees, head in hands. Headlamp beams travel over him as cars enter the roundabout.

"Where the hell have you been?" I say.

He looks up. "Nice," he says.

"No, really, have you been here this whole time?"

"Once the cavalry showed up, there wasn't much left for me to do." No, just everything left for *me* to do.

I sit next to him. "What're you over here for? The view?" I shield my eyes as the glare from a turning car sweeps across us. I blink fast, but tears make it through and fall down my face. *Shit.* I rub my cheeks.

He sits up. "Are *you* all right?"

"They found a body." I can't look at him. "I recognised her purple skirt. It was George's girlfriend. I talked to her today. She's dead."

His breath snags.

"Her head was banged up. Blunt trauma. Massive blood loss. If I'd checked on her after interviewing Dru . . ."

"You had no reason to. You'd solved it."

"I'd solved Grace Rhys. What about Mathilde Oliver? What about this woman? Her name was Juliet. Jesus Christ. It takes time to bleed out. Maybe I could have been here before she . . ."

"You're sure?" His voice is eager. "She died this afternoon?"

"No, Keene, no one's sure. But they're guessing from the blood loss in an upstairs bathroom and how far she got on the stairs. She must have lost track of which floor she was on; she kept going all the way to the basement. . . ." My voice cracks.

"But they think she was dead before we got here? That's what they think?"

"Why do you want me to say it again? Yes, she likely died hours ago. And I did nothing to stop it. Are you happy now?" I mean it sarcastically, but the question is bizarrely apropos. He's smiling. "What are you laughing at?" I say.

"I'm not . . ." But he is. It turns into a cough. "I don't know."

"Nothing about this is funny."

"Shit, Chloe, nothing's funny. Fucking nothing. I know that." Another headlamp streak prowls across his body. He doesn't move. "I knew she was there," he says.

"What?"

"I saw part of her through the window. I saw her, and didn't try to get her out."

"Jesus, Keene." On the stairs, when he hesitated. *He saw her.*

"I know."

"What's wrong with you?"

"I know. I know."

"You should have done something."

"I know what I should have done! I should have broken in. I should have taken a brick to the window, and got in, and pulled her out."

He could be sacked. He could be sued. "What the hell is wrong with you?"

"I don't know! I haven't been the same since coming back. I can't . . ." He doesn't finish.

"You can't what?"

"I didn't have a gas mask. I didn't want to suck that poison into my lungs. I had to make a call: her or me. I chose me."

"No one's asking you to be a hero all by yourself. I was there, Keene. I was on the other side of the stairs. You should have said something. You should have—"

"You don't get it, Chloe. I froze. I've lost my nerve. I—" He pushes out a long breath. "It took me by surprise the first time it happened. I drop out. I drop away when things get . . . I just see that knife coming at me."

"You're scared?"

He blinks, as if seeing the banality of it for the first time.

"I . . . yes. I was scared. A year ago I would have gone in. No hesitation. It's easy to be brave when you don't really know what it feels like, what it feels like *in your head,* to have a knife go in. I was open. I thought I was dead. Jesus Christ. I'll never go near that feeling again. I can't. I . . . I just can't."

He bends forward. I put my hand on his back.

He pants. "She was already dead. I didn't kill her. I didn't kill her." His shoulders bounce. He's laughing again, from relief. Maybe not laughing. Maybe that other thing, that thing we both hate to do.

"You got the neighbours out first. A spark could have caused an explosion. You made the right decision," I assure him.

"It wasn't a decision. A decision is a choice between two things you could do. I couldn't do it."

"Don't say that. You made the right decision." I put force on each word and raise my eyebrows at the end. He needs to stop saying these things out loud. Say them to a therapist, a priest, in bed . . . just not to a fellow officer.

He doesn't take my hint. "You know that accident, with my car?

When he came at me, I . . . I just, I let go. It's like I wasn't there anymore, and my car . . . it barrelled off the road. It wasn't my hand. I kept
saying that, remember? 'It wasn't my hand.' And everyone understood
that that meant it wasn't my fault, it was that man's, in the other car.
He came at me, it's true. But then *I* went off the road. . . . He didn't
push me there. I just, I stopped driving and the car rammed into the
fence. It wasn't my hand. It wasn't him. It was my head. Chloe, I'm not
right in the head anymore." He flips his hands palms up, like he's giving this to me, making a present out of more honesty than I want. "I
was a fucking magician: I kept everyone, including me, looking at my
hand so no one would look anywhere else. Couldn't hide it from you,
though. You're right. I'm not fit to be back on the job."

"If you need a break, take it," I say. "You were right, about George."
And if I'd followed up on that thread, Juliet might still be alive.

"She's dead; he's gone." He shrugs. "Being right's not so grand."

"We'll call Bristol. He may have headed home. We'll get him. I
didn't see it, Morris. You did. You were right." This is selfish, all selfish
on my end. I trust him. I depend on him. I want to keep doing that. I
want what I said to Cole to not be true. *Don't leave me, not like this.*

He shakes his head, and shivers down his whole body. "Lucky I
wasn't with you when you interviewed Dru. It could have hurt the case
if I'd been more involved and then I go back on medical leave."

Now it's my turn to laugh inappropriately. "Lucky, yeah," I joke. I
don't elaborate.

We walk back to my car. I have to move a pile of papers from the
passenger seat.

"I'm sorry you've been stuck writing up the case notes," he says.

"I don't mind."

"You do mind."

I crack a smile. "You're right. See? Right again."

He smiles, too. But he repeats: "I have to take a break."

"What will you . . ."

He waves his hand, as if dispelling secondhand smoke. He clicks
the seatbelt in, first time. He shivers.

"Where's your coat?" I ask, finally noticing.

"I left it in Richard's car."

I crank up the heat. He'll get his own car back from the garage soon. It could all go back to normal, if he'd just play along. Well, normal without his hand. Last-week normal, not last-year normal. Last-year normal is never coming back.

We wait our turn to enter the roundabout. Ahead of us, the ambulance moves slowly, no sirens, no flashers. No rush with a dead body. I suck in my breath as it passes. He asks if I'm all right.

"I'm fine," I say.

"Me, too." It's like a joke now. "We're fine."

CHAPTER 33

GEORGE HART-FRASER

I drove to Heathrow. I used my credit card. No point covering my steps; it was a race now, not hide-and-seek.

I knew some Spanish. I'd been there before, for the telescope. It's a beautiful country.

In Chile, the Milky Way is bright enough to read by. Even at night, a shadow hangs off me.

———

I slept on the beach until a widow invited me to her house. We make a pretence of me renting her spare room, though I don't sleep in it and don't pay for it. Her adult son gets me work, as a builder.

I'm fitting pipes, working alone.

"Esteban! Esteban Hart-Fraser!" They kick at the door. They probably have guns. South American police carry guns, don't they?

Gravity is a property of mass. All mass has gravity, with a pull matching its amount. My body has gravity, but not enough to affect anything. The Earth has gravity enough to keep us on it, and to keep the moon in orbit. Stars have gravity enough to hold planets spinning round them. Galaxies have gravity. They have a lot of gravity.

Gravity pulls on light, too. Very large objects pull on the light around them and distort our view of objects near that view path. Galaxies distort light enough to act as a natural magnifier, and even to give us a peek of objects behind them. The distortion drags hidden images out from behind and projects them as if beside.

There is no truly hidden place.

I'm not ashamed. The universe itself started with an explosion. This is just the beginning.

I twist two pipes apart. Gas stinks up the air.

"Stephen Hart-Fraser! You must come out now!"

Like the other men I work with, I've taken up smoking. I slide the lighter out of my jeans pocket.

Ages from now, from some spectacular distance, someone looking at just this spot on our long-dead planet would see a brief, dazzling flash.

CHAPTER 34

CHLOE FROHMANN

Keene's chill turned into walking pneumonia, which would have allowed him to take further medical leave without confessing his post-traumatic stress. I certainly didn't say anything about it. But he put it out there, asked for counselling, and has stepped away from the job for an undetermined time. He's been offered alternative work on the force—meaning desk jobs—but has not yet signed on for one.

There have been no overt repercussions for me tattling to Cole about Keene's state of mind. You'd think his voluntary leave would prove me justified, but some people blame me for driving him out. I look out for subtle punishments.

The family with the dark-haired runaway daughter—Ashley Abington—were convinced that the hammer, shirt, and hair applied to her and made lots of noise about it. For a while, that evidence got associated with her case. Then she turned up, with the actual teenage boy she'd met online, a real Romeo and Juliet, not the predator they'd assumed. That put the Brookside hammer and shirt in limbo and in storage, unattached to any case. The parents were thrilled to have her back unhurt and, I quote, "not pregnant."

In the absence of evidence otherwise, Mathilde Oliver's death has been classified an accident.

Grace Rhys's murder has only some paperwork left. I drive to Deeping House for a last visit. I need Dru's signature on the document that had been typed up from her recorded witness statement.

They're packing. There's a skip outside, full of rubbish and men's clothes. They're expunging him from their lives.

I stand in the doorway. On and under the wooden floor in front of me is where we'd found the blood. It had been cleaned up, of course. It hadn't been visible, but we'd made it so.

There's a rug here now. I walk over it.

Mrs. Bennet is carefully sorting the family photos into *with him* and *without him*. "For the skip," she says, gesturing to the *with him* pile.

Dru is wrapping dishes and mugs in newspaper to cushion them in transit. She rinses the ink off her hands and signs the papers for me.

"How are you holding up?" I ask.

She shrugs, and her gaze falls on her sister.

Max is wearing a curly brown wig studded with pink bows. She sprawls on the couch reading Enid Blyton. She yawns.

"Did you hear about the Finleys?" Dru asks, rolling a tall glass in newsprint, stuffing the jagged paper ends inside the lip. "He ran off with the nanny."

"Liliana?" I say, startled.

"No, a new one. A fat one." Ah, so Mrs. Finley got the middle-aged, overweight nanny she wanted. *Thought* she wanted. Dru lays another glass on the news in front of her. It's the horoscope page. I don't think much of fortune-telling; the predictions are either vague, wrong, or lucky. But stirring Max to think about a future, any living future, is a good thing.

I thank Dru and wish them well. Mrs. Bennet gathers up an armful of tainted memories and carries them out ahead of me.

I pause. A photo on the top of the keeper pile shows a happier day. Max and Dru on the London Eye, arms around each other's shoulders, the city fanned out behind them. I pick it up. Yes, that's the shirt from Brookside. Unisex, oversized on Dru, and with the same little pocket on the front.

Max has fallen asleep. The book rides her chest. Her dreams curve her mouth into a smile.

Dru watches me tuck the photo into my bag.

She runs out after me, catches me in the hall. "Inspector," she says, and it sounds incongruous to be professionally addressed by a child.

I face her. If she confesses, I'll run with it. If she's willing to talk, it won't matter that I scuppered the original interview and that it would be excluded from court. We could just forget about that. And it'll be good for her, too. Her youth, and her state of mind at the time of the crime, mitigate things. She'd just been raped; she was scared; she had sacrificed. Grace, in her kindness, had been about to rob them of Max's security. Surely a compassionate sentence would prioritise psychiatric care over prison. Surely she'll need it.

"You forgot these," she says, wide-eyed. The witness statement. I must have left it on the table after she signed it. She holds the papers out. Her father must have been small; she's littler than her mum, and looks up to me.

The B1040 has been reopened. I ride it over the Nene, now back within its banks. I drive to the recycling centre where Mr. Bennet had dumped the Christmas tree. I slip the photo into the black-bin waste for incineration.

ACKNOWLEDGEMENTS

It's been a privilege to interact with so many generous, knowledgeable people in the process of writing this book. Their expertise is certain; any errors or liberties are my own.

Regarding Cambridge University, thanks to: Dr. Lindsay King and Dr. Carolin Crawford, Institute of Astronomy; Dr. Simon Wadsley, Director of Studies for Mathematics, Homerton College; Ben Champion, Corpus Christi College; and Christine Jelbert, formerly of the Registrar's Office.

Regarding other aspects of the story and setting, thanks to: Dr. Steve Boreham, Caspar Bush, Alice Elfick, Alexander Finlayson, Gina and Dave Holland, Jeff Lewis, Katy Salmon, and Mick Wright, Dog in a Doublet lock keeper.

My early readers provided correction, insight, and encouragement. Thanks to Derek Black, Rachel Wadsley, and Susan Van Valkenburg for being picky about my British usage; to Renee Cramer, Mimi Cross, Eva Gallant, Sophie Hannah, and Amy Mokady for being picky about my story; and to Margaret Brentano Baker and Marianna Williams for overall impressions.

Thanks to my friends online for that last-minute, thought-provoking confab over word choice: Rebecca B, Melissa B, Steve C, George D, Kristi D, Theo F, Laura G, Catherine H, Lara K, Christina M, Estelle P, Caroline P, Dave P, Jo R, Danelle T, and others already thanked above. Good times!

Loving thanks to G, for many, many things, especially for spending Valentine's Day driving me all over the county to find a suitable place for a body dump. Affectionate thanks to S and W, for entertaining yourselves on the Wii while I was on deadline. You three are the loves of my life.

Thanks to Cameron McClure, for excellent agenting and excellent coffee. Also to Don Maass, for the counsel to take the time I needed.

Thanks to all at Delacorte Press, especially Kate Miciak, Randall Klein, and Loren Noveck. It's been a privilege and a pleasure.

ABOUT THE AUTHOR

EMILY WINSLOW is an American living in Cambridge, England. She's the author of *The Whole World* (published by Delacorte in 2010) and is at work on *The Red House,* both of which are set in Cambridge. Her training as an actress at Carnegie Mellon's elite drama conservatory is put to use in her multiple first-person narrators, and her years designing puzzles for *Games* magazine inform her playful, complex plot structures. She and her husband together homeschool their two sons in a house full of books.

www.emilywinslow.com

ABOUT THE TYPE

This book was set in Granjon, a modern recutting of a typeface produced under the direction of George W. Jones, who based Granjon's design upon the letter forms of Claude Garamond (1480–1561). The name was given to the typeface as a tribute to the typographic designer Robert Granjon.